Vampires Gone Wild

Also by the Authors

By Kerrelyn Sparks
Wild About You
Wanted: Undead or Alive

By Pamela Palmer
A Love Untamed
A Blood Seduction

By Amanda Arista
Nine Lives of an Urban Panther
Claws and Effect
Diaries of an Urban Panther

By Kim Falconer
Journey by Night
Path of the Stray

Vampires Gone Wild

SUPERNATURAL UNDERGROUND

Kerrelyn Sparks

Pamela Palmer

Amanda Arista

Kim Falconer

AVONIMPULSE
An Imprint of HarperCollinsPublishers

Excerpt from *Wild About You* copyright © 2012 by Kerrelyn Sparks.

Excerpt from *A Blood Seduction* copyright © 2012 by Pamela Palmer.

Excerpt from *A Kiss of Blood* copyright © 2013 by Pamela Palmer.

Excerpt from *Diaries of an Urban Panther* copyright © 2011 by Amanda Arista.

"V is for VampWoman" copyright © 2013 by Kerrelyn Sparks

"A Forever Love" copyright © 2013 by Pamela Palmer

"First Dates Are Hell" copyright © 2013 by Amanda Arista

"Blood and Water" copyright © 2013 by Kim Falconer

EPub Edition FEBRUARY 2013 ISBN: 9780062264978

Print Edition ISBN: 9780062264985

10 9 8 7 6 5

Contents

V is for VampWoman

Kerrelyn Sparks

Chapter One

AS A MAN of few words, Mikhail Kirillov never stated the obvious. His companions were smart enough to reach the same conclusion he had. Zoltan's snitch had double-crossed them, and now they'd teleported into a trap.

Mikhail quickly scanned the group of Malcontents as they emerged from the nearby forest and gathered on the moonlit meadow, snarling and thumping their fists against their shields. They were armed with swords, spears, and axes. A mortal might assume these vampire thugs were hopelessly stuck in the past, but Mikhail knew better. The Malcontents preferred their battles up close and bloody. The scent of blood in the air drove them wild.

He completed his headcount. "Thirty-six to four."

"Could be worse," J.L. whispered.

"We each take out nine," Jack said. "We can do it."

Zoltan nodded. "We should fight in a circle, so our backs are protected."

Mikhail frowned as his companions drew their swords. Zoltan's idea wasn't bad, but it would severely limit their mobility. And if there was one thing Mikhail valued, it was a life free from limitations.

Freedom from the ravages of time and disease. Freedom to live however he liked and fight however he wanted. In over six hundred years of battle, no one had come close to defeating him. As a result, he had become a fiercely aggressive warrior but never much of a team player.

Not that he didn't care about his friends. Just twenty minutes earlier, Jack had announced with a huge grin that his wife, Lara, was pregnant. Mikhail would single-handedly annihilate an entire army of Malcontents to ensure Jack returned to his wife even though it was unlikely that he would need assistance. Jack, aka Giacomo di Venezia, was probably the best vampire swordsman on the planet. Jean-Luc Echarpe would disagree, but he was too busy designing silly clothes, while Jack and Mikhail were helping Zoltan destroy a Malcontent human-trafficking ring based in Albania.

As Coven Master of Eastern Europe, Zoltan Czakvar could handle himself in a swordfight. It was J.L. Wang who had Mikhail concerned. The former FBI Special Agent was a young American Vamp and probably more comfortable with a pistol in his hand than a sword.

A metallic screech pierced the air as the Malcontents drew their swords. They shouted taunts across the field, no doubt feeling arrogantly secure in their superior numbers.

Time to improve the odds. With one swift move, Mikhail reached overhead to draw his weapon from the leather scabbard on his back. It was a huge broadsword, heavy enough that most mortals found it difficult to lift with two hands. With his left hand, he pulled a freshly sharpened battle-axe from his belt.

His roar boomed across the field, causing the Malcontents to flinch. As he charged toward them, he saw the calculations in their gleaming eyes. Just like the weathermen who watched incoming hurricanes, they were predicting where and when he would make landfall.

Dead center. The vampires in the middle lifted their swords and shields in anticipation. The ends of the battle line inched forward, hoping to close in and surround him.

Mikhail teleported to the right flank, and with one mighty swing of his sword, he lopped off three heads. Before the dead could fully disintegrate into three piles of dust, he teleported to the left flank and decapitated three more Malcontents. With one last stop at the center of the line, he took out three more, then teleported back to his companions. The entire maneuver had taken less than five seconds.

Shocked, the Malcontents fumbled about. A dozen succumbed to fear and teleported away.

Mikhail took a deep breath, then bellowed another war cry as he lifted his sword and battle-axe overhead. That alone was enough to make three more Malcontents piss on themselves before teleporting away.

Behind him, his companions chuckled.

"Now it's twelve to four," Zoltan said.

"Way to go, Mikhail," J.L. added.

"What are we waiting for?" Jack asked.

With a shout, they charged toward the Malcontents. Mikhail dispatched two with one swing of his sword, then spun around to take out a third with his axe. A quick glance assured him that his companions were doing well. Jack had killed two and engaged a third, an ugly guy with a scar down the side of his face. Zoltan and J.L. had each killed one and were fighting a second opponent.

That left two Malcontents. Mikhail spotted them attempting to sneak up on J.L. and Zoltan from behind. Typical Malcontent behavior. Stabbing someone in the back.

He teleported to the first one, turned him to dust, then glowered at the second Malcontent. "Boo."

With a squeak, the second Malcontent teleported away. Mikhail wedged his axe beneath his belt, then turned to watch the end of the battle.

A burst of music joined the clanging of swords. Mikhail tilted his head. The music appeared to be coming from Jack's jacket. A lively rendition of "That's Amore."

With a muttered curse, Jack lunged at his opponent, causing Scarface to jump back six feet. With his left hand, Jack pulled out his cell phone and glanced at it.

"You don't have to answer it," Mikhail muttered.

"It's Lara." Jack continued to fence with Scarface. "If I don't answer, she'll worry."

Mikhail snorted. Thank God he'd avoided the trap

most of his friends had fallen into. Marriage and children? *Never again.*

"Hello, *bellissima*," Jack answered the phone. His opponent tried to take advantage of his divided attention by rushing forward, but Jack easily drove him back.

"This is not a good time, Lara. Can I call you back in about twenty minutes?" Jack glanced to the side as Zoltan finished off his assailant. "Make that ten minutes."

There was a pause as Jack parried with Scarface. "No, there's nothing going on. We're perfectly safe." He deftly handled a well-aimed thrust. "That clashing noise? Oh, it's just a few of the guys doing sword practice."

Stifling a groan, Mikhail slid his sword back into the scabbard. J.L. Wang jabbed his opponent in the heart, turning him to dust. He joined Mikhail and Zoltan as they stood nearby, watching Jack.

"No, sweetheart, you don't have to wait on me for dinner." Jack jumped, missing a low swipe intended to slice through his knees. "I'll be home soon. Could you put a bottle of Blardonnay in the fridge for me?"

Mikhail rolled his eyes. With a resigned sigh, Zoltan sheathed his sword. Jack could have killed Scarface five minutes ago if he weren't so distracted.

"If you're hungry, go ahead and eat." Jack easily fended off another frenzied attack. "You're eating for two, you know."

Mikhail groaned. J.L. glanced at his watch.

"What? No, I don't think you're fat. I think you're— *merda!*" Jack leaped to the side to avoid disembowelment. "No, *bellissima*, I wasn't referring to you—"

"Enough!" Mikhail zoomed forward, caught Scarface's hand in his fist, and squeezed till vampire cried out in pain and dropped his sword. Then Mikhail punched him in the jaw, sending him flying back twenty yards, where he slumped onto the ground in a daze.

Jack gave Mikhail a grateful nod, then walked away a short distance to continue his phone conversation. "Lara, I think you're more beautiful than ever." He slid his sword into its sheath. "I know you miss working in the field, but we agreed you shouldn't be taking any risks right now. Yes, it's perfectly safe here, but—why is my voice echoing? Did you put me on the speakerphone? Lara—" He stopped as a form materialized nearby.

It couldn't be Lara, Mikhail thought, as a dark form took shape in the moonlight. As a mortal, Lara didn't have the ability to teleport.

This was a vampire and definitely female. Her head was covered with a black spandex cap that included a mask over her eyes. Whoever she was, she was stunning. Black leather boots and gloves, and the rest of her encased in body-hugging black spandex. Long, slim legs, nicely rounded hips, a trim waist cinched tightly with a leather utility belt, and breasts that were firm and full. Not too full, he amended his assessment, but full enough to fit nicely in his hands. Not that he intended to—

His thoughts screeched to a halt. Her body looked familiar. Only the lower half of her face was exposed, but that, too, seemed familiar. Where had he seen those lips? So pink and delicate. And the way she lifted her chin with a slight tilt, as if she could shrivel a man's balls with one arrogant, disdainful glance—he'd seen that before on a reality show on the Digital Vampire Network. He didn't usually watch television, but that was one show he hadn't missed.

Was it truly her? How many times had he imagined her naked on a pile of furs?

She twirled around, her black silk cape rippling through the air as she scanned the surroundings. Apparently convinced she was in no danger, she faced them, assuming a dramatic pose. Black boots wide apart, gloved fists on her hips, chest thrust forward, and chin lifted as she looked them over. She gave an imperious nod to Zoltan, then J.L.

Mikhail watched her closely as her gaze moved to him. Her eyes widened, then she quickly focused elsewhere.

It was definitely her. Her eyes were an odd shade of blue. Lavender blue. In over six hundred years, he'd never seen anyone with eyes quite like hers. She was the most beautiful female vampire in the world. Unfortunately, she was also the snootiest.

There had been many occasions over the years when he could have met her in person. He always spotted her across the ballroom at Roman's big parties. She would wear one of her wispy Regency-style gowns and pile her shiny blond hair on her head with a few curls trailing down her lovely neck.

Naked on a pile of furs. He'd always been careful to keep his distance, for he knew if he drew too close, he'd want to drag her off to a cave.

Not that he had a cave. There was just something about her that stirred the centuries-old Norseman in him, heating his blood till he was driven to conquer and pillage. No doubt, she wanted to perch on a satin chaise in an elegant parlor while she sipped hot Chocolood from a china teacup and engaged in witty conversation. He wanted her naked and wet on a pile of furs.

She had a long, fancy name, but he preferred to think of her simply as Pam. *Naked and wet and panting on a pile of furs.*

"Good evening, gentlemen," she addressed them with her crisp British accent. "Jack, you may inform Lara that I have arrived safely."

Jack lowered his voice. "Lara, what have you done?"

Mikhail leaned to the side to watch Scarface, who was still on the ground. The Malcontent's eyes were open, and he was leering at Pam.

"I know I said it was safe here," Jack continued, "but you shouldn't have let her come." He glanced at the woman in spandex. "Who the hell is she?"

Behind Pam, Scarface jumped to his feet. Mikhail tensed, ready to attack.

"I am VampWoman!" Pam gripped the edges of her cape and lifted her arms suddenly as if she planned to take flight. All she managed to do was clobber Scarface as he made a lunge for her.

"Oh, dear. So sorry." She glanced back at his crumpled body on the ground. She must have realized he was a Malcontent, for she swiveled to face them with a victorious flourish of her cape. "I meant to do that."

Mikhail snorted. Snooty as always.

She lifted her chin and attempted to glare down at him, an impossible task since he was a good foot taller than her. He stared calmly back until her cheeks flushed a rosy pink, and she looked away.

Zoltan stepped toward her. "Lady Pamela?"

She flinched.

"Who?" Mikhail asked, unable to resist goading her.

She shot him an annoyed look, then turned back to Zoltan. "This is a most unfortunate development since I had hoped to keep my true identity a secret. I did not anticipate that anyone would see past my clever disguise."

With a sigh, she waved a hand in the air. "In hindsight, I now realize that it is nigh impossible to conceal someone as well-known as myself." She cast another irritated look at Mikhail.

One corner of his mouth curled up, and she stiffened before turning back to Zoltan. "At any rate, it hardly signifies. Since we are all on the same team—"

"*We?*" Mikhail asked. Her eyes flashed at him. Damn, she was beautiful even when she was angry.

She turned away from him. "As I was saying before I was so rudely interrupted— since we are working together, I feel certain I can rely on your utmost discretion."

"Lady Pamela," Zoltan began.

"VampWoman," she corrected him. "I will thank you to address me properly while I am in costume."

"Lara, I'll call you back." Jack pocketed his cell phone. "What are you doing, Lady Pamela? Is this some sort of game where you masquerade as a superhero?"

She planted her hands on her hips. "This is not a game. I am quite serious, I'll have you know."

"Could be worse." J.L. grinned. "She could pretend to be a supervillain."

"I am not pretending," she insisted. "I labored for a fortnight on this costume. And I studied fencing and martial arts for six months. I assure you, I am quite prepared to battle evil."

"Why?" Mikhail asked.

She gave him an exasperated look. "Why not? I have my reasons, and they are of no concern to you."

While Zoltan launched into an explanation that six months of lessons hardly sufficed when the Malcontents had centuries of experience, Mikhail tilted his head to look around her. In the nearby forest, a large group of Malcontents were teleporting in. Apparently, the cowards who had fled earlier were now returning with reinforcements. There had to be over fifty of them.

"Weapons?" he interrupted Zoltan's lecture.

She gave him a frosty look. "When did you acquire the ability to speak more than one syllable at a time?"

He stepped closer. "Weapons?"

Her chin went up another notch. "Of course. I came well prepared." She flipped back her cape to reveal her utility belt. "I have a sword, an assortment of knives and ninja stars, an automatic handgun with extra clips, and several hand grenades."

"Hand grenades?" J.L. gave her an incredulous look. "Why would you want those?"

"They were on sale." She gasped when Mikhail grabbed at her waist. "Unhand me, you brute!"

He wrenched a grenade off her utility belt, ripped out the pin, and tossed it into the forest.

"How dare you—" Her voice broke off when he pulled her against his chest as he twisted around.

A loud explosion boomed, followed by screams. He hunched over her as branches and leaves rained down on his head and shoulders.

Zoltan, J.L., and Jack drew their swords and rushed to the forest to destroy any survivors. He needed to go with them, but Pam was clinging to him, clutching handfuls of his black T-shirt in her fists.

She was in his arms at last.

Naked on a pile of furs. He shook his head. He couldn't risk those thoughts right now. Too much lust, and his eyes would glow red. "Are you all right?"

She nodded, her face pressed against his chest. "What happened?" She lifted her head, and their eyes met.

Lavender blue. The color instantly sparked a surge of longing so intense he forgot to breathe. Time froze, and he was drowning as memories flooded his head, memories of love, joy, and everything that was beautiful in the world.

With a shake of his head, he squeezed his eyes shut. He couldn't fall into that trap again. The grief and guilt had nearly destroyed him.

"Oh, dear. Are you in pain? Were you injured?"

Yes, he was in pain, but it had been a slap in the face

he sorely needed. He'd vowed centuries ago never to involve himself with another vain and selfish woman. The damage from the first one had ravaged his heart, and he could never allow himself to be that vulnerable again.

His mind made up, he opened his eyes. Unfortunately, with one look at her, he was instantly rocked by another wave of lust. It gripped him by the balls and squeezed tight. Damn, he wanted her bad.

Grasping her by the upper arms, he moved her back a few inches. "I'm fine. Release me, so I can help the others."

She gave him a blank look, then gasped. "Oh! I didn't realize." She released her grip on his T-shirt. "Oh, dear, I've wrinkled your shirt. I do apologize." She attempted to smooth out the wrinkles.

He gritted his teeth at the feel of her hands rubbing across his chest. *Naked and wet on a pile of furs.* His groin swelled. *Not now, dammit!*

Her hands stilled. "Are you wearing body armor beneath this shirt?" Her gaze lifted and locked with his once more.

His leather pants bulged. "No."

"Oh." She stepped back, her cheeks blushing. "I beg your pardon. I didn't know a man could be so . . . hard."

You have no idea. He turned away abruptly as his vision turned pink.

"Oh dear, I must have offended you," she said in a rush. "Obviously, I don't make a habit of feeling men's chests. I don't recall my late husband being so . . . well, he was much more refined. A viscount, actually."

A candy ass. Mikhail willed his eyes to stop glowing, but it didn't work. Prim and proper Pam would be shocked.

"I don't believe we have been formally introduced," she continued. "I am Lady—"

"I know who you are." And why not shock her? Why not show her how he honestly felt? Was he such a coward that he intended to keep it a secret for another hundred years? He turned back to face her.

With a gasp, she stepped back.

She was tinted pink, along with her surroundings, a sure sign that his eyes were glowing red. There was no need to write a sonnet in her honor or woo her with fine gifts. No need to say a word. He could simply let the fire in his eyes blaze the message to her soul.

Yes, I want you. I lust for you. Deal with it.

He could hear her heart racing. She opened her mouth, but no words came out. For the first time in centuries, Lady Pamela Smythe-Worthing had been rendered speechless.

Chapter Two

"WE'RE DONE!" JACK ran up to them, followed by J.L. and Zoltan.

Mikhail turned away, so they wouldn't see his eyes. He gazed at the forest while he attempted to force his vision back to normal. "I originally spotted about fifty."

Pam gasped. "Fifty? Malcontents?"

Mikhail nodded. "Ready to attack."

"I think the blast killed about half of them," J.L. reported. "Most of the survivors teleported away, and we took care of the rest."

"Oh, dear," Pam whispered. "We were terribly outnumbered . . ."

"Any mission can suddenly become dangerous," Zoltan told her. "It was ill-advised for you to come here."

"I disagree," she replied with a stronger voice. "You should be thankful I came here so well equipped."

"Oh, yeah." J.L. chuckled. "Thank God for the holy hand grenade of Antioch."

"Actually, it came from Yorkshire," Pam explained. "It's amazing what you can find on e-Bay."

"My lady, the Malcontents could return any second," Zoltan insisted.

"I believe we are safe for the moment." Mikhail turned to face her, his vision now back to normal. "They'll think twice before risking another of milady's hand grenades."

She gave him a shy, grateful smile. "Thank you."

"So we have time for a few questions," Mikhail continued. "How did you find out about our mission?"

Her smile withered. "Does it matter?"

"Yes. You're not an employee at MacKay Security and Investigation, so you shouldn't have known—"

"You mustn't blame Lara," she interrupted, turning to Jack. "She worries so much about you. I went to see her at your villa in Venice, and I encouraged her to call you, knowing that I could use your voice as a beacon."

"How did you find out about our mission?" Mikhail repeated.

She fiddled with her glove and avoided looking at him. "It's a rather long story—"

"Then make it short, Pam."

That made her look at him again. Her eyes flashed. "That's Lady Pamela to you—I mean VampWoman."

His mouth curled up, and she turned away from him with a huff. "It all began when Maggie and Darcy went to Scotland to film Angus MacKay's castle and interview

Emma for their show, *Real Housewives of the Vampire World.*"

Jack groaned. "I can see where this is going."

"Yes." Pam frowned at him. "Your wife was quite devastated when you postponed your appearance on the show."

"I told her I could do it after we destroyed this human-trafficking ring," Jack mumbled.

"And that was six months ago." Pam glowered. "Maggie and Darcy have been waiting forever. After they finished up in Scotland, they dropped by to see me and the old harem girls in London. They told us how frustrated they were, waiting for you to complete your mission in Albania, and that's when I thought you might appreciate some help."

"From you?" Mikhail asked dryly.

Her chin lifted. "You weren't complaining when you needed one of my hand grenades."

"We do appreciate your help," Jack muttered. "But you should return home now."

"I think not. We may have defeated some traffickers, but where, pray tell, are the humans?"

She made a good point. Mikhail scanned the area, wondering where the human captives were being held. Scarface had regained consciousness and was attempting to sit up. He flopped about, groaning, his lips bloodied and both eyes bruised and swelling.

Mikhail zoomed over, grabbed his shirt, and hauled him to his feet. "Where are the humans?" he asked in Albanian.

Scarface sneered. "Why should I tell you?"

He pulled back a fist.

"Wait!" Scarface gasped. "Don't hit me again. There's a road through there." He waved at the forest behind them, then teleported away.

Mikhail drew his sword. "Let's go."

They ran through the forest. With his longer legs, Mikhail could have easily outdistanced his companions, but he held back, making sure Pam remained safe. *You fool, it's happening already,* an inner voice chided him. He was becoming vulnerable. Over another vain and selfish woman. He shoved those thoughts away.

After half a mile, they emerged on a dirt road, where a dented and rusty old camper truck was parked. Mikhail quickly circled the truck. No Malcontents in sight. He returned to the back door, where Jack was hacking at the chained padlock with his sword.

"I'll do it." Mikhail smashed through the chains with his battle-axe, then opened the door.

They were greeted by a dozen pair of terrified eyes. The girls, tied up and gagged, attempted to squirm farther back into the filthy recesses of the camper. Mikhail guessed their ages to be somewhere between twelve and twenty. More years than his daughter had lived. He pushed that errant thought aside. At least he hadn't failed these.

He climbed into the camper, and the girls cowered on the floor, whimpering behind their gags.

"You're frightening them." Pam quickly followed him into the camper, then knelt in front of the girls. "You poor dears, there is no need to be afraid. We have come to rescue you and deliver you safely home."

"My lady," Zoltan whispered to her. "These are humans. We should leave them to the human authorities. I'll call the local police—"

"And what?" Pam looked up at him, aghast. "Make them endure hours of questioning when we could easily take them home to their families? Haven't they suffered enough?"

"Our first imperative is always to keep our existence a secret," Zoltan whispered. "If we teleport them—

"They have bite marks," Mikhail interrupted, motioning at the girls. "The Malcontents were feeding off them. They already know about vampires. We should teleport them home, then wipe their memories."

"I agree." Pam gave him a grateful smile that made his heart squeeze in his chest.

He ignored it and moved closer to the girls, who were huddled together, trembling.

"There, there." Pam patted a girl on the shoulder. "I know he looks like a huge brute, but he won't harm you."

A huge brute? Mikhail winced inwardly. Even so, it seemed like a good thing that Pam was here. Her presence was comforting the girls. They had grown quiet, the terror on their faces melting into hope.

He leaned over one of the girls, and, using his psychic power, he delved into her mind to locate her home. Then he grasped her arm and teleported her back. With a happy squeal, she turned to thank him. He removed her gag and ropes while he wiped her memory of the last few days. When her face turned blank, he teleported back to the camper truck.

With all five of them working, it took only a few minutes to return the captives to their homes. After delivering a third girl, Mikhail reappeared at the camper to find it empty. He sauntered around the truck, making sure no Malcontents had returned. As he approached the back, Pam materialized.

She glanced into the camper, then, with a satisfied smile, turned away. "Not bad for your first night," she murmured to herself, then peeled the spandex cap off her head. Her blond hair slipped free, and she shook it out, the golden tresses falling in waves around her shoulders.

Good God, she is beautiful. He must have made some kind of noise, for she spun around to face him.

"Oh, you—you've returned." She glanced around. "The others haven't made it back yet." She winced. "I'm sure you already know that."

"Yes." He stepped toward her.

She brushed her hair back over her shoulder. "The cap was rather hot. Stifling, actually. I might have to reconsider my costume design."

He raked his eyes down to her boots, then back up to her breasts. "It looks good to me."

"Do you mind?"

"Hmm?"

"You're ogling my chest."

"There's a red mark there. It draws a person's attention."

She gritted her teeth. "That's a 'V.' It stands for—"

"Voluptuous?"

She scoffed. "Hardly."

"Viscountess?"

She winced. "No. VampWoman."

"I would never have guessed."

She gave him a dry look. "You may mock me, but I much prefer my new identity."

"What was wrong with your old one?"

She ducked her chin and fiddled with her gloves. "I'd rather not discuss it."

He stepped closer. "Why are you doing this? Why are you risking yourself?"

A pained look crossed her face. "I'd rather not—"

"What was wrong with Lady Pamela? I always thought she was beautiful."

"No!" She glanced up. "She's . . ."

"She's what?"

"She's . . . shameful." Her eyes glistened with tears, and she turned away.

His breath caught. She didn't sound as vain as he had expected. "Why do you say that?"

She sighed. "So many reasons. First, I married a vampire without realizing it. There were rumors about Maximilian. Plenty of clues. I never saw him eat, never saw him during the day. But like a fool, I ignored it all. I was too enamored with the notion that a viscount could love me and want to marry me."

Mikhail frowned. "That wasn't your fault. He should have been honest with you."

She waved aside his attempt to defend her. "I was

young and foolish. A few weeks after the wedding, Max asked me if I would like to wear beautiful gowns and go to lovely parties forever. I said yes." She brushed away her tears with an angry swipe. "Can you imagine giving up mortality for such a ridiculous reason?"

"Did you know he meant to transform you?"

"No." She gave Mikhail a wry look. "It was a bit of a shock when he attacked me."

Mikhail gritted his teeth. It was a good thing the bastard was dead.

"I was so foolish. I gave up my chance to ever have children."

Mikhail's heart squeezed as the memory of his daughter swept across his mind. "You wanted children?"

She nodded, and another tear rolled down her cheek. "Then I made the mistake of complaining to my father. I didn't go into any details, but it was enough to make him suspect that the rumors were true."

Her shoulders slumped. "I was a coward. I knew my father hated Max, but I did nothing to dissuade him. Max trusted me, and I let him down."

"So it was your father who killed your husband?" Mikhail asked.

"Yes. He staked Max while we lay beside each other in our death-sleep. Father left his ring in the ashes so I would know it was he. I feared that Max's vampire friends would avenge him by killing my father, so I begged him to flee to America. He asked me to accompany him, but I was too afraid to go. I abandoned him when he was in danger."

She sniffed. "I joined the Coven Master's harem in London, where I would be safe. Then later, when the Germans were bombing London, I fled to New York. As usual, I took the cowardly way out."

"That was self-preservation. The underground lairs were no longer safe."

"And then my friend, Vanda, was in danger. The Malcontents blew up our nightclub and wanted to kill her, and I left her. I went back to London." She turned to face him with tears running down her cheeks. "Don't you see why I'm ashamed? I'm a coward who fails the people who count on me. I abandon them when they need me the most."

Mikhail stared at her, stunned by the ferocity of her self-recrimination . Was she trying to earn redemption as VampWoman? She'd be lucky if she wasn't rewarded with an early death. "I can understand the need to make up for past mistakes, but what you're doing now, you're putting yourself in danger—"

"You don't approve." She dried her cheeks with an impatient swipe. "I shouldn't have confessed everything to you."

"No! I'm glad you told me."

"But you could never understand how I feel. You're so incredibly huge and fierce. I doubt you've ever lost a battle or ever let anyone down."

He flinched.

"Do you even know what it's like to be filled with guilt and regret?"

He pinched his eyes shut to avoid the memories that

flooded his mind. "Enough." He opened his eyes to find her staring at him.

"You do know," she whispered. Her hand lifted toward his face, but before she could touch him, she blinked and withdrew her hand. Her gaze dropped to his chest. "Then you do understand."

"I understand that each time you endanger yourself, it will scare the hell out of me."

"But you hardly know me."

That much was true. For almost two hundred years, he'd assumed she was selfish and vain. And why wouldn't she be, when she was the most beautiful vampire in the world? But instead of feeling superior, she had actually been ashamed of herself. She'd used the snooty image of an arrogant viscountess to hide her self-doubt and vulnerability.

With a small shock, he realized that Lady Pamela had been the masquerade. VampWoman was the true Pam.

"You're . . . Mikhail?" Her gaze lifted back to his face. "From Moscow?"

"You know of me?"

She blushed. "Everyone knows who you are. You're a full head taller than the other men, and they're rather large. Of course, the rumor is that you're some sort of fierce medieval Viking and that you came to Russia centuries ago to pillage and plunder."

"Is that what they say?"

Her blush deepened. "Well, I was in a harem for years. There wasn't much to do other than gossip about the men."

"I've always thought you were beautiful." He touched a lock of her hair. Now he realized she was just as beautiful on the inside. And he'd been a fool to avoid her all these years.

He moved closer.

Her eyes widened. "What—?"

He touched her cheek and wiped the moisture of her tears with his thumb.

"I-I should be going."

"So soon?" He grazed his thumb over her lips. They were as soft as he'd imagined.

She gulped. "I believe our work here is done."

He slid his hand around her neck and leaned over till his mouth was a mere inch from hers. "Pam."

"Yes?" Her rapid breaths puffed against his skin.

"Prepare to be plundered."

With a gasp, she teleported away.

Chapter Three

"COWARD!" LADY PAMELA yanked off a boot and threw it on the parquet floor of her bedchamber.

How could she have behaved so cowardly? Six months of planning and practicing to be a stronger and more fearless person, and what had she done? She'd run away just like she had in the past. With a disgusted groan, she tossed her other boot on the floor.

Perhaps it wasn't too late. Less than a minute had passed since she'd fled in fear. She could teleport back and . . . what? Allow that huge barbarian to kiss her?

A shudder skittered down her spine.

"Coward," she muttered. Instead of running away, she should have slapped the brute soundly. Or better yet, she should have used some of her newly acquired martial-arts skills to fling him over her shoulder.

Her breath caught. Was it even possible to fling such a man? He was so enormous. As immovable as a giant boulder.

And his eyes had turned red.

Her hands flew to her cheeks, and she felt the heat of a blush. His eyes had turned red.

When she'd first spotted him, she'd been shocked by the sheer strength of his presence. It felt like he had swallowed up her entire field of vision, so she could hardly even see the other men. Or hear them.

His eyes had turned red. Because of her.

Why, oh why had she told him so much about herself? What had possessed her to confide in such a huge brute? Although he had seemed rather attentive and understanding for a barbarian.

She chased that thought away. He *was* a barbarian. He had attempted to kiss her. *Prepare to be plundered.* The gall of the man!

She jumped when a loud pounding shook her door.

"Lady Pamela? Is that you I hear?"

That accent could only belong to Miss Cora Lee Primrose—a Southern belle, transformed just prior to the American Civil War, and one of Pamela's friends who shared the London townhouse.

"Yes, I have returned," she answered.

"Well, land sakes, come out of there and tell us how it went. We've been worried sick about you."

"I'll be down shortly." Pamela removed her utility belt and set it carefully on her bed so the various knives and ninja stars wouldn't snag her pink satin coverlet.

With a sigh, she unzipped the front zipper on her costume. Perhaps she shouldn't be overset by the night's events. After all, she did assist the men in defeating the traffickers and delivering the captives back home. The blast from the hand grenade had frightened her but not enough to make her run away. Apparently, the prospect of a kiss was more terrifying than an explosion.

She removed her cape, then peeled off her latex costume. No doubt *he* had imagined undressing her. How dare he ogle her like that?

His eyes had glowed red. How could a man's passion flare so hot so quickly?

"Posh." She slipped on a silk wrapper and tied the sash around her waist. The man was a barbarian. He probably ogled a dozen women nightly and leered at them all with glowing red eyes. Prepare to be plundered, indeed. Who did he think he was? A Viking warrior who ravished innocent women?

What if she had stayed? Where would he have touched her? And kissed her? No doubt a barbarian did wicked things a gentleman would never do. Goose bumps prickled her skin.

She rubbed her arms as she marched toward the door. "I will not give him another thought."

She was halfway down the stairs when she recalled his reaction to the camper full of pretty mortal girls. His eyes hadn't turned red for them. Like her, he had wanted to take them home, and he'd handled them gently to assuage their fears. He'd been surprisingly kind . . . for a barbarian.

"Thank the Lord you are alive and well!" Princess Joanna announced when Pamela entered the parlor.

"Santa Maria be praised," Maria Consuela added, and kissed her rosary.

"I'm quite all right," Pamela assured the ladies.

Joanna's title of princess was honorary since she was an old vampire, having been changed in Venice while en route to the Holy Land during one of the Crusades. Maria Consuela de Montemayor had been captured during the Spanish Inquisition when the authorities had feared that her fiancé was Jewish. Fortunately for her, he was also a vampire, and he'd teleported into the prison to rescue her. Both had been widowed centuries ago and had then transferred to a harem, where they could live in comfort and safety.

After appearing on a reality show for the Digital Vampire Network, Lady Pamela and her old harem friends had become modern enough to eschew the concept of needing a master. Still, in many ways, they held fast to their historic roots.

Princess Joanna settled in an easy chair by the fireplace. "Prithee, tell us all that has transpired."

"Oh, yes." Cora Lee walked in with a tray and set it down on the table. "We want to know everything." She poured four cups of steaming hot Chocolood, a mixture of synthetic blood and chocolate. "I do declare we were worried sick."

Maria Consuela shuddered. "It reminded me of being tortured."

"Please do not suffer on my account." Pamela sat, then accepted a cup from Cora Lee. "Thank you, dear."

The Southern belle perched on the settee next to Maria Consuela. "Were you able to find Lara's husband?"

"Yes. Everything went precisely as I had planned." *Not*

precisely, Pamela thought with a silent groan. Never in her wildest imaginings would she have foreseen herself in that man's arms.

"And who was there?" Princess Joanna sipped from her cup. "Giacomo di Venezia, of course. And Zoltan Czakvar?"

Pamela nodded. "They were quite shocked to see me when I arrived."

"I bet!" Cora Lee snickered. "Who else was there?"

"Two others. We hardly know them." Pamela took a sip from her cup. "One was that new chap, J.L. Wang."

"From Cathay?" Princess Joanna asked.

"I believe it's called China now, dear." Pamela set her cup down. "But he's actually American."

Princess Joanna waved a dismissive hand. "Those Americans are such a . . . boiling cauldron."

"I think it's melting pot," Cora Lee said. "Who was the other fellow?"

Pamela shrugged nonchalantly even though heat was invading her cheeks. "That . . . man from Russia."

"Russia?" Princess Joanna's eyes widened.

Cora Lee gasped. "You mean the huge giant with the icy blue eyes and the blond braid down his back? Land sakes, his hair is longer than mine!"

"Wicked," Maria Consuela whispered as she clicked through her rosary. "I know of whom you speak. He has eyes as cold as sin."

More like red-hot and glowing, Pamela thought with an inward wince. But the sinful part was probably accurate.

"Heaven forbid!" Princess Joanna pressed a hand to her chest. "You cannot mean that barbarian!"

Pamela started to lift her cup, but changed her mind for fear her hand would noticeably tremble. "He seemed to be a valuable member of their team. No doubt he's a fierce warrior."

Princess Joanna snorted. "Fierce, indeed. The man is one of those horrid Vikings."

"Evil," Maria Consuela whispered.

Joanna shuddered. "For centuries, they were a scourge on our countryside, always pillaging and plundering."

And she'd come close to being plundered. If Pamela had waited but a second longer, his lips would have touched hers. And being a barbarian, he wouldn't have stopped. He would have ravished her mouth entirely. Thoroughly.

Her skin pebbled with gooseflesh, and in a shocking burst of clarity, she realized it wasn't fear that was making her heart pound and her body tremble.

It was excitement.

Good heavens! Was she losing her senses? Such feelings could not be tolerated. The man was not her type at all.

"His name is Mikhail, right?" Cora Lee asked. She sipped from her cup. "I do declare he's always frightened me a bit. He seems so . . . cold and forbidding."

"Evil," Maria Consuela muttered.

"He is absolutely wrong in every possible way," Pamela said in a rushed voice. "Incredibly huge and muscular, with a chest like a rock. Not at all like my late husband.

Maximilian was a gentleman. Sophisticated and refined. He would have never said . . ." She paused when she realized that the three women were watching her curiously.

Cora Lee leaned forward. "What did he say?"

Pamela's face blazed with heat. "Nothing." *Prepare to be plundered.*

"You are comparing him to your late husband?" Princess Joanna asked.

Pamela shook her head. "Only to emphasize what a huge brute he is."

Cora Lee gave her a pointed look. "Maybe he's huge all over."

Pamela gasped. "I daresay that is . . ."

"Wicked." Maria Consuela zipped through her rosary at vampire speed.

Cora Lee shrugged. "I'm just saying it's been a long time since any of us indulged in a little romance."

"That is quite out of the question," Pamela snapped. "I have no intention of going anywhere near that brute—"

"*Huge* brute," Cora Lee interrupted with a smirk.

Was he really huge? Pamela shoved that disturbing thought aside. "We all know a man's size is totally irrelevant. What matters is his mind-control ability."

Princess Joanna nodded. "Indeed. We need to make the acquaintance of a gentleman who is skilled at vampire sex."

"Like Roman." Cora Lee sighed. "I do declare he could satisfy us all in ten minutes."

"Exactly," Pamela agreed. "It was very time-efficient. And wonderfully private. The entire experience is so much more refined when it's conducted purely as a mental exercise."

Cora Lee nodded. "We could stay in our own rooms. And we didn't even have to take off our clothes."

"And it was never messy, like physical sex." Pamela grimaced. "No grasping, sweaty hands pawing you all over."

Maria Consuela shuddered. "Evil."

"There was a time when I think I actually enjoyed real sex." Princess Joanna waved a hand in the air. "But that was centuries ago, and I have long forgotten."

"It is best left forgotten," Pamela said. The thought of having a man physically invade her body—it was far too shocking. Too raw and frightening.

But wasn't she trying to get over her cowardice?

"So what happens now?" Cora Lee asked. "Are you going to meet them tomorrow night?"

"Surely, one night of wild behavior will suffice," Princess Joanna said. "It is far too dangerous for you to continue with this folly."

Pamela swallowed hard. She had to be brave. She couldn't wallow in cowardice for another century. Or even another night. "VampWoman will return."

Chapter Four

"YOU SHOULDN'T HAVE come," Zoltan announced the next evening after Lady Pamela teleported into his parlor in Budapest.

With a silent squeal of triumph, Pamela congratulated herself on finding the men. Back home, while donning her costume, she'd worried about being able to locate them. But since Zoltan was the Coven Master of Eastern Europe, she'd decided his home was a good place to start. She'd been here before to attend a party, so the location was embedded in her psychic memory.

"Good evening." She smiled at Zoltan, who stood next to the fireplace. "Gentlemen." She nodded at Jack and J.L., who lounged in nearby chairs, frowning at her. A pile of sheathed swords and knives rested on a coffee table.

Where was . . . the back of her neck prickled as if touched by an icy breeze. Or was it the frigid glare of pale blue eyes? She spun about, her black silk cape rippling through the air.

Mikhail was leaning against the doorjamb, his arms crossed over his massive chest, his eyes glittering like broken shards of icicles. Heat spread like flames throughout her body, causing her face to flush. How could such a cold brute make her feel like she was melting?

A corner of his mouth curled up.

Arrogant oaf. How dare he assume he was the cause of her blush? Even though he was. But as annoyed as she was, she couldn't help but notice the dimple caused by his half smile. And what a wide, sensuous mouth he had. Finely sculpted lips, too. Lips that had come so close to kissing her. *Don't think about it!* With a blink, she forced her gaze back to his eyes.

Dear God, no. He was ogling her again, lingering over every dip and curve of her body. Her skin tingled beneath the black spandex, and the costume felt suddenly tighter, constricting her to the point she could scarcely breathe. His eyes met hers, and he slowly smiled.

With a flourish of her cape, she turned her back to him. *Blast him!* He enjoyed unnerving her.

He said something in a foreign language that made Zoltan chuckle. It must be Hungarian. She hadn't thought about it till now, but the oaf's English was quite good. And he'd spoken in Albanian to a Malcontent the night before. He was surprisingly well educated for a barbarian, and that unnerved her even more.

She squared her shoulders and adjusted her utility belt. "Pray tell, where will our mission take us tonight?"

"We're waiting for a report to come in from Dubrovnik," Zoltan replied. "We believe the Malcontents are hiding a group of human captives in a warehouse near the docks. We need to rescue them before they're loaded onto a ship."

A lump of alarm rose in her throat, and she swallowed hard. This mission could easily turn violent. But wasn't this what she had trained for? She took a deep breath to steady her nerves. Tonight, she would prove she was no coward. When her companions needed her, she would not turn tail and run.

"As soon as we get the call, we're leaving," Zoltan continued, then gave her a pointed look. "And you will not be coming with us."

"Of course I will. I'm part of the team."

"No, milady, you are not," Jack said softly.

"You don't work for MacKay S and I," J.L. added.

"I'm a free agent," she insisted. "I'm here to help you, and I will not be dismissed!"

"Lady Pamela." Zoltan gave her an exasperated look. "We only wish to keep you safe."

"Your presence could endanger us all." Jack stood and selected a sword from the coffee table. "If we're forced to protect you—"

"I can take care of myself." She planted her fists on her hips. "I am up to the challenge."

"Are you?" a deep voice spoke behind her, and she pivoted to face him.

Mikhail walked toward her, watching her with a predatory gleam in his eyes. "If I remember correctly, you frighten very easily."

Her heart sped up, pounding in her chest.

His gaze dropped to her mouth. "Are you certain you won't . . . disappoint?"

Was he alluding to their almost kiss? How dare he! She lifted her chin. "I will not abandon my teammates."

He focused on her breasts, which made her even more breathless and tingly. "You're afraid. I can hear your heart racing."

"That's not fear! It's—" Good heavens! She stopped herself in the nick of time.

His eyes met hers in a flash, and the intensity of his look took her breath away. He tilted his head, searching her face.

She jumped when a phone rang.

"That should be my informant." Zoltan pulled a cell phone from his jacket pocket, while Jack and J.L. quickly armed themselves. "I'll turn on the speakerphone, so we can teleport to his voice."

Excellent! Pamela faced him, mentally steeling her nerves for battle.

The phone rang again, and Zoltan frowned at her. "Mikhail, get her out of here. I'll call you in sixty seconds, so you can join us."

"What?" Pamela gasped when Mikhail grabbed her from behind. Before she could react, everything went black.

As soon as she materialized, she jumped into action. A sharp jab in his ribs with her right elbow as she spun to face him, then a left punch in the—"Ouch!"

The man's stomach was like a slab of concrete.

"Are you all right?" He grabbed her hand.

Before he could remove her glove, she yanked her hand away. Balling her fists, she bounced back on the balls of her feet, then aimed a quick roundhouse kick at his chest. He nabbed her ankle and tugged, making her lose her balance. As she started to fall, he grabbed her and pulled her hard against him.

"Oof." She caught her breath, her nose pressed against his chest. He smelled surprisingly clean for a barbarian. As she splayed her hands against his stomach, preparing to shove him away, she realized he wasn't as smooth and cold as a concrete slab. He was warm and rippled. With muscles.

He held her tight, his arms banded around her shoulders. She resisted an urge to snuggle against him. It was tempting, so tempting. What if he wasn't a barbarian after all?

She glanced up at him. "What did you say to Zoltan that he found so amusing?"

A corner of Mikhail's mouth lifted, causing the dimple to reappear. "It was a compliment."

"About me?"

"Of course." His left hand slid beneath her cape and down her spine to her utility belt. "I was admiring you from . . . behind." His hand curved around her rump.

"Stop that!" When she attempted to push away, his hand flexed on her buttock, pulling her closer. How could she have ever doubted he was a barbarian? "How dare you!"

He gave her another squeeze.

If only she could slap that amused look off his face, but both her arms were pinned against his chest. She stomped her boot on his foot.

He merely looked annoyed. "Do I need to tie you to the bedpost?"

"You wouldn't dare—*bedpost*?" She glanced over her shoulder and flinched. A massive, canopy bed dominated a room filled with bookcases and tables and large leather chairs. "You—you brought me to your bedroom?"

"This is the cellar of my hunting lodge."

She glanced at the huge bed again. Of course it was huge. The man was huge. "This is highly inappropriate."

"I had to take you somewhere."

"You should have taken me to *my* bedroom."

His mouth twitched. "Is that an invitation?"

"No! I meant my home. In London." She scanned the room once more. This was a hunting lodge? It was as well furnished as her townhouse. And he certainly owned a great number of books . . . for a barbarian.

He released her and stepped back. "If I knew the way to your home, I would have taken you there. You should go there now."

And give up on her dream? "No, I'm coming with you."

"No. You're going home, where you'll be safe."

"I refuse." She lifted her chin. "I will not take the coward's way out."

His eyes hardened like ice as he stepped toward her. "Then you'd better be brave because if you're still here when I return, I will tie you to the bedpost. After I strip you—" His phone rang.

Her heart thundered in her ears so loud, she couldn't hear him answer the phone. He would strip her? And tie her to the bedpost?

"Pam!"

She jumped when she realized he was talking to her.

"The guys need me. Go! Quickly!"

The guys were in need? She vanished and materialized silently behind Mikhail.

"Okay, she's gone," he said into the phone. "I'm coming."

She leaped on his back just before he disappeared.

DAMN IT TO hell! As soon as Mikhail materialized, he pried away the hands that were gripped around his neck. She was the most stubborn, disobedient woman he'd ever met. He should have tied her. And stripped her. She wouldn't have pulled this stunt if she were naked. But then he wouldn't have answered the phone . . .

"*Merda*," Jack whispered. "Why did you bring her?"

He gritted his teeth as he turned to glare at Pam, who stood behind him with a defiant look on her face. "You little—" His anger froze when he spotted several dozen armed Malcontents streaming through the double doors of the warehouse, headed straight toward him and his companions.

A quick scan of their surroundings confirmed the gravity of the situation. They were blocked on three sides by heavy metal containers. They could fight or flee. Zoltan, Jack, and J.L. had their swords drawn, ready to fight, but Pamela's sudden appearance was making them hesitate.

She drew her sword. "Let's do it."

Mikhail noticed a second-floor balcony to the right. He grabbed Pam and teleported her onto the balcony.

As soon as they materialized, she hit him on the chest and opened her mouth to berate him.

He clapped a hand over her mouth and turned her so she could see the men below. "I didn't take you away," he whispered. "Stay here, stay hidden, and keep out of trouble."

He unsheathed his broadsword and teleported quietly behind the group of Malcontents. With a war cry, he attacked from the rear. Zoltan, Jack, and J.L. charged from the other end. The warehouse echoed with the clanging of swords and screams of the wounded.

Wounded? Mikhail tended to kill the enemy so quickly, there was no time for a scream. And he'd learned from experience never to leave wounded in his wake, for they could rally and attack from the rear. The screams appeared to be coming from the middle of the Malcontent pack.

He spotted flashes of silver metal streaking down from the balcony. It was Pam! She was hurling ninja stars down at the Malcontents. The crazed woman! It was only a matter of time before one of the Malcontents teleported up there to terminate her actions. By terminating her.

With another war cry, he accelerated his attack, lopping off heads at vampire speed. He needed to keep the Malcontents focused on him, so they would forget the wild woman on the balcony.

When less than a dozen Malcontents remained, his worst fear happened. One of them vanished and reappeared on the balcony. Mikhail's heart lurched when he saw the Malcontent's sword slash down at Pam. She dodged the blow, then jumped back and readied her sword.

Mikhail teleported beside her. "Stay back." He shoved her behind him and lunged forward to attack the Malcontent. He jabbed him in the heart, dusting him, then heard an ominous crash behind him. He spun about to find that another Malcontent had attempted to stab him in the back. Pam had deflected the blow, but it had taken both her hands to wield her sword and all her strength to knock aside the thrust meant for him. The Malcontent took instant advantage and sliced her left arm with his knife.

With a cry, she fell to her knees. Mikhail beheaded the Malcontent, then grabbed her as she crumpled on the floor.

"Why?" he gasped as he slapped a hand over her wound. Blood seeped between his fingers. "Why couldn't you stay hidden like I asked you?"

Her face paled to a deathly white. "I—I will not abandon my teammates."

Crazy, foolish . . . beautiful woman. The pain clouding her lavender-blue eyes struck a blow to his heart more sharp than any sword. If it took an eternity, he'd make sure she was never injured again. He would protect her. And love her. And if it made him vulnerable, so be it. He would not give her up.

A quick glance below assured him that his companions were close to winning the battle. They wouldn't miss him.

He gathered her close to his chest. "I'll take care of you. Trust me."

Everything went black.

Chapter Five

PAMELA SNUGGLED DEEPER under her pink satin coverlet, her mind drifting in a foggy haze. Three hours had passed since she'd been wounded, but thanks to Mikhail's doctoring and a whole bottle of Blardonnay, she was feeling no pain.

With a smile, she remembered the look on his face when he'd taken care of her. The furrowed brow, the tortured eyes, as if her pain hurt him more than her. He'd teleported them to the cellar of his hunting lodge, then taken her up the stairs to the kitchen.

After setting her in a chair next to the table, he'd poured her a glass of Blardonnay. "Drink it all. You've lost too much blood."

She drank the mixture of synthetic blood and Chardonnay, then removed her gloves and pulled the cap off her head while he covered the table with an impressive array of medical supplies. "Where did you get all this?"

"From Dr. Lee. He's too far away in Texas for me to see him whenever I get injured, so he taught me the basics."

"I can't imagine anyone's managing to wound you."

"Minor cuts and scrapes." With an apology for destroying her clothes, he used scissors to cut through the spandex at her shoulder before easing the sleeve off her arm. He apologized again while cleaning her wound, wincing when the sting made her gasp.

She tried not to think about the pain, and so took advantage of the chance to study him up close. Even though his hair was a golden blond, his eyebrows were brown, and his eyelashes dark and thick. He was remarkably handsome . . . for a barbarian. And gentle. It would be so easy to fall for him. She gulped down the rest of her Blardonnay.

He filled a syringe. "This is a painkiller."

"Should I have that when I'm drinking wine?"

"I'd rather see you tipsy than in pain." He gave her the shot, then applied a row of butterfly bandages along her wound. "These will keep it closed till it can heal during your death-sleep. You might end up with a small scar."

"That's all right."

He'd looked at her then, his icy blue eyes glimmering with pain like fractured icicles. "It is not all right. If the wound had been deeper—"

"I'm fine."

"You're beautiful. If I had known how beautiful you were inside, I would have never . . ." His voice drifted off as he wrapped her upper arm with a thick bandage.

"Never what?" she whispered.

Frowning, he fastened the bandage. "I wasted so much time." He glanced at her. "It will be different now."

Was her mind already befuddled? She wasn't following him. "What will be different?"

"You and me." He brushed her hair back from her brow. "You were injured trying to protect me. Don't ever doubt your bravery again."

Her heart squeezed in her chest. He thought she was brave. And beautiful inside. "You protected me, too."

The corner of his mouth lifted, revealing his dimple, and she thought she might melt.

He kissed her brow. "You should go home now, so you can rest, and I can return to the guys. They might need me."

"Of course." She winced inwardly. They'd left the other guys in the middle of their mission. She eased to her feet, and the room swirled. "I—I'm a bit woozy."

He caught her when she stumbled. "I'll take you." He swept her up in his arms. "But you'll have to let me into your mind for a few seconds, so I'll know the way."

Into her mind? Vamps dove into the minds of mortals whenever they wanted to, without any hesitation, but they tended to be much more protective of their own mental privacy. No vampire wanted to be controlled by another. Normally, they only lowered their mental defenses to have vampire sex. And even then, they tended to keep all their secrets and past torments locked away. No one wanted to reveal a weakness that might later be used against them.

A mind meld with Mikhail. It was a chance to see inside him. If he let her. "All right."

He cradled her against his chest, leaning his head forward till it touched hers. "Let me in."

She opened her mind, and he slipped inside with a gentle, persistent strength, burrowing straight through her thoughts to the location of her bedroom. He was quick and efficient, his mind well-ordered and disciplined. He was holding back, she realized, making sure he didn't overpower her, but even the strength in his restraint was impressive.

In those few seconds before he teleported her, she searched his mind, digging past the structured intelligence to see what lay beneath. A deep sadness. Past that, a swirl of strong emotion, then a shocking clarity as he revealed his feelings.

He loved her. He'd loved her for almost two hundred years.

As soon as they arrived in her bedroom, he exited her mind and placed her on her bed. Still stunned, she stared up at him, speechless.

He strode to the door and opened it to call her friends, so they could take care of her. They rushed in, gawking at him and fussing over her. She hardly heard them, her thoughts still reeling from the mind meld. *He loved her.* And he'd wanted her to know.

He leaned over her, kissing her brow once again before teleporting away.

Now, three hours later, it still dominated her thoughts. Mikhail Kirillov was not a barbarian. And he loved her.

She stretched under the pink coverlet and glanced at the empty bottle of Blardonnay on her bedside table. Cora Lee had insisted she drink the whole thing. She was fuzzy-headed, but her mind still functioned enough to recall the strength of his passion.

"Mikhail," she whispered.

The door opened, and Cora Lee entered with another bottle of Blardonnay.

"How are you, dear?" She set the bottle next to the empty one.

"I'm drunk." *And I'm hopelessly attracted to Mikhail.*

Cora Lee perched on the edge of the bed. "You gave us the biggest fright. When we saw that huge man in your bedroom . . ." She pressed a hand to her chest. "Are you sure he treated your wound properly? Do you want a real doctor?"

"I'm fine. He took very good care of me." *And I think I care for him, too.*

"Land sakes." Cora Lee waved a hand in front of her face. "I do declare that man simply oozes with virility. The way he kissed you. And looked at you. I don't know if he wants to worship you or devour you. Both, I suppose."

Pam gulped. *Good heavens, I think I might love him.* Her heart was yearning to see him, simply to talk to him or be in the same room with him. Her short glimpse into his mind had revealed a deep, dark pit of sadness. Grief. There was a tragedy in his past, and she wanted to be the one to console him. Wasn't that the beginning of love? And if more happened . . . her heartbeat quickened. "I—I think I want to be with him."

Cora Lee's eyes lit up. "Vampire sex? Oh, gracious me. I have a feeling he would be very . . . adept."

Pamela nodded. "I believe so, too."

"Land sakes." Cora Lee glanced at the clock on Pamela's bedside table. "What are you waiting for? It's two in the morning."

"It should be five in Moscow." And still dark. She could teleport to his hunting lodge. If she dared.

AS SOON AS Mikhail turned off the water in the shower, he heard a noise in the bedroom next door. He stepped silently from the shower stall and picked up the battle-axe he'd left on top of the laundry hamper. As far as he knew, no Malcontent knew where his hunting lodge was located.

"Mikhail?" a soft voice called from the bedroom.

Pam? He cracked the door open. Her eyes instantly widened, and he realized he most likely looked like the brute she thought he was. His hair was loose and wet, his body still dripping, and his groin hidden behind a battle-axe still stained with blood from the recent battle.

She turned to face a bookcase, her cheeks flushed.

"Are you all right?" he asked. "Did you need more painkiller?"

"I'm fine." She fiddled with the sash at her waist. "If this is a bad time, I could come back—"

"No." What was she wearing? Some sort of night robe? He was suddenly glad the battle-axe was concealing his ever-growing reaction. "Don't go. I'll be right out."

When she nodded, he closed the door. What was she doing here? The sun would rise in about forty minutes. Her visit would have to be quick . . . unless she was intending to stay here for her death-sleep. In his bed.

He toweled off and grabbed a pair of jeans. No, too tight. His groin was already swollen. He pulled on a pair of flannel pants. Grabbing his towel, he stepped into his bedroom.

She'd found his treasure box and was peering through the glass lid.

His heart stilled. Out of all the books and mementos on his bookcase shelves, she'd zeroed in on the one thing that meant the most to him. Had she glimpsed it in his thoughts for the brief time their minds had been connected?

He pulled his hair over his shoulder and dried it with the towel. "Don't open it."

With a start, she put the box back on the shelf. "I beg your pardon. I didn't mean to pry."

He tossed the towel into the bathroom. "I've managed to preserve those flowers for over six hundred years."

"That's amazing." Her gaze drifted over his bare chest, then shifted back to the dried flowers in the box. "They must be very important to you."

"They are." He approached slowly. "My daughter picked them for me. She died that night."

Pam gasped. "I'm so sorry."

"The color has faded, but the flowers were a beautiful shade of lavender blue." He stopped beside her. "The same color as your eyes."

She winced. "I remind you of losing your daughter?"

"You remind me of the most joyful days of my life."

Her eyes widened. "Can you . . . tell me about her? What was her name?"

"Anya." He touched the glass cover on the box, tracing the outline of the stems and flowers. "She was bright and beautiful. Blond with blue eyes."

"Like you," Pam whispered.

He nodded. "She was murdered. Along with my wife."

Pam gasped and touched his arm. "I'm so sorry."

With a grimace, he stepped back. "Don't waste any sympathy for my wife. She invited the vampires in. She wanted them to transform her, so she could stay young and beautiful for all time."

He turned away from Pam's shocked face and paced across the room. "When the vampires invaded our house, they attacked me and tied me up. I was one mortal against ten vampires. I couldn't defeat them."

"Of course not."

He twisted his hair, wrapping it around his fist. "I couldn't protect my daughter. They fed on her, drained her dry. She was only six years old."

Pam approached him, her eyes glistening with pink tears. "I'm so sorry."

"My wife had made a deal with them. She sacrificed our daughter, an innocent child, in exchange for eternal life. But the vampires double-crossed her and laughed over her corpse. Then they told me to enjoy my pain for the rest of my measly life."

Pam shook her head. "I don't know how a mother could do that."

He sighed. "I blamed myself for centuries. I should have seen the evil in her. I should have taken my daughter somewhere safe."

"You mustn't blame yourself."

He smiled sadly at her. "Like you? You've been blaming yourself for past mistakes."

She nodded with a resigned look. "So what happened?"

"I spent three years hunting the vampires, but eventually I realized I couldn't compete with them as a mortal."

Pam grimaced. "So you became one of the creatures you hated?"

"It was the only way to avenge my daughter."

Her eyes glistened with tears. "You loved her so much."

"Don't cry." He touched her cheek. "It was a long time ago. And I've managed to kill a lot of bad vampires in the last six hundred years. That's a good thing, right?"

"Yes." Her tear-filled eyes regarded him with tenderness. "You are a good man, Mikhail."

His mouth twitched. "I thought I was a huge brute."

"No. You're . . . lovely." A tear tumbled down her cheek, and he caught it with his thumb.

"Pam." He leaned forward and pressed his lips against hers. She sighed sweetly against him, a sign of surrender, so he gathered her in his arms and kissed her thoroughly. By the time he was done, she was clinging to him and breathless.

"Mikhail," she whispered, leaning against his chest.

He rubbed a hand down her back. No undergarments that he could feel. Was she naked beneath her night-clothes? His groin twitched. "Pam, I want you."

With a gasp, she stepped back. "Really? You-you mean, tonight?"

"Yes. We have less than thirty minutes, but—"

"Oh, that's fine." She waved a hand. "Ten minutes is usually quite enough for me."

"Ten?" Ten hours could hardly suffice. Not when he'd wanted her for almost two hundred years.

"Yes." She pressed a hand to her chest and blushed. "I daresay this is rather exciting."

His vision turned pink. "We haven't actually started yet, but I appreciate the enthusiasm."

Her eyes widened at the sight of his eyes, now red and glowing. "Good heavens." She glanced around the room. "Do you mind if I make myself comfortable on your bed?"

His groin tightened. "Be my guest."

"Thank you. And if you could retire to another room— perhaps upstairs?"

"Excuse me?"

"I prefer to be alone."

His vision popped back to normal. "What?"

She winced. "I suppose I'll have to explain. You see, I . . ." She blushed. "This is rather embarrassing, but I don't like anyone to see me when I reach that . . . certain moment. I have an unfortunate tendency to thrash about."

He stifled a grin. "You . . . thrash?"

"In a most unseemly manner." She ducked her head, her blush deepening.

"I want to see that."

She gasped. "No! Absolutely not! Just because we're having sex, it doesn't mean you can invade my privacy!"

"*What?*" She wanted to have sex in two different rooms? Oh, hell no. He gave her an incredulous look. "Are you talking about vampire sex?"

She huffed. "Of course. We're vampires, aren't we?"

"We're a man and a woman."

"Obviously." She waved a dismissive hand. "But surely you agree that vampire sex is the only dignified way—"

"To hell with dignity. I want you naked. With me."

With a gasp, she stepped back. "But—but mortal sex is so . . . so . . ."

"Barbaric?"

"Invasive." She retreated another step. "You-you would expect to touch me."

"That's only the beginning." He stepped toward her. "I plan to caress you and kiss you and taste you all over. I want to hear you moan and scream. I want to see your face when you climax." His mouth curled up. "And I damn well want to see you thrash about."

"Good heavens," she whispered.

He gathered her into his arms and kissed her brow. "Let me make love to you."

"This is so much more than I expected." She splayed her hands on his chest. "I would be so . . . vulnerable."

"No more than I."

She gazed at him in wonder. "You're so fierce. How could I possibly make you vulnerable?"

"Pam, you have my heart."

She touched his cheek. "Oh, Mikhail."

"Is that a yes?"

When she nodded, he swept her up in his arms and carried her to his bed.

Chapter Six

"I HAVEN'T DONE it like this in ages," Pamela whispered, as he untied the sash on her silk wrapper.

"It's been a while for me, too." Mikhail peeled back the wrapper to reveal the sheer nightgown she'd worn underneath. "I can see through this." He brushed his fingers over a nipple.

She gasped, and her skin pebbled beneath the sheer fabric.

His mouth curled up. "Naughty woman, I think you came here to seduce me."

She had, but with vampire sex in mind. She was getting more than she had bargained for. Her breath caught when he unbuttoned her nightgown with vampire speed.

"I wish we could spend hours on this, but we're short on time." He lifted her into a sitting position.

"I understand." Even so, she felt extremely self-conscious when he slipped her wrapper and nightgown off her shoulders. He was very careful with her wounded arm, but it hardly registered. She could only think that her bare breasts were now exposed to his red and glowing eyes. No one had seen her naked since her late husband two hundred years ago.

And no one had confessed to loving her, either, in all that time. "I-I saw how you felt when our minds were connected." Would he say the words out loud? She would feel much more at ease if he did.

He said nothing, only pushed her back onto the bed and tugged her clothes down her hips and legs.

She covered her eyes, imagining his glowing eyes examining every inch of her body. What would he do next? Would he invade her without warning, like Max had done? And then after a few uncomfortable thrusts, it would all be over.

For the first time, she wondered if her late husband had been a selfish lover. She'd been completely innocent up to the wedding, so she'd had no one to compare him to. She only knew that in recent years, she'd enjoyed vampire sex more than anything he had done.

"Pam?"

She peeked between her fingers and found Mikhail stretched out beside her, studying her face.

His cheek dimpled. "Why are you hiding? Don't you know how beautiful you are?"

She lowered her hands. "I feel so exposed."

"You are." He brushed her hair back from her brow. "And I love you more than ever."

Her heart swelled. "Oh, Mikhail." She touched his

face, and blond whiskers tickled her fingertips. "I never knew you felt that way. Why did you keep it a secret?"

"You're so beautiful, I assumed you were selfish and vain like my late wife." He grimaced. "You should slap me for being a fool. I lost so much time when I could have been loving you."

She traced the outline of his strong jaw, then brushed a finger over his beautifully sculpted lips. "We can still have centuries together."

The red in his eyes darkened. "Good. For once I have claimed you, I will not give you up."

Her heart felt like it would burst with longing. "Mikhail." She wrapped her arms around his neck.

He kissed her tenderly and thoroughly till she grew comfortably relaxed with him, warm and pliant. Then his hands began to roam. And his mouth. The comfortable feeling quickly flamed into a fiery passion that sizzled through her veins, making her hot and frantic.

He was true to his word, kissing and tasting her all over. She moaned as he suckled on her breasts, gasped when his fingers discovered the wet heat between her legs.

He did things with his fingers she had never imagined. Soon she was thrashing about and not even caring. And when he burrowed his head between her legs, she cried out in shock. How barbaric! How . . . wonderfully wild. She writhed beneath him till she shattered with the strongest climax she'd ever experienced.

She was still pulsating with aftershocks when she felt the first tug of death-sleep. The sun was rising, and they were running out of time.

"Mikhail," she panted, reaching for him. He'd spent all their time pleasuring her. How could she not love such a dear man?

"Damn sun." He ripped off his pants and settled between her legs.

She gasped. He *was* huge. But even as fierce and powerful as he was, he couldn't keep the sun from rising. Another tug of death-sleep pulled at her.

He collapsed beside her and pulled her into his arms, his erection pressed against her stomach. "Tomorrow, you will be mine."

A sharp pain squeezed her chest as death-sleep claimed her. *Tomorrow,* she thought, as she fell into darkness.

THEY BOTH JOLTED awake at the same time.

Pam stared into his face, only inches away, and the enormity of her actions stole her breath away. She'd given herself to a man she hardly knew. True, the sex had been beyond her wildest imaginings, but she'd done more than have sex. She'd given him her heart.

His mouth curled up as his eyes turned red. "Shall we pick up where we left off?"

With a gasp, she felt his manhood swelling against her belly. "I-I should eat first. I'm quite peckish when I awaken."

"Then bite me." He pulled his hair over one shoulder to expose his neck.

She gulped. She'd never bitten a vampire before. Not

even her late husband. And Mikhail was six hundred years old. No doubt his blood would be extremely rich and powerful. It was shocking that he'd even offer it to her.

What a sweet and generous man he was. No wonder she'd fallen for him so quickly. Still, it was frightening to think how vulnerable she was now. "Don't—don't you have some bottles in your fridge?"

"Yes." He tickled her breasts with the tail end of his hair. "But I want to keep you in bed all night."

"Don't we have a mission to go on?"

"We'll take the night off." He kissed her mouth, then trailed kisses down her neck to her breasts.

She shivered when he drew a nipple into his mouth. How could she resist such a man? But if he claimed her, he would never let her go. He'd said so himself.

A frisson of panic skittered through her. Was she ready for this? Mikhail might have waited two hundred years for this, but for her, it had only been a few nights. "I-I should go home to . . . freshen up."

"It's still daylight there." He shifted to the other breast.

Oh, bother. He was right. It would be a few hours before she could teleport to London. "I should have brought my costume with me."

"It's missing a sleeve." He nibbled a path to her belly button.

She shivered. "I have a spare."

He lifted his head. "A what?"

"A spare costume. And another box of ninja stars." She gasped as a hunger pain cramped her stomach.

"Here." He offered his wrist.

"No." She shook her head. "I don't want to weaken you before our mission."

"There is no mission."

"You mean you finished destroying the human-trafficking ring last night?"

"No, I mean you won't be doing any more missions."

"*What?*" Another hunger pain seized her, doubling her over.

"Wait." He jumped out of bed, and returned a few seconds later with a bottle of Blardonnay and two glasses. He filled a glass and handed it to her.

She guzzled it down fast.

"Better?" He refilled her glass.

She nodded and drank some more. As the pain subsided, she let her gaze wander over him. She'd been too overwhelmed with passion the night before to get a good look at him. He was beautiful, golden and muscular. He drank from his glass, his head tilted back, his long hair loose down his back.

She stroked a hand down his hair, and a wave of desire swept over her. It would be so easy, so tempting to fall back against the pillows and let him make love to her.

But he'd said she wouldn't be going on any more missions.

He set his empty glass on the bedside table, then reached for her. "Where were we?"

"I'm afraid we were about to quarrel."

His mouth twitched. "I thought we were going to make love." He leaned toward her to kiss her.

She stopped him with a palm against his chest. "You said I couldn't go on any more missions."

"Pam." He brushed her hair over her shoulders. "You're not trained well enough for battle."

"I disagree. I studied at the premier fencing academy in London. And I took classes three nights every week at a martial-arts—"

"You're not ready. You were wounded last night." His hand skimmed over her bandage. "There's no need for you to risk yourself."

She scooted back. "There is a need. I explained it to you before. I thought you understood."

"I do understand. You wanted to prove that you wouldn't abandon your friends. You did that. You showed us how brave you are."

"Once isn't enough! I don't intend to scurry back to my parlor and embroider handkerchiefs for another hundred years. This is the new me—VampWoman!"

His jaw shifted. "The new you will end up getting killed."

"I will not. The other women fight evil, so I can, too. Jack lets Lara help out. Olivia assists Robby. And Emma does things, too."

"Lara was a police officer; Olivia was with the FBI; and Emma was with the CIA. They have years of training. If you want to go about this safely, you will join MacKay S and I and get the training you need. But even then, if you're not ready for battle, you will not be allowed to fight. I know for a fact that Lara and Olivia do not engage in vampire battles. They work more in the area of investigation."

With a sigh, Pam reached for her wrapper. "I did apply at MacKay S and I. Six months ago. They turned me down."

Mikhail sat back. "I didn't know."

She slipped on the wrapper. "That's when I decided to be a free agent and take care of my own training. I suppose if you won't let me fight with you, I'll have to go solo."

"What?" He grabbed her arm. "Are you suicidal?"

"I'm determined."

His grip tightened. "I won't allow it."

She pulled away from him. "You don't own me!"

"No, I don't." He gritted his teeth. "But I cannot bear for you to be injured. The last time I lost someone I love, it nearly killed me."

Tears blurred her vision. "I'm really sorry about your daughter, but I can't give up my dream and do nothing for the rest of my life. I thought you understood how important this is to me."

"I thought you understood how important you are to me. You have my heart."

"I didn't ask for it!" She winced. Oh God, she shouldn't have blurted that out. He had instantly flinched and let go of her.

He climbed out of bed, his face harsh and his eyes cold. "My apologies for burdening you with something you do not want."

He stalked off to the bathroom and shut the door.

Her chest seized with a sudden pain. What had she done? She hadn't meant to hurt him. She only wanted go on missions with him. She wanted to prove herself strong and brave. What was so wrong with that?

Instead, she'd proven herself a terrible fool.

Tears ran down her cheeks. What should she do? Apologize and tell him she loved him? Did she?

Oh, God, yes. She must love him for this to hurt so horribly.

She slipped out of bed, ready to dash to the bathroom and confess her love. But what then? Would she be expected to give up her plans?

She wandered to the bathroom and knocked on the door.

No answer.

"Mikhail?" She knocked again. "Can we . . . talk?"

No answer.

She opened the door, and the room was empty. He must have thrown on some clothes and teleported away. He was probably at Zoltan's, getting ready for the next mission.

She was tempted to follow, but how could she show up there, wearing nothing but a thin wrapper? Besides, she didn't know what to say. He wasn't likely to back down, and she didn't want to give up her dream. They were at an impasse, and she didn't know how to fix it.

All she knew was that she loved him. She wanted an eternity with him.

But she might have discovered it too late.

Chapter Seven

A week later . . .

"HAVE A SEAT." Angus MacKay motioned to an armchair in the parlor of his London townhouse.

"Thank you." Pamela sat and wedged her small handbag into the chair next to her. After receiving a brief phone call and invitation from Angus's wife twenty minutes earlier, she'd quickly dressed in a modern, professional-looking suit designed by Jean-Luc Echarpe. She wasn't sure what Angus and Emma wanted, but since they were the owners of MacKay Security and Investigation, and he was Coven Master of the British Isles, she wanted to look her best.

Angus paced across the parlor, his blue-and-green-plaid kilt swishing about his knees. "I hear ye've been busy of late, helping the lads in Albania."

"Yes." So this was the purpose for her sudden invitation. The men must have complained about her interference with their mission, and Angus was going to berate her over it.

She gripped her hands together. Was Mikhail behind this? Was this how he intended to keep her safe at home and hopelessly bored for the next few centuries?

Angus stopped pacing and frowned at her. "I heard ye were injured in battle. Are ye all right now?"

"I'm fine. Thank you." Pamela shifted in her chair. "How are you and Emma?"

"We're very well." Emma strode into the room, carrying a tray. "Would you like a cup of hot Chocolood?"

Pamela nodded. "That would be lovely. Thank you."

While Emma poured two cups from a teapot, Angus helped himself to a glass of Blissky at the sidebar.

"Here you are." Emma passed her a cup, then sat near her on the settee. "I'm sure you're wondering why we invited you here."

"Yes." Pamela sipped some Chocolood, then set her cup down before her trembling hands could betray her.

Angus plunked his glass of Blissky on the coffee table, then sat next to his wife. "We received a detailed report on your recent activities." He arched a brow. "Vamp-Woman, ye call yerself?"

"Yes." Heat invaded her cheeks. She'd thought her idea excellent for the past six months, but now she feared others would see it as an irresponsible prank. She steeled herself for the berating soon to begin.

"I'm afraid we made a mistake not hiring you before,"

Emma said with an apologetic smile. "We didn't realize how determined you are."

Pamela blinked. She wasn't in trouble?

Angus leaned forward, his elbows resting on his knees. "We'd like to hire you now if ye're still interested."

Her mouth dropped open.

"Of course, we doona think ye're properly trained for battle," Angus continued.

"But we will train you," Emma added. "Vigorously. Are you up to that?"

Pamela snapped her mouth shut and nodded. Her pulse quickened. She was going to work for MacKay S and I!

Emma took a sip from her cup of Chocolood. "You worked as a bartender at Vanda's club in New York, correct?"

"Yes."

"How do ye feel about spying?" Angus asked.

Pamela's heart skipped a beat, but she sat up straighter. "How soon can I start?"

Angus chuckled. "Let me explain the plan first. The Malcontents are in disarray, with Casimir and Corky gone. No clear leader has surfaced, and information is scarce. We know of a nightclub in Moscow they like to frequent, so there's a good chance we could gain valuable information there."

Pamela nodded. Good heavens! Did they expect her to work in Moscow?

"It's a tragic place." Emma grimaced. "The mortals who go there are enthralled to the point that they enjoy being fed on. Eventually, they run out of blood and are cast aside like empty milk jugs. And regrettably, there are more mortals ready to take their place. You would have to witness that but do nothing to help them, or your cover would be blown. Then you would be in serious trouble."

Pamela swallowed hard. "I understand."

"Ye would work at the bar, serving the puir mortals, and listening in on the Malcontents," Angus said.

Pamela slumped. This wasn't going to work. "I'm afraid I can't help you. I don't know any Russian."

"That's why you're perfect for the job." Emma gave her an encouraging smile. "The Malcontents will feel free to discuss their affairs in front of you."

"They will most likely test you to make sure ye doona understand them," Angus warned her. "They might say some verra nasty things to you to see if ye react."

"Just ignore them and go about your job, serving the mortals," Emma said. "You'll be wired, so their conversations will be heard by our Russian operative."

Pamela's heart lurched. "You mean . . . Mikhail?"

"Aye," Angus replied. "He'll be yer partner."

She shook her head. "He'll never agree to it. He doesn't want me doing anything dangerous."

"Dear." Emma reached over and touched her arm. "This was Mikhail's idea. He's the one who convinced us to hire you."

Pamela sat back, stunned. Mikhail was behind this?

"He'll be listening in while you're at work," Emma added. "If there's an emergency situation, he can teleport to you instantly."

Angus stood. "What do ye say, lass? Do ye want the job?"

"I . . ." Her heart thundered in her ears. A job with Mikhail? Night after night?

"Perhaps you would like to discuss the matter with him first?" Emma asked.

"Mikhail!" Angus shouted.

Pamela gasped. He was here? She glanced at the entrance to the parlor just as his large frame filled the open doorway.

Her heart clenched with longing. How many tears had she shed the past week, believing she'd lost him forever? Even now, her eyes filled with tears, and she squeezed them shut. This was not the time to fall apart. She needed to show Angus and Emma how strong she could be.

Taking a deep breath, she opened her eyes and eased to her feet. Mikhail strode into the room, his eyes focused on her with an intensity that made her skin prickle with gooseflesh.

Emma grabbed her husband's arm and pulled him toward the entrance. "We should give them some privacy."

"They're staring at each other something fierce," Angus whispered.

"Shh." Emma herded him through the door and shut it.

Pamela drew in a shaky breath. Over the past week, she'd envisioned meeting Mikhail many times. Sometimes, she imagined herself fussing at him and taking a tough stance. Other times, she would confess her love and throw herself into his arms. But far too often, she had burst into tears for fear he would never want to see her again.

Now the time had come. He was here, and she didn't know what to say.

He stopped about ten feet away. "You look thin. And pale."

She blinked away the tears in her eyes. Dear Mikhail. No false flattery from him, just the blunt truth. It was one of many things she loved about him. He was thinner, too. His cheekbones and the line of his jaw were sharper, and his eyes had a haunted look about them. "I didn't realize you were in London."

"I arrived an hour ago to present the plan to Angus. He told you about it?"

She nodded. "He said we would be . . . business partners."

His mouth thinned. "That would be a start."

A start for what? "I suppose I might need to live closer to the bar where I'll be working."

"I have a townhouse in Moscow. You're welcome to live there." A pained look crossed his eyes. "There's a spare bedroom."

She winced inwardly. "Then this is a . . . business proposition?"

"Yes."

She shook her head, confused. "I don't know why you're doing this. You made it clear you didn't want me doing anything dangerous, but now you've—"

"You don't know why?" He stepped toward her. "Isn't it obvious? I'm trying desperately to get you back into my life. I'm so desperate I'm willing to put you in a dangerous situation that will scare the hell out of me every night. And I'm willing to endure that torture just so you'll be near me."

Her heart swelled. "Mikhail—"

"I know I rushed you. I've been in love with you for almost two hundred years, but it was new for you. I should have courted you, waited for you." He slashed the air angrily with his hand. "I *will* wait for you. No matter how long it takes."

"Mikhail." Tears ran down her cheeks. "The wait is over. I love you."

His eyes widened, then he grabbed her and pulled her into his arms. "Oh, God, Pam. I thought you hated me. I thought I'd messed everything up."

"No, I messed up." She touched his face. "I didn't mean to hurt you. I'm sorry."

He wiped the tears from her cheeks. "I love you so much. I should have never let you go."

"It's okay." She wrapped her arms around his neck. "I didn't realize how much I loved you till I had lost you."

He kissed her brow. "We can't let the Malcontents know you're with me. It would blow your cover. So we'll have to keep our marriage a secret."

She blinked. "Marriage?"

He winced. "I keep going too fast. Don't worry. We'll take it slower this time."

She shook her head, smiling. "I'll beat you up if you stick me in that spare bedroom. I can do it, you know. I'm VampWoman."

With a laugh, he hugged her tight. "You're *my* woman."

A Forever Love

Pamela Palmer

Chapter One

"CATCH IT, CATCH it, catch it, *yes!*"

Elizabeth Bryant jumped from her seat as the Washington Redskins scored on a beautiful touchdown pass in the last ten seconds of the game to win. "Hail to the Redskins!" she sang at the top of her lungs, joining her friends. At the Skins' win, high fives exploded around the small apartment living room, followed by several victory kisses between her girlfriends and their husbands and fiancés.

Elizabeth's date, Tim, grabbed her around the waist and pulled her close, laying one on her. She stiffened before she could catch herself, then forced herself to relax and kiss him back. It wasn't the first time they'd kissed— she'd been dating him for about a month, but the tender he-man assault was just too much like something Lukas would have done. She didn't appreciate the attempt or the reminder. She'd *belonged* in Lukas's arms. She didn't belong in Tim's. And the thought made her chest ache.

Pulling away, she made a quick excuse and headed for the kitchen. *Damn you, Lukas Olsson. Why can't I forget you?* And she *needed* to forget him. Two years ago, he'd left her, suddenly, without so much as a good-bye. She should be completely over him by now. She ought to hate him.

The trouble was, deep inside, the flicker of hope that he'd someday return refused to die. Because Lukas Olsson had been full of secrets. When she'd asked what he did for a living, he'd only ever given her vague answers—the kind of answers top secret types always offered in this town. CIA. NSA. Not only was Washington, D.C., overrun by politicians; it was crawling with spies.

In the eight months she and Lukas had dated, she'd only ever seen him late at night. And while, logically, she knew that that probably meant he'd had another girlfriend, or even a wife, hidden away somewhere, and that he'd left her at the risk of getting caught, she couldn't let go of the hope that he'd been sent on some last-minute top secret assignment that demanded communication silence, a mission that was taking longer than he'd expected. And that someday he'd waltz back into her life, sweep her into his arms, and kiss her senseless.

But with each passing month, it became harder to hold on to that hope. The likelihood that their relationship had never meant as much to him as it had to her became greater and greater. In all probability, Lukas had taken the coward's way out and disappeared rather than facing her with that truth.

Logic said that he was gone and wasn't coming back, and the sooner she accepted that and forgot about him,

the happier she'd be. But the heart was a hopelessly il-
logical organ.

As she entered the kitchen, Steph caught up with her,
her eyes at once sympathetic and a little frustrated.

"I thought you liked this one," she whispered.

Elizabeth shrugged. "Tim's a great guy."

"But he's not Lukas." Steph's warm fingers closed
around her forearm. "Sweetheart, *no one* is ever going to
be Lukas."

Elizabeth's lips twisted ruefully. "Trust me, I know
that." There would only ever be one Lukas Olsson. With
the blond hair and blue eyes of his Nordic ancestors and
the build of a linebacker . . . or Viking marauder . . . Lukas
had been gorgeous in a powerful, masculine, wholly un-
civilized way. And that smile of his . . . oh, that smile
could whip an entire roomful of women into a frenzy of
delight or jealousy, depending on who was on the receiving end.

Elizabeth sighed. "There's no spark with Tim, and I
can't keep pretending there is." And, Heaven help her,
there'd been sparks with Lukas. Fireworks bright enough
to light up the night sky.

She'd thought he adored her. He'd acted as if he
adored her, as if he'd been every bit as much in love with
her as she'd been with him, even if they'd never actually
said the words. They'd dated, made love, and spent every
night together for almost eight months.

Damn him. She *knew* he'd cared for her, at least a little
bit. No man was that good an actor for that long. But he
obviously hadn't cared enough.

Releasing a hard sigh, she grabbed a Corona and the bottle opener.

Steph watched her open her beer, her expression soft. "I can't believe I'm going to say this, but there's more to life than sparks, sweetie. Tim's nice, he's good-looking, and he's a lawyer. And let's face it, a lawyer's salary would go a long way toward balancing your teacher's pay."

Elizabeth snorted. There was that.

But as Tim walked her back to her apartment an hour later, Elizabeth knew she couldn't see him again. They'd dated a month, and she'd put off having sex with him as long as she could. She'd already learned from experience that there was nothing lonelier in the world than sharing that ultimate intimacy with the wrong man when she knew there was a right one.

Even if, in all probability, the right one was gone from her life for good.

When Tim tried to take her hand, she feigned ignorance, and a chill she didn't feel, and crossed her arms instead. At the base of the stairs to her apartment building, she turned to him.

Wry disappointment twisted his expression. "This isn't working, is it?"

"I'm sorry. I like you, Tim, but . . ."

He nodded. And sighed. "I know."

Giving in to impulse, she kissed his cheek. "You're going to be a great catch for the right woman. I'm sorry she can't be me."

An hour later, ready for bed, Elizabeth eyed the drawer of her bedside table. *Don't touch it,* she urged herself.

Leave it alone and go to sleep. But the temptation was just too great, and she lifted out the framed picture that Steph had snapped the weekend before Lukas disappeared. With a beer in one hand, he'd pulled Elizabeth against him in that way that screamed *mine*. She'd looked up, laughing. And the expression on his face as he'd grinned down at her had been so full of adoration. Of *love*.

How could he have left her without a single word?

"Damn you, Lukas Olsson." As she stared at his beloved face, her heart squeezed, tears burning her eyes. "Why do I still miss you so much?" She'd found that most wonderful and elusive of treasures—a forever love. Then lost it, lost *him*, in a haze of mystery, questions, and uncertainty.

Despite that, if she had it to do over, she wouldn't change a thing. Knowing Lukas, loving him, even for that short time, was worth all the doubts and misery and loneliness that had followed. A loneliness, she feared, that might well last a lifetime.

Chapter Two

STEPH WAS WAITING in front of Elizabeth's apartment the next morning, two Starbucks lattes in her hands. The September morning was just cool enough to hint at autumn's impending arrival, the sun bright, the sky a brilliant cobalt. Elizabeth's cotton cardigan felt good, though by the time school was out, she wouldn't need it.

With a grin, she adjusted her purse on her shoulder and took one of the lattes. "You are the best friend, *evah.*"

Steph laughed as the two started down Wisconsin Avenue NW toward Georgetown and Adams Middle School, where Steph taught music and Elizabeth math. The weather was lovely, the road narrow and tree-lined, the architecture quaint, filling her with pleasure despite the heavy traffic and morning crush.

"I figured the morning after a breakup deserved something special."

"And how do you know Tim and I broke up?" Elizabeth asked primly. Steph always knew what Elizabeth was going to do before she did it.

"The writing was on the wall. You did break up with him, didn't you?"

"Yeah." Elizabeth sighed. "I did."

They walked side by side, past the Naval Observatory, the sidewalk crowded with people heading to work, or looking for coffee, or just meandering with a dog on a leash.

"What are you doing after school?" Steph asked. "I'm thinking about checking out the new health club. Come with me. We can ogle the hotties together."

Elizabeth snorted. "You're married."

"Yeah, but I'm not dead, girlie. Garrett doesn't mind in the least if I work myself into a lather. Not as long as I come to him for relief."

With a smile, Elizabeth took a bracing sip of hot latte goodness. Hazelnut, just the way she loved it. "I'm up for a workout as long as you don't try to fix me up with anyone." Before Steph could profess innocence of any such plan, Elizabeth continued, "I didn't have time to check the news this morning. Anything interesting that I missed?"

Steph sobered. "Another person's gone missing, this one down by the Navy Yard. He was on his way to a Nats game, and his friends say he just disappeared. Which is impossible, of course."

"What does that make, now? Fifteen, sixteen?" People all over the city had disappeared over the past few months, some in broad daylight. Some purportedly into thin air.

"Nineteen. The most popular theories are space-alien abductions, or the rapture, though if it's the latter, it's taking forever and leaving most of the superreligious behind. They're pissed. Garrett's worried, but I keep reminding him that nineteen out of well over a million means my odds of being snatched are small enough to be approaching zero."

"You sound like the math teacher."

"Am I right?"

"You are. Still, I feel bad for the families left wondering where they went." She had a sense of what that felt like, the void a missing loved one created in one's life. The never knowing where they'd gone or why, or if they were ever coming back. It had crossed her mind that Lukas's disappearance might be related though it seemed unlikely, given that the spate of disappearances had started only a couple of months ago.

"So share the deets on the health club," Elizabeth said, steering the conversation to a less depressing topic.

"They've got a grand opening special . . ."

As Steph talked, and they walked the mile to school past colorful Georgetown row-house shops, Elizabeth sipped her latte and drank in the sights and sounds of the hectic morning rush, consciously embracing all that she loved about her life. And there was much to love— her friends and family, her math kids, the teaching itself, and the constant, familiar bustle of the city she'd grown up in.

For eight months, she'd been more than just happy. She'd felt . . . complete . . . as if her world and her life had finally snapped into full, brilliant focus. Though, if she were honest, that brilliant focus had always suffered more than a handful of shadows. Shadows in the form of Lukas's secrets. She'd never called him on his unwillingness to share more about himself, hoping that eventually he'd trust her with the truth. Instead, he'd left without a word. And she'd never quite be the same again. Not with her heart now missing an elemental piece.

If she was lucky, someday another man . . . *the right man* . . . would come along and fill the hole Lukas had left. But deep inside, her heart stubbornly insisted that Lukas Olsson was the only *right man* for her.

As they reached P Street, the crosswalk flashed with the red-handed "wait" sign, and Elizabeth took another sip of coffee. Steph had a way of shifting conversational directions on a dime, and they were now talking about the new fall television season.

"You've got to see it," Steph enthused about yet another amateur singing hour.

Elizabeth smiled. "I'll set it to record on my DVR when I get home."

The light changed to "walk," and they started forward again. But halfway across P Street, a cool draft of air shivered over Elizabeth's skin.

And with her next step, the lights went out.

Chapter Three

ELIZABETH FROZE. HER pulse took flight as the darkness, *the silence,* pressed in all around her. She could see nothing. Hear . . . *nothing.*

How? *How . . . ?*

A second ago, she'd been walking across P Street beside Steph in the bright sunshine. Now . . . *this.* Had she passed out? Was she having a seizure, or a stroke? Good grief, had she . . . *died?*

No. Not unless her latte had traveled with her. Her Starbucks cup remained clasped warm in her hand.

"Steph?" Her voice cracked with fear.

Out of the corner of her eye, something coalesced from the darkness. Slowly, a landscape began to materialize around her. No, no, it was just her eyes beginning to adjust to a dark that was not, as she'd first thought, complete—the dark of a dangerously stormy day. Or dusk.

All around her stood buildings. Not the buildings that should be here but something entirely different—small houses and large, a general store, a . . . *stable*? It looked like a ghost town from a bygone era, deserted. Crumbling.

Trees rose among the buildings and houses, as if trying to reclaim forest once stolen by the town. But the trees were winter bare, twisted, some half-disintegrated, as if they, too, had been left to die.

What is this place? A chill skated over her skin, part shock, part true chill, for the air was much cooler here than it had been in . . . the place she belonged. *How in the name of all that's holy did I get here?* It smelled different— woodsy in a dry, aged way, and dusty. Dust overlaid with decay.

Clutching her Starbucks cup with both hands, she turned around slowly, her heart trying to break its way out of her chest.

This can't be happening. "I have to get to class," she murmured, as if whatever mysterious hand had plucked her out of her life would say, "Oh, sorry. Of course I'll send you back."

Is this Heaven?

A sound caught her ear, blasting through the panic pounding at her eardrums. *A man's scream.*

Maybe it's Hell.

Her heart thudded so hard, her entire body began to quake. She felt light-headed, dizzy. *Don't pass out. You can't pass out.*

Another sound broke through, the dull clip-clop of

horses. Multiple horses, much closer than the scream. Were the ghosts of this place coming for her? If so, she'd be the one screaming soon.

The warmth seeping into her now-shaking hands reminded her that she still held her latte. Gripping the precious cup, she sipped gingerly, relishing the tasty slide of warmth down her throat. The familiar taste grounded her, if only a little, reminding her of Steph, of their walk, of their discussion . . .

The nineteen missing.

Oh my God. I'm number twenty.

Her face turned to ice. Her head began to pound as one thought broke free of the dozens swirling inside. If Lukas finally came back, he wouldn't find her. Now she was the one who'd disappeared.

"No," she breathed, her mind turning to steel. "I'm not staying here."

There had to be a way back home.

And she had to find it.

Chapter Four

ELIZABETH TOOK ANOTHER bracing sip of her quickly cooling coffee, then started forward. No good could come of standing in the middle of the street, especially with the sound of the horses drawing nearer. Instinct urged her to find a place to hide until she saw what manner of people . . . or creatures . . . rode those horses. But where?

She had no idea what this place was. The streets were laid out just the same as Georgetown's, but the buildings were all wrong. They appeared not only decrepit but *old*. As if the buildings she knew had been replaced with their predecessors. Or as if they'd never replaced their predecessors at all.

How is that possible?

As she neared the sidewalk, another thought occurred to her. If she was one of the missing, where were the others? Were they the ones on horseback? Or the ones screaming?

Her stomach quivered.

The sound of the horses grew louder, and she stepped up her pace, running toward the nearest door, praying it offered sanctuary and not greater danger. But when she reached for the knob, she found it locked tight. Glancing at the windows, she shied away. They'd been shattered, leaving deadly, jagged edges like razor-sharp teeth ready to devour anyone foolish enough to try to climb through.

Strikeout. She'd have to hide behind the house instead. But as she retraced her steps to the sidewalk, three horses and their riders turned onto the street. She saw them. Worse, they clearly saw her, for they rode straight toward her, closing the distance fast, the beasts' hooves kicking up dust in the twilight air.

Her primal self screamed at her to run. Her logical mind scoffed at the notion. She didn't stand a snowball's chance in hell of outrunning them. Not only were there three of them, on horseback, but they knew where they were. And she didn't have a clue.

Sometimes, the best defense was a good offense. Sometimes, it was the only defense. Swallowing hard, she crossed her arms over her chest, careful not to spill her coffee, and waited for their arrival as if they were three young students late to class, and not . . . whatever they really were.

The men slowed their mounts to a walk as they reached her, fanning out around her as they pulled up, eyeing her with smiles and speculation that made her skin crawl. At least it was nice to know her instincts . . . the ones that had told her to run . . . had probably been correct. If only she'd stood a chance of getting away.

Taking a studiously nonchalant sip of her coffee with a badly shaking hand, she studied them, trying to hide just how scared she really was. Two of the men were dressed alike in what appeared, in the low light, to be tan pants and long-sleeved black shirts with tight cuffs and billowing sleeves, reminding her of pirate garb from some old movie. Adding to that image were the swords strapped to their waists. But other than their garb and weapons, those two looked nothing alike. One had skin as black as night, his hair hanging long around a face pierced in more than a dozen places—through the eyebrows, the nose, the lip. A face devoid of softness, devoid of humanity. The other's skin appeared pale as moonlight though most was hidden beneath a full, bushy, black beard.

The third rider . . . *holy cow*. His hair glowed. *Glowed* like a black opal. He appeared considerably younger than the other two, maybe no more than early twenties, and he, at least, watched her with something approaching sympathy. Which meant she probably needed it.

Oh, she was in trouble.

"You're a pretty one," the dark-skinned swordsmen said, then suddenly . . . *literally* . . . disappeared off his horse. Before her jaw could drop, he reappeared an arm's length in front of her.

Elizabeth jumped back with a squeak, nearly dropping her latte. Her entire body began to quake.

The man threw his head back with a look of such pleasure that she wondered what kind of drug he was on. Or what he was imagining doing to her. Her breath lodged in her throat, and she started to back away. The nicker of a horse at her back reminded her there were three of them, and she was going nowhere.

"I think I'll claim you for my own, pretty one," the male in front of her said, his head straightening, dark lashes sweeping up to reveal . . .

The Starbucks finally slipped through her fingers, but she barely noticed, barely heard the splat or felt the splash of liquid against her pant legs as she stared at his eyes . . . dark eyes now centered with a perfect white circle, a white pupil.

Her shock apparently pleased him, for he grinned, revealing long, sharp incisors. *Fangs.*

Her breath left her altogether. "Who are you?" she gasped, her voice quavering like a twelve-year-old boy's in the presence of a twelve-year-old girl. "What is this place?"

The man's smile widened, his look of pleasure deepening, his fangs growing longer still.

"I'm your new master, pretty one. And this place? Washington, V.C. Vamp City."

Chapter Five

"*VAMP . . . ?*" ELIZABETH STARED at the man with the white-pupiled eyes. *And the fangs.* "As in *vampire?*" Her voice shot up, nearly to a squeak.

This isn't happening. Vampires aren't real. Everyone knows they're not real.

Suddenly, an arm snaked around her from behind, pinning her back against a hard chest. The brush of beard against her hair told her which of the other two had her.

Elizabeth struggled against his iron hold, his arm pressing so hard against her shoulders she gasped with pain. "You're hurting me." But he didn't seem to care.

The pierced man's white-pupiled eyes lit with fury. "Mine," he snarled.

"I say she isn't," the man at her back growled. "But I'm willing to share. Let me take the first bite."

Bite? Elizabeth felt the blood drain from her face

and was almost glad for the arm restraining her because without it, she feared her knees were going to fail her.

The hoofbeats of another horse caught her attention.

"Hold!" The voice, not the youth's, called from a short distance. A voice that sounded wonderfully, achingly familiar, as if she'd conjured it up in this desperate moment.

A tiny flare of hope had her head snapping up as the fourth horseman approached, deep in the twilight shadows. All she could make out was a form big enough and broad-shouldered enough to be Lukas's. As he drew closer, she could tell the hair was a little longer, in need of a haircut. Logic told her it wasn't he, it couldn't be. Her agitated mind was merely attempting to overlay his image on the male who approached, the image of a savior. A hero.

It wasn't Lukas.

But as he drew closer, and she finally saw the strong jaw and high cheekbones of the face that had haunted her for two years, her knees gave way.

"Lukas," she gasped.

How was this possible?

He was dressed in a black shirt and tan pants, the same as the other pair, two swords strapped to his back, their hilts rising from behind his shoulders like wings.

The man she loved pulled his horse to a stop beside the male with the pierced face and stared at her with an expression she'd never seen, his mouth hard, his eyes at once cool as frost and angry as hell.

Her heart began to shatter.

"I've been searching for you, Elizabeth," he snapped.

Her eyes narrowed with confusion. "What? *Here?*"

"No way," the male at her back exclaimed, tightening his hold on her until she cried out with the pain shooting through her chest and shoulders. "You're not claiming her, Lukas. She came in on the sunbeam, and don't try to deny it—she's got Starbucks. She didn't get *that* in Vamp City."

"She was my slave in the real world," Lukas said smoothly. *Slave?* "I expected her to find her way to me before this."

"She's not your slave."

"She knows my name, doesn't she?" His expression was so hard. Cold blue eyes pinned her. "Are you mine?"

She stared at him, her heart thundering. Yes, she'd been his. The old Lukas's. She did not know *this* man.

"You left me." The words came out unbidden, as raw as the pain in her heart.

For a swift second, she thought she saw that pain mirrored in his eyes, but a moment later, he stared at her once more through hard, blue crystals.

"*Are you mine?*"

"Yes!"

"Yes, *master*," he snapped.

This was *not* the man she knew. Yet at the very first sight of him, her heart had begun, very slowly, to unfurl, to blossom, and it continued to do so.

Her heart was an idiot.

"I saw her first," the pierced male grumbled. "I should at least get a taste of her."

Lukas swung down off his horse far slower than the

bearded man had, his movements deliberate, threatening. And she didn't think the show was for her.

"Release her." Lukas's gaze pinned the man at her back. "No one touches what is mine."

In the blink of an eye, the arm across her shoulders disappeared. In the blink of another, Lukas was beside her, his hand gripping her upper arm. Too fast. Either she was suffering some kind of head trauma, or they were moving *too damned fast.*

Her head felt suddenly full of helium, and she began to sway. Lukas swept her up as if she weighed nothing, and she grabbed at her purse as it slipped off her shoulder. He strode to his horse, deposited her on its back, and swung up behind her.

As his arm slipped around her waist, as he pulled her back against the chest she'd once loved so much, she finally found herself in the one place she'd longed to be for two years. Once more in Lukas's arms.

But instead of the joyous reunion she'd imagined, she was shaking with shock. And fear. Lukas Olsson was not the man she'd thought he was.

She wasn't certain he was a man at all.

Chapter Six

"BACK TO OUR search," Lukas commanded, as if he was the leader of this bunch. "We don't want to be anywhere near this block if the sunbeam breaks through again."

The two males who'd threatened her mounted, and the four horsemen started down the road, Lukas in front, Elizabeth snug against his chest.

She was so confused, her mind a tangle of conflicting emotions. She was furious, and hurt, and terrified. And yet her heart refused to be silent as it rejoiced that she'd found Lukas at last. Part of her wanted to turn around and kiss him senseless; another part wanted to punch him in the mouth. And the biggest part wanted to leap off the horse and run like crazy.

The arm pinning her ensured she did none of those things. All she could do was pray that the man she'd fallen in love with—the kind, loving Lukas who'd been so good to her—hadn't been a complete lie, that he was still in there somewhere. Whatever soft feelings he might have once felt toward her might be her only chance of survival.

"Do you really think we're going to find the sorceress all the way out here?" Pierced-face grumbled. "We're in fucking nowhere Georgetown. No one's lived here in decades."

So they really were in Georgetown? In what dimension?

"Which would make it the perfect place to hide," the bearded one countered. "We've already flushed a dozen runaways out of hiding. We could still get lucky." The lurid tone in his voice sent another chill down Elizabeth's spine.

They took a right on . . . M Street? It would be M Street if this really were Georgetown. The streets were definitely laid out the same, but the buildings weren't right. Not at all. What happened to the colorful row houses that were the hallmark of Georgetown?

She stared around in consternation. What *was* this place?

They rode another block before Lukas pulled up. He dismounted, then turned to her, his back to his companions. As his gaze caught hers, emotion flared in those once-beloved blue eyes—anger and dismay, and something more. Something softer. Something that gave her hope that the man she'd loved wasn't entirely gone.

Her breath turned shallow.

Breaking eye contact, he pulled her off the horse and set her on her feet beside him. "Give me your purse." When she did, he stuffed it into one of his saddlebags.

"Spread out," Lukas commanded. The two older males each headed for a different deserted, crumbling house along the street. The kid with the glowing hair accompanied the pierced one. Lukas took her wrist as if she were a difficult student in need of a chat with the principal and led her across the street toward what appeared to have been some kind of general store.

Once upon a time, he'd have taken her hand, lacing his cool fingers between hers. The thought flared with new meaning, with fresh understanding. He'd always been cool to the touch—his hands, his face, even his body, though he'd always assured her he didn't feel cold.

No wonder he'd only ever come to her after dark. Vampires couldn't handle sunlight.

Dear God.

Memories continued to cascade through her mind— the way he was always gone by morning. Always. *The marks on her neck . . .*

Her fingers rose, her flesh going cold, as she remembered how she'd often . . . *always?* . . . awakened with a couple of red spots on the side of her neck when she was dating him. They usually faded by noon, then reappeared the next morning. She'd never figured out what they were. Then Lukas had disappeared and, with him, the spots.

Bite marks?

How could any of this be real?

Lukas tried to open the door, but it was locked. Without a moment's hesitation, he lifted a foot and kicked in the door as if it were made of cardboard. He ushered her into a room that, in the dim light, did appear to have once been a store though the goods had long since been removed.

None too gently, Lukas pulled her around the corner and pushed her back against the wall, staring down at her with a look as different from the one he'd given her on the street as a look could be. The coldness, the hardness, fell away like a mask. The longing in his expression almost brought tears to her eyes, and suddenly he was kissing her as if it had been hours since he'd last seen her and not two years, as if they'd met one another at the theater and not this . . . this godforsaken place.

As if he weren't a vampire.

Turning her head, Elizabeth broke the kiss. "Stop," she gasped. "I don't even *know* you."

Cool, gentle fingers gripped her chin, turning her back to face him. "You know me, Lizzy. I haven't changed."

"You're a *vampire!*" Did she really say that out loud? "When, Lukas? When did you become a vampire?"

"Centuries ago."

Her head dropped back against the wall with a thud. "The least you could do is laugh at me and tell me there's no such thing."

Cool fingers slid into her hair, caressing her scalp. "I'm sorry, Lizzy-mine. You should never have found out this way. I never wanted you to know at all."

She pushed away from the wall, from him, her mind awhirl. *Centuries ago.* He'd been turned *centuries ago.* All this time, she'd thought he was human. She'd thought he was falling in love with her, as she'd fallen in love with him. A *vampire*.

"I think I'm going to be sick." Reaching out blindly, she touched his arm, felt his hand close around hers, and she snatched it back, pulling away. "You bit me. When we were dating, you bit me." She turned back to him slowly, his face faintly illuminated in the twilight from the back window.

He smiled, but in his eyes she saw only regret. "Your blood was sweet. And you loved it, Lizzy girl. You came and came and came when I sucked on your neck like that."

Speechless, she stared at him. "God." Her cheeks turned to flame. "Why don't I remember any of it?"

"I took your memories. Only the ones that would damn me." His eyes pleaded with her to understand. "I never hurt you. I would never hurt you, my Lizzy." He reached for her, but she jerked her hands out of his reach and stepped back.

"Don't. I'm not your Lizzy. I'm not your anything." The heat in her cheeks deepened, not from embarrassment now but from utter humiliation. She'd thought he loved her, when all she'd been to him was food.

At the sound of footsteps outside, Lukas moved between her and the door.

The pierced one poked his head in through the doorway. "I'm hungry."

Lukas scowled. "You have your own slave."

"I've been sharing with you. I think it's time you returned the favor."

"And I think you should get back to work." Lukas turned and started walking toward the stairs. "Come, Elizabeth," he snapped, holding out a hand for her.

She glanced at the hungry eyes of the other vampire and flew to Lukas's side, sliding her hand into his, gladly. His cool fingers closed around hers, and he led her up the stairs, warning her to watch her step. As one of the stairs splintered and crumbled beneath her foot, he pulled her clear as if she weighed nothing.

Finally, at the top of the stairs, he released her hand. "Wait here." Then he disappeared, or moved away from her so quickly that he might as well have. She sensed rather than saw him dart in and out of the upstairs rooms. And then he was back at her side, his strong hand once more closing protectively around her own.

"You're looking for a woman?" Elizabeth asked, as they started back down the treacherous steps.

"Yes. Or evidence that anyone's been hiding here."

Pierced-face was waiting for them when they returned to the shop level, his pupils white as snow, his fangs elongated as he watched her hungrily, making chills race over her skin.

"Have you told her the way of things around here, Lukas?" he asked silkily. "Does she know that we don't just need blood to survive, but various emotions? Have you warned her that Butch is a pain-feeder, that he's watching her, waiting for the chance to snatch her away from you and hurt her?"

"He's not going to touch her," Lukas growled.

But Pierced-face continued as if Lukas hadn't spoken.

"My guess is he'll rape her and probably sodomize her. But he might go the quick route and just yank out a couple of her fingernails."

Elizabeth's blood turned to ice.

Pierced-face threw back his head in delight.

Lukas's grip on her arm tightened. "Ignore him, Elizabeth. The asshole is a fear-feeder, determined to scare you. Butch won't touch you." His voice rose, turning hard as granite. "Neither of them will if they want to live."

Pierced-face grinned. His words had hit their mark, and they all knew it.

"Come," Lukas said, tugging her past the prick and out the door.

Elizabeth's grip on Lukas's hand tightened. Lukas might be a vampire who'd fed on her without her knowledge, but she still trusted him a thousand times more than she did his companions.

As they walked toward the next building, a small house, Pierced-face remained close behind them, apparently hoping to scare her again. Her mouth tightened in annoyance even as her spine tingled and crawled as if, at any moment, she might feel a knife plunge between her shoulder blades. Or fangs sink into her neck from behind.

She fought the scaremongering, struggling not to succumb. Hardening her jaw, she glanced at Lukas. "Do vampires really feed off emotions?"

He met her gaze, his blue eyes touching something deep inside her even in that brief and hooded look. "Emoras do. We're just one race of vampires, but we're the predominant race in Vamp City."

"Do you have any idea how much this is twisting my mind?"

His hand squeezed hers gently. "I have some idea."

She peered at him. "What emotion do you need?"

Meeting her gaze, his mouth tightened, then turned rueful. "Pleasure."

"Your own or others'?"

"Mostly others'." His voice lowered to a whisper. "I fed well from yours."

Her breath stuttered, the thought incredibly . . . *hot.* No wonder he'd lavished such sweet attention on her body. She'd thought him the kindest, most thoughtful lover any woman had ever had. He'd loved to make her come—before he entered her, while he was inside her, over and over and over. Then yet again when they lay close and sated and complete. He'd told her he got as much pleasure from her orgasms as she did.

Apparently, that was, quite literally, true.

Bastard.

She pulled her hand from his, her stomach clenching with yet another spasm of betrayal. He hadn't brought her to orgasm for *her.* He hadn't done it to make *her* happy. He'd done it for the simple, cold reason that he'd needed to eat.

"You used me," she said, her tone flat. Hurt.

"You were my slave, Elizabeth," he said coolly. "Even if you didn't know it."

Her jaw clenched shut. Damn him.

As they reached the crumbling front walk of the house, Pierced-face spoke. "Just wait until he gets you back to the stronghold, Elizabeth. Just wait until all those pain-feeders get their fangs . . . and cocks . . . and knives . . . into you."

Lukas released her and whirled, his sword suddenly free of its sheath. "Go. Now. Before I cut off your idiot head."

Pierced-face grinned. "She's not as fearful as many new arrivals, but she's been a sweet little snack." A moment later, he was gone.

As Lukas led her up the rotting steps, he said quietly, "I never used you. I never enslaved you. I . . ." He didn't finish, and she wondered what he'd almost said. "It doesn't matter. All that matters is that no one realize that I have feelings for you, Lizzy, or we're both going to suffer."

As he led her inside the old house, and they were finally alone, she turned to him. "Do you? Do you really have feelings for me?"

With a sound of misery, he pulled her into his arms, tight against his chest. "You have no idea, woman. You've no idea how I've suffered not being able to return to you, knowing you thought I'd abandoned you." He pulled back, cupped her face in his hands. "I have thought of you, *missed* you, every minute of every hour of every day for two solid, miserable years, Lizzy-mine. Yes, I have feelings for you."

As he kissed her softly, tenderly, his words slowly soaked into her mind, her heart, her soul, like a warm, summer rain on parched earth. Could she believe him? Did she dare believe him?

Her heart said yes. Her mind insisted on reserving judgment.

Finally, he pulled back and took her hand. "Come. I have a job to do. And it's critically important."

As they began to search the fully furnished, if decrepit house, she glanced at him. "This sorceress you're looking for. Is she real? I mean . . . magic?"

"So they say."

"Why do you need her?"

"Because she's the only one who can save us."

She looked at him sharply. "Save you from what?"

His expression turned grim. "In 1870, a powerful wizard created Vamp City, an exact duplicate of a portion of Washington, D.C. at that time. It was billed as a vampire utopia, a place where the sun never shone and where vampires were free not only to come and go as we wished but to bring in humans for whatever purposes we desired. An arena was built for games to be played only by vampires, where we were free to use all of our skills, all of our strengths, without fear of discovery by the far-too-prevalent humans. And for 140 years, it has been that—utopia. Until two years ago, when the magic started to fail. Those of us within Vamp City at that moment became trapped here."

Her eyes widened. "That's why you never came back."

"Yes." He pulled her against him, kissing her hair. Then he stopped and turned her to face him, his hands gripping her shoulders, then cupping her cheeks, a plea in his eyes. "I never would have left you willingly. There are millions who can provide me sustenance of the body, my Lizzy. It is you alone who feeds my soul." The pain in his voice soaked into her heart, nourishing the song there that had already begun, once more, to sing.

"When the sorceress is found, will you be free?"

"We hope so. We hope that she'll be able to renew the magic and save Vamp City."

"And if she doesn't?"

His thumb stroked her cheek. "Those of us trapped are tied to the magic. If the magic dies . . ." He shrugged. But she heard his unsaid words, and they ripped the heart right out of her chest.

If the sorceress failed to renew the magic, Lukas's immortal life was over.

Chapter Seven

ELIZABETH ACCOMPANIED LUKAS back outside, her hand firmly tucked in his. She was so confused. *So* confused. For two years, she'd ached, mourned, railed at Lukas for leaving her without a word of explanation. She'd felt humiliated, angry, and sad. At times she'd even wondered if he'd died, and no one had known to contact her.

Now she'd found him gloriously alive. Or, at least, thoroughly undead. And he claimed he'd never stopped caring about her, that he'd been unable to return to her. That he was trapped and in danger of dying, this time for real.

She didn't know what to think. Worse, she didn't know what to feel. Her heart sang at his nearness, at his touch, as it always had. And it trembled now with fear that he might once more be ripped from her life, this time for good.

But, my God, he was a *vampire*. A bloodsucker who'd fed on her the entire time they'd been dating, then wiped her mind clean of the memory each time. And he'd not only fed on her blood but on the pleasure she'd found in his arms. He'd used her in the most despicable of ways. Yet he claimed he cared. That he'd always cared.

What on Earth was she supposed to believe?

"We have to get you out of here," he said quietly, as they left the house and started toward the next one on the street. "Tell me what you remember. How did you get here?"

She glanced at him, her heart melting a little more at the beauty of his face and the intensity in his eyes. "I was walking to school with Steph. Between one step and the next, right in the middle of P Street, everything changed. Everything went dark. Silent. I heard the sound of horses, then your friends came riding around the corner. And then you," she added softly.

His mouth turned grim. "You came in on the sunbeam. I figured as much. The sunbeams are the places where the real world is breaking through. As the magic crumbles, the real world breaks through more and more often and in more and more places. Every now and then, a human will slide into Vamp City through one of those breaks between the worlds. How, we don't know. Most can't. Most pass unaffected through the breaks and never sense them at all."

"So why me?"

"I don't know. But you have to promise me something." His grip on her hand tightened. "If I get you out of here, you must never return to the area of D.C. overlaid by Vamp City, or you could walk right back in again through another sunbeam."

"How will I know where that is?"

"I can give you some directions. Your apartment is safe. It's just outside. Your school, unfortunately, is just inside. You can't go back to Adams Middle as long as the worlds are bleeding through this way. Not until the magic is renewed."

"But I . . ." She stopped, swallowing her automatic objection that she had to get back to school. One step at a time. First, she had to get home.

The rumble of a vehicle engine sounded in the distance, cutting through the unnatural stillness of this world, surprising her. The sound was so . . . anachronistic.

"You have cars here?"

"Some." Lukas stopped at the base of the front steps. At the sound, he'd tensed. "Come on. He changed directions, heading back toward the street. "SUVs are the only ones that can manage what pass for roads in this place. Most of us ride horses."

As they started down the street the way they'd come, Elizabeth listened to the approaching vehicle. There were so few sounds in this place. "I haven't seen a single bird," she mused. "Or heard one. Not even any insects."

"When the sorcerer created Vamp City, he duplicated the physical aspects of D.C., but nothing living conveyed. No plants, no animals. The only creatures here are the ones we've brought in. Horses, humans, and a handful of cats and dogs. All foodstuffs and supplies have to be brought in from the real world."

Lukas and Elizabeth joined Lukas's companions as they converged in the middle of the street.

"We're about to get company," Lukas said. From the tense looks on the faces of the vampires, she could tell that wasn't a good thing. "Ricky, take Elizabeth and hide in one of the houses. Keep her safe."

"That's my slave you're ordering," Pierced-face commented. His gaze slid to her. "There will be a price for his services."

Elizabeth shuddered before she could stop herself, knowing her fear would only please him. He wanted her blood. Maybe even her body.

"You're not touching her," Lukas replied evenly. "But if you want my attention on the fight, and not on guarding what is mine, Ricky must protect her."

Pierced-faced watched him, his displeasure evident. But, finally, he nodded. "We'll discuss payment later." He turned to the kid with the glowing hair. "Take her and hide in that house," he said, pointing to the one they stood in front of.

"Yes, master." Ricky motioned to her with his head and started toward the front steps.

Lukas stepped in front of her, blocking her view of the other men, hiding his own expression from his companions. "If you're in danger, scream. I'll come."

"Be careful." Was she really telling a vampire to be careful in a fight? Apparently, she was.

Lukas's beautiful eyes crinkled at the corners, warming to the blue of a summer sky. "I will. Now go."

He released her and stepped back. But as she hurried

past the other two vampires, she felt their gazes following her, thick as tar. They made her skin crawl, both of them. If anything happened to Lukas, she was going to have to run.

Ricky waited for her in the doorway of the house she and Lukas had already inspected. When she stepped inside, he closed the door and headed for the dimly lit stairs. "We'll get a better view from an upper window."

"Watch the rotted step," she warned.

She followed him up the stairs and to one of the windows looking down on the street below.

"So you're a slave?" she asked. "Are you . . . ?"

"Am I what?" His tone was hard and not particularly nice. "Human?" He snorted. "Yes, I'm human. After a couple of years in this place, the magic turns humans immortal, and our hair starts to glow. They call us Slavas. Once we become a Slava, we can never go home." His tone was too matter-of-fact. As if he'd long ago gotten over it.

"I'm sorry. How long have you been here?"

"Almost eighty years."

Her eyes widened, her jaw dropped. *Eighty years?* No wonder he was over it. He'd have nothing, and no one, to go back to.

As she watched out the window, she saw the vehicle, a black Cadillac Escalade, pull into view, trailed by a cloud of dust. The moment it came to a stop, four males alighted with inhuman speed and grace.

The one in front curled his lip. "York scum. This is Gonzaga territory."

Pierced-face scoffed. "Does Cristoff Gonzaga attempt to claim all of the Nod, now? We're nowhere near Gonzaga lands, and you know it."

The Gonzaga vamp pulled his sword. "As long as we're searching for the sorceress, wherever we choose to search is ours."

"And what if we find her first?" the bearded one, Butch, drawled.

The Gonzaga vamp scoffed. "And what good will she do any of us in your hands? Cristoff is the only one who possesses the ritual to renew the magic. Without it, she's useless."

"You don't know that," Pierced-face said.

A second Gonzaga vampire pulled his sword. "Be on your way, scum. Or would you rather die here?"

Lukas's companions drew their swords. Lukas drew two.

Elizabeth caught her breath, glancing at Ricky. "Are they really going to try to kill one another?"

"Of course. The York and Gonzaga kovenas are enemies."

Even as he spoke, the seven vampires all but disappeared, flying at one another so quickly that she lost sight of them. Four against three. Only Lukas took on two opponents at once, swinging his swords in an incredible display of strength and dexterity. She'd often thought he should have been a Viking. Now she wondered if he'd actually been one. Her fingers gripped the window frame, her breath turning unsteady. Watching him fight was at once terrifying and thrilling.

Lukas, dammit, you'd better not die.

"If this battle turns against us, I suggest you run," Ricky said beside her.

If Lukas and his friends died. "Do you think the other vamps will find us up here?"

"If any of them are fear-feeders, I guarantee they will."

The thought chilled. "Where would I run to?"

"I don't know." He made a sound of amusement as if it was all a joke. A sick one, but a joke. "There's no escaping this place. Once you're brought to Vamp City, you're here for life. For most people, that's not very long. For a few of us, it's very long indeed. Just run. Maybe you'll get lucky. The very last place you want to be taken is to Cristoff Gonzaga's castle. He's a pain-feeder of the worst kind."

As her gaze remained glued on Lukas's faster-than-lightning moves, a yell turned her attention briefly to the other two battles. She watched as Pierced-face's head rolled from his body and hit the dirt with a thud.

Elizabeth gasped, clutching the window frame.

"Well, hell," Ricky muttered. "He was my master. Sorry, chickadee, you're on your own. I'm leaving." Without a backward glance, he darted out of the room. Escaping.

For one pregnant moment, Elizabeth wondered if she should follow him. But, no. Not as long as Lukas was still alive.

Her pulse racing with fear for Lukas as much as herself, she turned back to the window just as a second head rolled, this one belonging to one of Lukas's opponents. The battle was now three against two, but Lukas once more battled two at once. How long could he keep that up?

In the street, the remains of the two dead vampires exploded suddenly, one after the other, raining down around the fighting vamps like ash, leaving nothing visible behind. And then a third head rolled as Butch took down his opponent, at last, leaving only Lukas fighting two Gonzaga vamps.

Elizabeth expected Butch to go help Lukas. Instead, he disappeared.

Had he run? The coward!

But a moment later, she knew exactly where he'd gone when she felt a strong, unwelcome arm grab her from behind and yank her away from the window, that bushy beard scraping against her temple.

"What are you doing?" she cried. "Why aren't you helping him?"

"He'll be fine. And I'm hungry." He struck, his fangs impaling her neck like two red-hot spikes.

Elizabeth screamed.

Chapter Eight

ELIZABETH GASPED, STRUGGLING against the vampire's iron hold, moaning with a pain far worse than any she'd ever known. Her vision began to waver, her stomach started to roll. Lifting her foot, she drove her heel back into her attacker's knee, but he didn't even grunt. With her arms pinned to her sides, she was helpless. And he was draining her blood!

God, *so much pain*. Tears ran down her cheeks, tears of agony, of fury, and of frustration that she couldn't do a thing to stop him.

"Lukas." She tried to scream his name, but the word came out as little more than a gasp, her vocal cords all but immobilized.

The vampire released her suddenly with a furious growl, the fire in her neck increasing tenfold as she felt her flesh rip. She cried out, stumbled forward, then turned to find not one vampire but two in the room with her. The one who'd bitten her. And Lukas.

She sank back against the window with relief.

Lukas looked like a berserker of old as he stared at his companion, his eyes burning with rage, the sword at his side dripping with blood.

"I just wanted a taste." Butch lifted his hands like a kid caught swiping a cookie off a classmate's lunch tray.

Lukas blurred. His sword whistled. A second later, the bearded one's head rolled with a thud to the floor.

Elizabeth's legs gave way, and she slid down the window until she was crouched low, shaking, a warm stream of blood running down her throat.

Lukas whirled toward her. His eyes dark with concern, he started forward, wiping off his sword and sheathing it.

But she shook her head. "Stay back." The words were but a whisper. She was so cold. Still in so much pain.

"You're in shock, sweetheart." He reached for her slowly, his voice low and soothing. "I won't hurt you. You know I won't hurt you, Lizzy-mine, but I have to do something before you lose too much blood."

She started to list sideways, and he caught her, sweeping her into his arms and pulling her tight against the hard body that she'd once known so well. The smell of battle clung to him, but beneath it was the familiar and beloved scent of Lukas, and she sank against him, curling her arm around his neck.

She held on tight as he carried her downstairs and laid her on the leather sofa. As she looked up at him, he stroked the hair back from her face with a featherlight touch, his eyes pained.

"I won't hurt you," he murmured, sinking to his knees on the floor beside her. "I promise, sweetheart." Then he dipped his head to her bleeding neck.

"Lukas?" She stiffened, tried to push him away, but like the other vampire, he was impossible to move.

She went rigid in anticipation of more pain, but she felt only the tickle of his soft hair against her jaw and a featherlight brush of lips. And then the strange sensation of tugging, of pulling. Had he bitten her? She'd felt no hot, stabbing spikes this time. No stabbing at all.

Little by little, the pain began to lessen, then ebb. With the realization that Lukas had bitten her without hurting her, as he'd promised, the tension began to leave her body, only to be replaced, moments later, by a tension of another kind.

An erotic, intense, pleasure began to build low inside her.

"What are you doing?" she gasped, her voice normal once more.

He didn't answer, and how could he when his mouth was fastened to her neck? But his hand lifted to stroke her hair, his touch calming her, as his bite stole the last of the pain and filled her only with a pleasure that made her gasp, that made her body hot and restless.

"Lukas, stop." She tugged at his head. "Please stop."

Slowly, he did, lifting his head, looking at her behind a monster's mask. His pupils had turned stark white, his incisors had lengthened and thickened and sharpened to fine points. And they were covered in blood. Her blood.

She stared at him in horror. He closed his eyes and

turned away. Lifting her hand, she felt the stickiness along her neck, but her fingers encountered only sores, not the open flesh wounds she knew should be there.

"What did you do?" she asked quietly, this time reaching for him, touching his jaw.

He turned back to her, his eyes once more normal, but guarded. Sad. His mouth was closed, his fangs no longer visible, if they were still elongated at all.

"I've initiated your healing," he said simply, and she saw that his fangs were about half the size they'd been before. "Vampire saliva contains healing properties that rush into your bloodstream with my bite."

Pressing her hand against his cool cheek, she shuddered. "Thank you for saving me."

His eyes warmed slowly, his mouth softening to something close to a smile. "You mean the world to me, Lizzy. I hate that you were brought here. This is no place for you." Pulling her close, he pressed his cheek to her hair. "But I've missed you so much." His words were filled with such pain, such a depth of longing, mirroring the misery she'd lived with these past two years.

It didn't matter what he was or how he fed. He was her Lukas.

Snaking her arms around his neck, she buried her face against him. "I've missed you, too. I thought . . ."

Her voice cracked, and he pulled her tighter, stroking her hair. "You thought I'd left you. That I'd walked away. *Never*, Lizzy-mine. *Never*." Slowly, he pulled back until she could see his face. He ran his thumb along her cheekbone. "If there had been any way to return to you, I would have."

The depth of emotion in his eyes rocked her, filling her heart until she thought it might overflow. "I believe you. Deep inside, I could never accept that you'd intentionally left me without even saying good-bye."

"*Never.*" His cool palm stroked her cheek. "A hundred times I thought about sending word to you. But I could think of no logical reason for my staying away without telling you a truth that would be impossible for you to believe. All along, we've held out hope for a sorcerer or sorceress who would save us. I told myself that once I was free, once I knew my life would not end here, I'd find you and try to make it up to you."

Her brow furrowed. "How could you get word to me if you're trapped here?"

"Not all vampires are trapped within Vamp City. Some can still come and go as they please. I have a friend, Micah, whom I would have trusted to give you a message. He's the only one I trust to get you safely out of here if I can get word to him." He kissed her softly, passionately, then pulled back, his eyes shining with so much emotion, the same emotion that pulsed inside her.

"I want you safe, Lizzy-mine. I love you," he said tenderly, his eyes aglow. The words she'd waited so long to hear.

Tears sprang to her own eyes. "I love you, too, Lukas. I have almost from the beginning."

He kissed her again. "I know," he whispered against her lips. "The way you used to light up when you saw me warmed me in a way nothing and no one has in centuries. I tried to harden my heart against your sweetness, not wanting you to know of my world or the sordidness of it. But I failed, Lizzy. I failed within days of meeting you and fell head over heels in love with you."

Tears began to leak out of the corners of her eyes, her chest so full she thought it would burst. She buried her fingers in his hair, pulled his mouth back to hers, and kissed him deeply, drowning in his taste, in his scent, in the sheer joy of his love.

Her hands slid down to his massive shoulders, to the hard muscle that played along their sculpted breadth. "I want to touch you."

He pulled back, a smile playing at his mouth, then sat up and pulled the black shirt over his head, revealing the most beautiful male chest ever made. As her fingers found his abs and began an upward slide, luxuriating in the feel of the hard planes beneath her palms, his own fingers found the buttons of her blouse and began unbuttoning it with slow deliberation, as if he savored every new glimpse of her skin.

When he had her shirt undone, he parted it slowly, his gaze intent as he reached for the front clasp of her bra and flicked it open. With cool fingers, he parted the cups, freeing her to his gaze. His eyes feasted.

"I've missed you so much," he breathed, reaching for her, claiming her breasts with his fingers, his palms, and, finally, his mouth. Cool lips closed over one taut nipple and he sucked her fully into his mouth making her moan and arch with pleasure. Her hands slid once more into his hair, and she held him close, loving the feel of him in her arms again. Loving him, fangs and all.

"Lukas?"

He lifted slowly, licking across her nipple, tightening things low inside her body. His gaze flicked up to meet hers. "Hmm?"

"When you bite me, do you ever hurt me?"

"Never."

"Then promise me something. Please?"

"Anything."

"Don't enthrall me anymore. Don't take my memories, again. Not unless I ask you to. Please?"

He leaned up, kissing her mouth thoroughly before pulling back. His gaze bore into hers. "I promise, Elizabeth. No more secrets between us." His eyes turned tender, a boyish smile lifting his mouth as his expression took on a look of wonder. "I was so afraid for you to learn the truth."

"That you're a vampire?"

He kissed her again. "It's not an easy thing to overlook."

She laughed. "No, I suppose it's not." Lifting a hand, she stroked his beloved cheek. "You're still my Lukas."

"Always." He turned and kissed her palm.

"Lukas, do you ever . . . ?" Her cheeks began to heat, making him smile. "Do you ever bite me . . . places other than my neck?"

His eyes warmed, heated. "I haven't, no, though I've wanted to. I wouldn't engage in that kind of intimacy with you when you weren't fully aware."

"But you still drank from me."

"Yes. I brought us both incredible pleasure."

"Why didn't your bite hurt me, when Butch's fangs . . ." She shuddered. "They burned, Lukas. It was horrible."

His eyes darkened. "He's . . . he *was* a pain-feeder. It was his gift to cause pain with his bite. My gift is to offer only pleasure with mine."

"I'm glad." She smiled shyly. "Perhaps we can take it one step at a time since this is all so new to me."

His eyes crinkled at the corners. "We'll take it however you wish, Lizzy-mine." His fingers went to the button of her pants. "But I need to taste you again, if only with my tongue. Will you let me?"

Heat rushed through her body. "Yes."

As he tugged off her shoes, she shrugged off her shirt and bra, then watched as he slid her pants down over her hips and legs, pulling them off, leaving her in nothing but a pair of silky black panties.

A growl of need rumbled in his throat, the corners of his mouth lifting as he shot her a look of pure masculine approval. His blue eyes flashing with white heat, he held her gaze as he dipped his head between her legs, then licked her right through the silk. His rough tongue made her arch with pleasure.

"Oh, Lukas, how I've missed you, too."

With a low laugh, he slid one finger beneath the edge of her panties, pulling the crotch aside, then laved her bare flesh with his tongue, making her cry out with joy. He was teasing her, playing with her, and, as she watched him, his eyes once more began to turn white where his pupils should be black.

"Why are your eyes changing?"

His lashes swept down.

"Don't, Lukas. No secrets."

He looked up again, worry in that beautiful face. "I'm a pleasure-feeder though no one's pleasure has ever pleased me more than yours. When I taste it, the need inside of me, the hunger, awakens. And that's when my eyes change."

"And your fangs lengthen?"

"Not always at the same time, but soon, yes." His expression turned achingly tender. "I will never hurt you, Lizzy. Do you believe me?"

"Yes." Then she gasped again as his hand moved, his finger sliding deep inside her. "Oh, yes. Oh, Lukas."

Tired of the game, he pulled her panties down and off, then eased her legs apart, eyeing her with a hunger that stole her breath. His face lowered, his mouth kissing her, licking her, sucking at the core of her pleasure until she was rocking against him, gasping, her head thrown back. His hands caressed her hips, her thighs, as the pleasure mounted, as her body tightened, rising, rising.

The orgasm broke over her, shattering in its brilliance, her body clenching and contracting deep, deep inside in a glorious explosion of joy. And then his mouth was on her abdomen, rising to suckle her breast.

Her fingers dug into his hair. "Inside, Lukas," she gasped, still riding the aftershocks. "I need you inside me."

When he lifted his head, his pupils were still white, his fangs long and sharp, though she'd felt no prick, no pain. But those inhuman eyes gleamed with love, and she wasn't even the slightest bit afraid.

"Did you bite my breast?" she asked, curious.

"No. You'll know when I do." He smiled. "You'll enjoy it."

Pulling away, he stood beside the sofa, unbuckled his belt, then removed his boots and socks, and pushed his pants down over lean, hard hips, revealing white Jockey shorts that barely held his massive erection.

Her thighs dampened, a low moan escaping her throat as he pushed down his shorts and that erection sprang free. It was huge, straight, thick, and gorgeous. Oh how she'd missed this man.

Lowering himself over her, his bare chest brushing the tips of her breasts, he slowly positioned his big body until the tip of him pressed at her slick gates. Resting on his elbows, staring into her eyes, he slid firmly, yet gently inside her.

His eyes nearly rolled back into his head. Her own almost did the same as the thickness of him stretched her, claimed her, thrilled her.

Her breath left on a groan as he pulled most of the way out, then slid in again and again, setting up a gradually escalating rhythm until he was pounding into her, and she was thrusting against him, needing him deeper, deeper.

Fingers in his hair, she watched him, loved him.

"Give me your neck, Lizzy-mine."

His words shivered through her on a thrill of danger, but she didn't hesitate. The dark thought rose that if she were going to die, this was the way she wanted to go.

She tipped her head sideways, giving him access,

then tensed ever so slightly as his head dipped, as his lips kissed her neck, as his fangs sank into her flesh.

As he'd promised, she felt no pain at all, just a weird and wonderful sensation of . . . connection. And then his lips closed onto her skin and he sucked, pulled, and she cried out with the incredible erotic pleasure. How she felt it *there*, she couldn't begin to guess, but with every pull of his mouth, she felt the tug more strongly between her legs. Again and again he sucked, and she cried out, her body rising, climbing, preparing to shatter all over again.

He rode the crest with her, driving into her harder and harder, his body straining toward that ultimate release. And, suddenly, they were flying together, soaring, shattering, then floating slowly and blissfully back down to Earth.

Lukas lifted his head, then managed to roll them over on the sofa until he was on the bottom, and she was lying atop him, cradled in his arms, her head tucked against his chin.

"Did I hurt you?" he asked quietly.

"No. I never imagined anything so wonderful." As she stroked his chest, she wondered how this male could be real. And how, even if he lived, they could ever have a life together, coming as they did, from such totally different worlds.

Chapter Nine

LUKAS STROKED THE warm, silken back of the beauty in his arms, the precious darling of a woman who'd stolen his heart the first time she'd smiled at him. Sweet and beautiful, his Lizzy. Never had he known anyone so full of life, so full of love.

"You are mine," he said quietly, wonder in his voice that she could love him at all, let alone after he'd revealed himself completely—his fangs, his eyes, his need for blood.

Lifting up, she propped her forearms on his chest and met his gaze, softness glowing in her lovely brown eyes. "As you're mine, Lukas Olsson. Since you can't leave here, neither will I."

His heart clutched. "No, sweetheart." His hands slid down her back to her buttocks, reveling in the feel of her soft curves, then up again. "You must go, Lizzy-mine. You aren't safe here, and I can't keep you so. Too many vampires within Vamp City have lost hold of their consciences. Too many want only to feed off your fear or your pain. And if I try to protect you and fail, too many will enjoy hurting you just to get at me. I've never been a fan of the kovena to which I've been forced to pledge allegiance, and many know it."

He reached for her hand, pulled it to his mouth, and kissed it. "Somehow, I will find a way to set you free, then you must go. For me."

That stubborn light ignited in her eyes, and as much as he wished it hadn't—not over this—he loved that she treated him no differently than she ever had, even knowing what he was.

"I won't be separated from you again," she insisted.

He gripped the back of her head and lifted his own, kissing her. When he pulled back, he found tears in her eyes, and they were almost more than he could bear. "I would give anything to keep you by my side, Lizzy-mine, but my mission is to hunt for the sorceress, to find her before Cristoff Gonzaga's vamps do. My master's own liege wishes to control the power, and, at the moment, the sorceress *is* that power."

She nestled against him again, her cheek pressed against his heart. He stroked her hair, his heart melting.

"Vampires don't sleep, Lizzy. We work day and night, hunt day and night. I haven't stopped in more than a week. What would I do with you?" His fingers weaved into her silken hair. "I would have to hide you, but then I wouldn't be able to protect you. And there are far too many here who would do you harm."

He placed a kiss against her hair. "You have to go back

to the real world. Then I want you to leave Washington and not come back until I contact you."

"What?" Her head popped back up as she frowned at him. "You said I needed to stay out of the Vamp City area. Not all of D.C."

"I know. But you'd be safest far away from both Washingtons. Outside the Vamp City area, you won't accidentally walk in through a sunbeam again, but there are still those who hunt humans to sell at the slave auction. You'd be safest away from here." He held her gaze, willing her to hear the truth of his heart. "I couldn't bear it if anything happened to you, sweetheart. I couldn't bear it."

Her gaze turning pained, she tucked her precious head once more beneath his chin, then plucked gently at his nipple with her fingers, making him smile even as he stifled a groan. His body began to stir all over again, but hers was softening in that way it always did when she was tired and ready for sleep.

"You have to come back to me, Lukas," she said quietly.

He kissed her hair. "That is my only life's goal, sweetheart."

Her hand stilled, tucking beneath her chin. Peace enveloped him, a peace he'd never known in Vamp City. A peace woven with steely resolve to keep her safe.

Love pulsed inside him as he held her, stroking her back, listening to her precious heartbeat. If it was the last gift he gave her, if it was the last good thing he did in this too-long life of his, he would see this woman safely out of Vamp City once and for all.

Even if he could never follow.

Chapter Ten

SEVERAL HOURS LATER, Elizabeth rode nestled against Lukas's chest through a dimly lit forest on their way to meet someone. A vampire named Arturo. Lukas's arm curled around her waist, his thumb gently stroking the underside of her breast. The ride itself wasn't particularly comfortable, but there was no place she'd rather be than here, with Lukas. The thought of saying good-bye to him again filled her with an aching misery.

Forcing her mind on other things, she studied the twisted, gnarled trunks of the trees all around them, trees totally lacking in foliage despite the fact that it was only early September.

"The trees look dead," she murmured.

"They are dead. They grow that way."

"That isn't possible."

"Magic, dearest," he said, giving her waist a gentle squeeze.

Magic. The evidence of it continually boggled her mind. And yet this world's very existence was the greatest evidence that it did. She was glad to be getting the opportunity to see a little more of Vamp City before she left. Assuming Lukas could really get her out of here. As badly as she didn't want to leave him, neither did she want to make his existence an ordeal, as she could if he were forced to constantly try to hide her. He needed to be able to concentrate on finding the sorceress who would save him so that he could come back to her.

A couple of hours ago, they'd left Georgetown, stopping at a small house in Foggy Bottom that, for a change, had been occupied. Lukas had bought a small loaf of freshly baked bread and . . . of all things . . . a cold can of root beer from the owner. Then he'd given the man a hefty amount of cash to deliver a message.

Afterward, they'd headed back toward Georgetown, this time riding down to the Potomac, where they'd dismounted and wandered around the fascinating ruins of the nineteenth-century waterfront while she devoured the bread and washed it down with the root beer. Mounting again, they'd headed into the woods just north of Georgetown, where they'd been watching . . . and waiting . . . ever since.

Arturo was apparently a friend of Micah's, the vampire Lukas trusted to help her. Unfortunately, Arturo lived somewhere Lukas couldn't take her. And without cell phones, hand-carried messages were the only form of communication, as unreliable as they might be. Arturo might never show up. For all she knew, they might have to wait for him for days.

"Do you hear that?" Lukas asked.

The sound of a vehicle, a Jeep, if she wasn't mistaken, carried faintly on the breeze. "Is that him?"

"I hope so." He lifted her onto the horse and mounted behind her but stayed within the questionable shelter of the trees.

Down one of the streets, Elizabeth caught a glimpse of what looked like a Jeep Wrangler. Moments later, it came fully into view. Yellow, she thought, though it was impossible to tell for sure with so little light.

As the Jeep came to a stop, Lukas urged the horse forward.

The driver cut the engine and alighted, walking toward them with long, confident strides. He had the look of the Mediterranean—his hair and eyes dark. With a name like Arturo, he was certainly Italian.

"Lukas," he said.

"Arturo. Thanks for coming."

Arturo dipped his head. "You claimed it was urgent?"

Lukas tensed slightly. "I need to get a message to Micah. I'm in need of his assistance."

Arturo looked at him for a long moment, then began to smile. "What is this about?"

"Forgive me, Arturo, but you are one of Cristoff Gonzaga's most trusted. The favor I would ask of Micah is a task I can only entrust to one I've worked with many, many times."

Arturo watched him for several moments more, then

dipped his head, as if conceding the point. "What do you want Micah to know?"

"I need him to meet me at the Boundary Circle. As soon as possible."

Arturo's gaze flicked to her, his eyes narrowing in speculation. "I see." Slowly, he nodded. "Be at the Rock Creek entrance at midnight. Micah will be there."

"Thank you." With that, Lukas turned the horse and headed back into the dead woods.

"He's Gonzaga," Elizabeth said with disbelief. "And you trust him?"

"Not really, no. But I do trust Micah, who is also Gonzaga. Arturo's the only one who might be able to get word to him."

"So this could all go south."

"It could, yes. But Micah's our one chance."

And if Arturo didn't come through? What if he betrayed Lukas and sent more Gonzaga vampires to kill him, instead?

"I don't like this plan," she whispered.

Lukas kissed her hair. "It'll work. It has to work."

Elizabeth sighed. The thought of going with any vampire who wasn't Lukas made her queasy. But apparently only a vampire could set her free. And Micah was the one Lukas trusted.

Her bigger fear was that in his determination to see her safe, Lukas was risking his own life. And that scared her most of all.

Chapter Eleven

"IT'S GETTING DARKER." Elizabeth peered into the woods around her, barely able to see the shapes any longer. "Either that, or my eyesight's going."

"Night is upon us."

"Then I'll really be in the dark."

Lukas pressed a kiss to her hair, his arm around her as they rode the horse. "Once the moon rises, you'll be able to see. For now, though, I'm taking you someplace where I can get you a decent meal and a soft, warm bed with clean linens. You need some sleep."

"With you?"

"Of course."

"Then you just described Heaven. And where is this miraculous place?"

"It's in the Cleveland Park area. Though in V.C., it's still country. The house is owned by a couple of vampire friends of mine, neither of whom are likely home. Their

Slavas will feed us and give us a room where we can pass the evening."

"You trust them?"

"I do. Both vampires and Slavas. Unfortunately, they're all as stuck in this place as I am."

Through the trees, Elizabeth thought she saw lights. Soon, a house became visible through the night's shadows, an old-style two-story farmhouse with a wide, wraparound porch. The flicker of candlelight or hearth flames were visible through several of the windows.

Pulling up in front, Lukas dismounted and tied up the horse, then he swung Elizabeth down and led her up the steps to the shadowy porch. He rapped on the front door, and, several moments later, a woman appeared.

"Lukas, welcome!" An attractive woman of perhaps forty stepped back and let them in. "The masters are out. What can I do for you?" Her hair, while blond, glowed with that same shimmery shine that Ricky's had.

Lukas smiled at the woman fondly even as he curled his arm around Elizabeth's shoulders and pulled her close. "Cyn, this is Elizabeth. She's newly arrived to V.C., human, hungry, and in need of a soft bed for a few hours."

"Hi, Elizabeth." Cyn's expression turned sad and sympathetic. "I'm sorry you got caught here." Her gaze swung back to Lukas. "Would you like her to eat with me, or shall I bring a tray to her room?" Her knowing look said she knew exactly what Lukas was about.

"A tray to her room would be preferable."

Cyn smiled. "I'll give you the back room to the left of the stairs. It's the only one ready for company."

Elizabeth looked around with interest. The house was actually very nicely furnished if a bit old-fashioned—150 years old-fashioned. The living room sported a wide, blazing hearth with a beautifully carved mantel, a velvet sofa, and a couple of chairs. A writing desk sat against one wall, and against the other . . .

Elizabeth laughed. "A foosball table?"

Lukas snorted. "You haven't time-traveled, woman though it might feel that way."

Cyn chuckled. "I don't know about that. The majority of the vamps in this city haven't left in decades. Some not since 1870. There aren't that many of you who feel comfortable in the twenty-first century, Lukas."

"I suppose that's true."

"Go on upstairs," Cyn said cheerily. "I'll bring your tray. One meal or two, Lukas?"

"Just one."

Cyn's smile turned knowing again, and she turned away.

As Lukas led her up the stairs, Elizabeth eyed him curiously. "I didn't think to offer you some of my bread earlier. But you eat food, don't you? Of course you do. When we were dating, I was always feeding you, or you were taking me out to dinner." She looked at him with confusion. "I thought vampires only drank blood."

"I don't need food to survive, but I've always enjoyed it."

"You're not hungry?"

He took the hand he held, lifting her wrist to his mouth and slid his tongue along the veins there. "Not for food," he said huskily.

Elizabeth shivered. And not from fear.

"But you'll eat first," he murmured, placing a kiss on her sensitive wrist before lowering her hand. "Then we'll see to . . . my appetites."

"I'm beginning to realize just how much I don't know about you."

As they reached the top of the stairs, he turned left toward an open doorway. "What would you like to know?"

A hundred things. A thousand. "Where are you from? When were you turned?"

He ushered her into a small, if neatly furnished, room that looked as if it could have been modeled after one in her great-grandmother's house. A double-spindled bed sat in the middle of the room covered in a colorful, patchwork quilt. Small throw rugs lay scattered across the hardwood floors, while calico valances hung atop windows that appeared . . .

"Are the windows painted?" she asked in surprise.

"They are. Many have taken to painting the windows black or boarding them up in case a sunbeam breaks through outside."

She sat on the bed. "So?"

He lifted a brow, a smile hovering at the corners of his mouth as he sat beside her. "So . . . what?"

She broke into a full smile. "Are you avoiding telling me how old you are?" The funny look he gave her made her laugh, and she nudged him with her shoulder. "Give it up, old man. No secrets, remember?"

With a pained sigh, he took her hand and started

playing with her fingers. "I was born in Sweden. The best I can figure, since we didn't keep track of time the way people did in the Roman lands, it was around the tenth century."

"A.D.?" she asked.

He scowled at her. "Yes, A.D. I'm not *that* old."

She gaped at him. "You're . . ." The breath escaped her lungs on a whoosh. "You're a thousand years old. More."

"A little more."

"And here I thought you were close to my age. Were you a Viking? I've always thought you'd have made a wonderful Viking."

He curled his arm around her neck and pulled her close. "Sorry, baby. I was only a hunter, my tribe nomadic."

"Have you had many wives?" she asked quietly, not really wanting to know. Of course he had. *A thousand years.*

"A few. Not many. None in the past few centuries. Vampires make lousy wives—I'd never take one as my mate—and wedding a human is complicated and difficult, requiring tremendous amounts of subterfuge. And they die," he added quietly, the pain in those last three words radiating out, sucking the laughter out of the room. He rested his cheek against her hair.

The impossibility of their sharing a future hit her fully for the first time. She would age, grow old, and die. And, assuming Vamp City was saved, he never would. They'd have two or three decades together before she started looking like his mother. Unless . . .

"You could turn me." The words were out of her mouth before she even gave them any thought.

Lukas straightened, turning her to face him, his hands firm on her shoulders, his eyes suddenly deathly serious. "I love you, Elizabeth Bryant. More than I've ever loved another." She heard the great big *but* hanging like a noose at the end of his words.

"Lukas . . ." she said miserably. "I wasn't serious." The last thing she wanted was to force him to try to explain that while he might have feelings for her now, they wouldn't last.

He gripped her chin. "*I'm* serious, Lizzy. I have loved before, don't get me wrong. Or I thought I had. But with you . . ." He shook his head. "With you, it's different. It's as if I've always known you. It's as if you were made just for me. There is nothing I want more than to keep you close to me."

"But . . . I heard the *but*, Lukas. You can say it."

His mouth softened. "Sweetheart, there is no *but* concerning my love for you. The problem is, turning a human is extremely dangerous. Most don't survive."

"Oh."

"And for some reason, the women who do survive often lose their souls in the process. Or they act like they have." He gripped her face in both hands, tipping his forehead against hers. "If I were to try to turn you, I would lose you, Lizzy-mine. Either in death, or by turning you into a woman incapable of love. I would kill the you I love, either way, and I can't do that to you, or to the people who love you. Or to me."

He pulled back to where he could see her clearly, his hands still cupping her face. "I'd rather know that you're living your life as you should be than to know I destroyed the most beautiful soul I've ever encountered."

"Will you share my life with me? At least until I start to get too old?"

His expression turned pained, and yet unbearably tender. "I can't give you children, Lizzy. I can't go near sunlight, not even daylight. That means no picnics, no trips to the beach, no running errands together, or going out to lunch. You've seen the kind of life I have to give you. You lived it for eight months, seeing me only at night. That will never change and it will never be enough."

She stared into those sad, beloved eyes. "Don't you understand?" she asked softly. "Without you, my heart stops singing. My soul goes silent. My world is more colorless than Vamp City. I would rather live my days alone than my life alone, Lukas. I know I'll turn old someday. Just give me the years you can, please?"

"If you truly want me, I will give you all the years of your life, Lizzy-mine. Without you, my life is meaningless."

Cyn's footsteps sounded on the wood stairs. Lukas kissed Elizabeth softly, then rose and met Cyn at the bedroom door, taking the tray from her.

Elizabeth joined him, and Cyn smiled at her. "If you're still hungry when you're done with this, I'm happy to fix you something else."

"Thank you, Cyn."

Lukas set the tray on the desk and pulled out the chair

for Elizabeth. Cyn had prepared a large bowl of hot beef stew with carrots and potatoes, blueberry muffins, and a small pot of butter. A pitcher of cold water completed the meal.

"Look good?" Lukas asked, relaxing back against the wall.

"It looks delicious." She devoured the meal in no time, and when she was done, Lukas pulled out her chair for her, turned her to face him, and began undressing her.

"It's my turn to feast," he said huskily.

Chapter Twelve

ELIZABETH REACHED FOR Lukas as he reached for her, each unbuttoning the other's shirt, pulling it from the waistband, pushing it off the other's shoulders.

"The door," Elizabeth said on a laugh.

Lukas pressed a hot, lingering kiss to her bare shoulder, then moved away to shut the door. On his way back to her, he pulled his arms out of his sleeves and tossed the shirt on the back of the desk chair. She did the same with hers, and they came together, chest to chest, his arms curling around her waist, hers around his neck, as their mouths found one another's, tasting, licking, stroking.

The kiss turned hot, his taste nectar, the feel of his cool, hard body, like Heaven. He smelled of winter nights and warm fires, and never, *never* did she want to be parted from this man. How was she ever going to return to being alone?

Lukas pulled back, his gaze soft and sad, as if he'd felt

the change in her mood, as if he shared it. "We'll be to-gether again, Lizzy-mine. I promise."

"You can't promise that. You have no idea what will happen."

He swept her into his arms and deposited her on the bed, following her down, lying halfway over her, his face inches from her own. In the glow of the lamplight, his eyes gleamed with soft blue fire.

"Then I'm going to willfully ignore that fact for now. I'm going to believe that nothing will keep us apart. I'm going to love you tonight. And in a few weeks, after the equinox, after the sorceress has renewed the magic of Vamp City and those of us trapped are free to leave again, I'll come to you and crawl into your bed, and I will love you again. For the rest of your life."

She lifted her hands, framing his beloved face. "I'm going to hold you to that." Her fingers slid up into his hair. "Now love me, my vampire. I need you."

He smiled the sweetest, sexiest of smiles and dipped his head to her neck, licking and kissing his way slowly up her throat while his hand slid down her chest, cupping one breast, then the other, caressing, tweaking, then moving down, his palm sliding over her abdomen to the waistband of her pants.

And all the while, he rained kisses over her jaw, her cheek, her forehead, her nose.

"Lukas," she sighed, stroking his shoulders, his neck. The play of muscles beneath her hands delighted her.

His fingers, deft as ever, unbuttoned her pants, un-zipped the short fly, then burrowed beneath the waistband of her panties, sliding down into her dampness, into her body.

With a gasp, she arched into his touch, driving his finger deeper. "*Lukas.*"

"Come for me, baby," he whispered against her temple, as his finger stroked in and out, his thumb flicking her clitoris. "Come for me."

"Bite me, Lukas. It felt so good."

He rose over her slowly, his gaze catching hers, his eyes already white-centered, his fangs elongating as she watched. And all she felt at the sight was a thrill of excitement and anticipation.

Tipping her head to the side, she gave him access to her throat. His eyes crinkling at the corners, he dipped his head, kissed her neck, and sank his fangs into her flesh. As he took the first pull, she cried out at the pleasure, shocked by the orgasm that was already beginning to build low inside her. As his finger moved in and out, his thumb working its magic, his mouth pulling at her neck, she exploded in a fiery shudder of intense, wonderful, pleasure.

As she floated back to Earth, Lukas removed the rest of her clothes and his own. Opening her arms and her thighs, she welcomed him to her.

"Love me, Lukas."

"Always, Lizzy-mine." Then he slid into her body, and she rose to meet him as they came together, one, driving each other up, gasping and straining and loving, until release broke over them in a brilliant fragmenting, a blinding blaze of ecstasy, a rapture beyond comprehension.

Finally, they lay together in a tangle of sheets and limbs, exhausted, replete, and thoroughly loved. Tucked tight against Lukas's chest, Elizabeth drifted toward sleep.

This was the only place in the world that she wanted to be. And it was the one place she couldn't stay.

Chapter Thirteen

ELIZABETH WOKE TO the stroke of cool fingers along
her cheek, followed by a soft, sweet kiss.

"Wake up, Lizzy-mine. It's time to go."

She rose groggily, and dressed, Lukas helping her. He
was already fully clothed and wide-awake. Then again, by
his own admission, he never slept.

"Will it take long to get there?" she asked, putting on
her shoes.

"No. Not usually." But his tone held a grim note she
didn't like.

"What aren't you saying?"

His jaw tensed, but he met her gaze. "There are dan-
gers in Vamp City. As you've seen."

"And the place we're going is dangerous?"

"Every place is potentially dangerous. Less so nearest the outer boundary of the city, but in recent weeks,
wolves have been spotted even there."

"Wolves? I thought there were no animals in Vamp City that you didn't bring in."

He grimaced. "Werewolves."

Her jaw dropped. "Oh, that doesn't sound good."

"It's not."

When she was fully dressed, he ushered her downstairs and out the back door. Cyn was nowhere to be seen, but given that it was midnight, she was probably in bed.

Lukas lifted Elizabeth onto the horse, swung up behind her, then headed out across the open ground to the trees beyond. The night was dark, but the moon was bright and illuminated the landscape nicely, turning the dead trees white.

They rode in silence for a time, the knowledge that they were about to part again thick between them.

"Lizzy, I have money," Lukas said out of the blue.

"That's nice."

He snorted. "That wasn't a random comment, woman. I'm telling you I can support you since you can't return to your school. And with extra money, you can afford to leave. Fly to Hawaii or something. Get out of D.C., sweetheart, please? Just get away."

"My parents moved to Florida a few years ago. I can go visit them."

"That's good. Then later, if I don't get out . . ."

"You will."

But he continued. "Over the centuries, I've accumulated far more wealth than I could spend in a dozen human lifetimes. And if I can't use it, it's yours, sweetheart. Micah can access it and give you all you need. All you will ever need."

Money, more than she could ever spend. The thought offered her a measure of comfort but little more. Because without Lukas, she would have nothing that mattered.

"If I need money, I'll let Micah know."

Lukas released a less-than-happy breath. "Fair enough."

They continued in silence, Lukas's arm tight around her waist, his breath teasing her hair. Finally, he said, "The Boundary Circle is just ahead."

Oddly, the moonlight only extended another thirty or forty yards, then darkness enveloped the land.

"The shadows? Is that where the world ends? This world?"

"Yes. They're not shadows. It's a wall of magic. Until two years ago, I could walk right through it and find myself in the real world."

"You had to be careful to do that only at night."

"You'd be right about that." His arm tightened across her middle, his body turning suddenly rigid.

"What's the matter?" she breathed.

"We have company. And I don't mean Micah."

She looked right and saw nothing, but when she glanced left, she saw them. Three massive, hulking beasts stalking them like prey. Wolves.

Werewolves.

Chapter Fourteen

ELIZABETH STARED AT the hulking werewolves, her heart beginning to pound. As she watched, one of them began to slowly change shape. Moments later, where the wolf had been, now stood a large, very naked man. With his hair long and unkempt, his beard full and scraggly, she suspected he didn't spend much time human.

"Give us the woman, and we'll let you pass, vampire."

Elizabeth's heart stuttered.

"You come near us, and I'll kill you, wolf," Lukas countered. "I'll kill you all."

"You can try," the werewolf said grimly. "But we're hungry. And we *will* eat tonight."

Elizabeth's mind seized. "*Eat?* They eat *people?*"

"When they're starving, they'll eat anything that moves. Hold on to the reins, Lizzy." He thrust them into her hands.

"Lukas, I don't ride."

"You don't have to. I'm staying right here, but I need room to swing my swords. Just hold the reins, lean forward, and hug the horse tight. And whatever you do, keep your head down."

As she walked her hands forward up the horse's maned neck, Lukas gripped her waist until she was fully prone. She did as he said, clutched the reins and hugged the horse tight, its coarse mane scratching her cheek and tickling her nose. The horsey smell overpowered her senses.

Her stomach churned with fear.

Behind her, she heard the metallic swoosh of Lukas's swords breaking free of their scabbards. Out of the corner of her eye she caught the gleam of a blade rising high, ready to cut down the nearest foe.

A moment later, one of the wolves leaped. As the horse shied, Elizabeth gasped and tightened her grip. "Easy, horse. Easy boy. Or girl. It's okay. It's okay."

Another flash of gleaming silver, another whistle of steel as Lukas swung, catching the beast in the face, knocking it back. But while the wolf whined and growled, it only lunged again.

Over her head, Lukas's blades sang, whipping back and forth faster than her eye could track. Vampire fast. She heard a beast's howl of pain, another's growl of fury. Yet still they attacked. And, somehow, Lukas managed to keep his horse from bolting.

Over and over, the blades whistled. Her muscles tensed, quivering, as she half expected, at any moment, to feel teeth sinking into her flesh. It was terrible being able to see only one direction, not knowing if she was about to be attacked from the other. But Lukas continued to fight them, and all she could do was hold on to the horse and trust Lukas to keep her safe.

"Here, Fido!" a male voice called from a short distance away.

A hand landed lightly on Elizabeth's back, and she jumped.

"Stay on the animal," Lukas said behind her. "But you can sit up. You're safe now."

She felt him dismount. Her pulse still racing, Elizabeth rose slowly, finally able to rub her nose and scratch the itch. As she gazed around warily, she saw one wolf lying dead on the ground nearby. The other two were still fighting, leaping at Lukas and another man, the one who'd made the Fido quip, she assumed. A male Lukas clearly trusted. Micah?

A wolf leaped at Lukas, jaws open wide as if it meant to bite off Lukas's head. Her breath caught as she watched her vampire strike as if in slow motion, his blades swinging as one. In fascinated horror, she watched as that furred head flew up into the air, separated from its body.

Lukas turned toward the other vampire just as the third werewolf, too, lost its head.

A moment later, Lukas was at her side, his eyes full of concern. "You're unhurt?"

"Yes. I'm fine."

He reached for her and pulled her down, then pulled her purse out of his saddlebag and handed it to her. Once she'd slung it over her shoulder, he pulled her against his side and led her to the stranger.

"This is Micah," he told her.

Micah was a big man, though not as big as Lukas. He was nice enough looking except for the scar on his cheek, but his eyes were kind, if a bit surprised.

"Elizabeth wandered in on a sunbeam," Lukas told him. "Fortunately, I was nearby."

"I'll take her home."

Lukas nodded. "I owe you, Micah. Show her the boundary, if you would, so she can steer clear of it until this is over. And transfer a healthy chunk of my funds into her account. If the sorceress is not found, transfer all of it."

Micah didn't seem the least bit surprised by the directive.

"Thank you, Lukas," she said quietly. He certainly didn't need to give her his money, but he clearly intended to do it anyway. And she'd be lying if she said she wasn't grateful.

"I'll give you two a few minutes to say good-bye, then we'll leave." Micah smiled at her, his eyes soft with sympathy.

This was it, the moment she'd been dreading. Turning to Lukas, she felt as if her heart were being ripped from her chest all over again. Their gazes collided, misery thick between them.

"I don't want to go," she whispered.

He cupped her face with one hand, his eyes wells of pain. "I don't want you to go. But I want you safe." Holding her face in both hands, he pressed his forehead to hers. "If I don't come back, live for me, Lizzy. You are my heart, the only heart that has beat firmly and fully in my chest for more than a thousand years."

Tears began to run down her cheeks. "I love you, Lukas Olsson."

He pulled her into his arms and kissed her soundly, thoroughly, stroking her hair, her back, her head, as she drank of his cool winter taste and immersed herself in his strength, his scent, the feel of his arms around her.

When he finally pulled away, she stroked the hair at the nape of his neck. "I don't want to live without you."

"Nor I you, my love. Nor I you. I love you, Lizzy-mine." He kissed her softly, sweetly.

"Come back to me, my Lukas."

He nodded, but made no promises.

Finally, pulling her against his side, he led her to where Micah waited. Micah held out his hand to her, and Lukas let her go. Elizabeth shuddered with the need to cling to him. Instead, she slid free of his hold, turning to meet his gaze one last time.

"I love you," she whispered.

"I love you," he whispered back, a gleam of moisture in his eyes.

Turning away, she placed her hand in Micah's. The vampire led her forward three steps, four, five. Her skin felt queer, trembly. And suddenly noise and light exploded all around her.

"Hey!" someone growled, and Micah pulled her out of the way of a couple of youths they'd nearly run into.

She looked around, the sounds of the normal world a shock. Welcome, and yet . . .

"Elizabeth." Micah tugged on her hand, and she followed him to a black sedan parked nearby. He handed her into the passenger side before sliding into the driver's seat.

"Do you think the sorceress will be found?" she asked, as he pulled into traffic.

"She'll be found. I'm certain of it."

"Good. I hope you're right."

He glanced at her, his expression rueful. "Unfortunately, the sorceress has very little magic. Her name is Quinn Lennox, she's about your age, and she didn't know she *was* a sorceress until a couple of weeks ago. Whether or not she'll actually be able to save Vamp City is very much up in the air." He glanced at her. "I'm sorry, Elizabeth. But I think it's best that you know the truth. I have friends who are doing all they can to save V.C., but the only thing most of us can do is hope."

With her heart so heavy, it was minutes before Elizabeth realized that Micah was heading straight for her apartment building. And he'd never asked her how to get there.

"How do you know where I live?"

He glanced at her with a small smile. "Lukas may not have been free to come to you, but that doesn't mean he forgot about you these past two years."

She looked at him askance. "He told you to watch me?"

His smile softened. "He asked me to keep an eye on you—to watch over you and let him know how you were doing."

"You're not trapped by the failing magic."

"No. I wasn't in Vamp City the night the magic began to fail. I can still come and go as I always could. Like Lukas and the other vamps used to be able to." He gave her a wry look. "I wanted to run off your dates, but Lukas wouldn't let me. He didn't want you to be alone, especially if he could never return to you." His expression tightened. "If there'd been a bad one, you wouldn't have seen him again. But you have good taste in men, Elizabeth. They were all good guys. Just not the right ones for you."

"You met them?"

"A few. Most I just kept an eye on."

She sank back against the seat, raking a hand through her hair. "My very own vampire guardian angel."

He grinned at her. "You could do worse."

Shaking her head, she returned his smile, feeling a bit dazed. "Maybe instead of spying on me, you could come by for dinner sometime. Food dinner. Human-food dinner."

He grinned. "I'd like that."

And so would she. He could bring her news of Lukas and of the hunt for the sorceress.

A short while later, Micah double-parked in front of her apartment building, escorted her upstairs to satisfy himself that her apartment was secure, and to show her on a map precisely where the Boundary Circle lay. Then he said good-bye.

Alone, Elizabeth took a long shower, then pulled on her pajamas, marveling that she'd been gone less than twenty-four hours. Steph . . . Poor Steph. She was sure to think Elizabeth had joined the ranks of the missing. Her friend wouldn't be sleeping tonight, she knew that.

Steph answered her call on the first ring. "Hello?"

"It's me. I'm home."

"Oh my God, Elizabeth. Are you okay?"

"I'm fine. It's been a long day."

"You disappeared! You were there, then you disappeared. What in the hell happened?"

"It's a long story, and I'll tell you everything tomorrow. I saw Lukas," she added softly. "He loves me, Steph."

"Oh, sweetie." She sighed deeply. "I'm just so glad you're safe. You're home? Are you going back to class tomorrow?"

"Yes, I'm at my apartment. No, I'm not going back to school for a little while. I can't. Long story, like I said. Come over as soon as class is over tomorrow."

"Like hell. I'm coming over now. I'll be there in ten. You don't have to tell me a thing tonight if you don't feel like it, but I have to see you. I have to see for myself that you're okay."

Her heart full, yet heavy, Elizabeth set down her phone and reached into her nightstand drawer to pull out the picture of her and Lukas. The love that shone in his eyes as he smiled at her wrapped around her all over again, filling her with warmth and longing and warm certainty.

With her fingertip, she traced his beloved likeness.

"Come back to me, my warrior. My vampire." The tears slipped down her cheeks. "My love."

She gazed at Lukas's face until the doorbell rang, then she slipped the picture back into the drawer and prayed that someday soon he found his way back to her arms.

First Dates Are Hell

A *Those Who Wander* Story

Amanda Arista

Chapter One

VALIANCE WALKED UP behind the Prima as she lounged at her favorite table. Six. There were six ways he could attack her while her back was to the main entrance of the coffee shop.

He looked around. The space hummed, pulsed with life. Even under the coffee's aroma and the espresso-soaked floors, he could smell the life of this place, the life of every person in here. His stomach growled.

This was a test of some sort. Prima Violet was famous for them, pushing everyone the extra step to make them better. Scheduling his monthly meeting here instead of in his own place of business was a test. Her directive to be unarmed was a test. And judging by the uncomfortable nakedness between his shoulder blades and the pressure of the others' energy, he wasn't going to pass this one.

But he could at least teach her something. Make *her* better.

Finding the ebb and flow of the life around him, he moved toward her, in sync with the others in the café. Their heavy steps along the wooden floor covered the sound of his boots as he slid up behind her. He wasn't going to ignore the irony of stalking a were-panther.

Valiance knelt slowly and whispered in her ear. "You could be dead."

The tall woman jumped in her seat and turned around almost as fast as he could blink. Then she laughed as she smiled down at him. "You really shouldn't stalk people like that, Val."

"You really shouldn't sit with your back to the door."

Prima Violet pointed to the amulet above the door. "Most powerful charm in existence. Nothing bad is getting through these doors, Val. You're safe here."

He exhaled. Her faith was going to be her downfall, but he would fall with her for the faith she had put in him. "You still shouldn't make a habit of it."

"Lesson learned, Solider boy. Sit."

Valiance slid into the seat across from her, folding his hands on the table between them. From this vantage point, he could see everything. At least one of them should be on the offensive, no matter how protected the Prima thought she was. Better a thousand times safe than once dead.

The Prima finished a text message and put the phone on the table. She swept her dark hair over her shoulder and settled her content moss green eyes on him. "So how is my favorite vampire this evening?"

His gaze darted to the surrounding tables to see if

anyone heard her. The café had become the primary haunt of the Wandering community, the magical taking refuge in the haven the Prima had created, but he still wasn't used to the openness. He'd spent a hundred and sixty-seven years trying to hide what he was from everyone, other Wanderers included. Violet was the only one in the pack who had reached out to him, who took a moment to realize that he wasn't the monster from the movies.

"I am fine, Prima."

She rolled her eyes. "You rolled around in ghoul guts with me. You can call me Violet."

He nodded. "Yes, ma'am."

She leaned forward on the table. "And you're not fine. You're pale, gaunt even. Have you been feeding?"

He nodded again, keeping his eyes to the table between them. He bounced his leg to relieve some of the pressure down his unprotected back.

"Valiance, look at me."

For a moment, her burnt magnolia scent, laced with pure concern, swirled around him like a warm, spring breeze. He drew his gaze up to clear eyes practically glowing with power and licked his suddenly dry lips.

"What's wrong? And remember my policy on honesty. Are you eating?"

Valiance nodded. "Once a month. Just like we talked about. They don't remember anything."

"Then what is it? You look like a ghost."

Valiance adjusted in the seat, knowing it wasn't the seat that was uncomfortable. "Nothing. Life is very . . . quiet," he finally said.

His Prima smirked. "I don't understand that word. *Quiet*. What is this *quiet* that you speak of?"

The smile crawled slowly across his mouth until he was smiling with her. The Prima's infectious humor. Some days it was more powerful than the panther that lived within her.

Prima Jordan was rarely alone, constantly bombarded by her pack mates. If it wasn't the minutiae of their everyday lives, it was the demon last August that had to be beheaded or the invasion of imps that swarmed Dallas until they were netted and sent back through the Veil. She always called him in for the fight, but after all the action, she went home to a full house, and he went back to an empty apartment.

Violet reached across the table and rested her hand over his knotted fingers.

The action startled him, and his entire body tensed. In the connection, he could feel her power and the slow rhythm of her heart. It was strong, steady, and echoed in the vastness of the energy undulating around them.

Violet only tightened her grip with his flinch of protest. "I can't even begin to imagine how hard it was for you after your Clade up and left you. But now, you've got to be brave again."

Valiance looked up. "Another demon?" For a moment, his heart raced with the thought of battle. A purpose for him and his blade. Something to draw him away from the stillness of his life.

Violet laughed. "No, but good one. You've got to start living. Get out of the shop, get an assistant. Take up quilting. Hell, take a vacation and come back to tell me what it's like."

And here it was. This entire evening was a test. He knew it. A test to see if he was capable of rejoining the human race or, at least, walking beside them again.

She leaned back in her chair, her hand and her power retreating. "Do anything new lately that didn't involve sneaking up on people?"

The monotony of his life flashed through his mind in a matter of moments. "Bought some sheets?"

She raised her dark eyebrow sharply. "That was your big adventure? You're killing me, Val. I expected romance, intrigue, danger." She leaned forward again and lowered her voice. "You're a vampire. That's got to get you into some trouble. Hell, being so blasted good-looking should get you into trouble."

"I thought you wanted us to stay out of trouble."

"No, I want you to stay out of danger. Living life comes with trouble."

Life was uncomfortable, like a wool sweater he hadn't gotten used to wearing. But there was one softer moment he could remember, where it didn't feel like life was trying to suffocate him. "There was this girl."

Violet's energy sizzled around them, and she smiled. "Girls are always trouble."

Valiance shook his head. "It was nothing."

"If you mentioned it to me, she was something. Let me guess. Tall and exotic? No, wait. I bet she's a redhead with legs for days." She leaned forward, her chin in her hands. "Tell me a story."

Valiance couldn't believe he was about to tell this to his leader, the one he followed into battle. But frankly, he didn't have anyone else to talk to about the girl. Maybe if he talked about her, she wouldn't keep circling around in his head. "Complete opposite. The girl who sold me the sheets. Dark hair. Brown eyes."

"Name?"

"Esme." Saying her name out loud only coalesced all the thoughts of her into something bigger and brighter.

"List three reasons you didn't ask her out right then."

The first one screamed through his brain every time he thought about the petite brunette: she was human, fragile and human. Valiance leaned back in his chair, letting his hands drop to his lap. He pinched the flesh on his ring finger and watched the near-bloodless skin slowly smooth out. "This is ridiculous. You're my Prima, for Christ's sake. You shouldn't be worried about my personal problems."

Violet sat up straight in her chair. "Valiance No-Last-Name, my entire job is to make sure you choose your own problems, and they don't come after you. You don't need me like the others do. I still can't figure why you don't have a Clade of your own. So if you need me to be an ear so you can talk about a girl, I'm right here. And if you need Chaz to hunt her down, I can lend him to you for an evening."

His eyes flicked up to his Prima, and she was smiling. In the past six months, he'd learned she meant every word she said, after you got through the Violet-speak. Frankly, she was the closest thing to a friend he had in

Dallas since his Clade brothers left him there. Left him because he took a stand for their future in Dallas. Left him because he showed an ounce of spine in a moment of crisis. He looked down at his hands in his lap only to find his fists, white and bloodless.

"Will we see you at the full moon?"

He wriggled his fingers to get the little blood left in him flowing again. "Are you going to hassle me about dating?"

Violet shook her head. "No. Maybe. Do you want to go to the full moon? You can bring your sword. I've been practicing a little. Might give you a run for your money this time."

He actually had to think about the question. Did he want to go? Sitting on a porch being lonely around other Wanderers didn't really seem like a great way to spend a weekend. He knew they saw him as the worst of their kind, something that stole the life they fought for. Alone with his thoughts, he saw himself like that most days.

But if he didn't go to the full moon, he knew Violet would just drag him someplace else. "I need to return Chaz's whetstone."

Violet smiled. Just as he thought she was going to hound him more about his current activities, her phone began to vibrate. She grabbed the dancing device, looked at the screen, and rolled her eyes. As she rose, she answered the line but didn't talk.

Valiance stood with her. He knew his manners were outdated for this century, but there were certain habits he could not break. Stand when a lady enters and exits. Always carry a handkerchief, and be on time.

She almost looked him straight in the eyes. "Don't make me worry about you, Valiance."

"No, ma'am."

Violet just winked at him as she left the coffee shop, taking the next caller in a long line of people who needed her help.

He sighed and sat back down at the table. His Prima had just told him to "Get a life." How pathetic was that?

"EXCUSE ME, SIR. I'm looking for Esme?"

Her skin prickled. It started on the back of her head and shimmered down her spine. She'd never heard that before. Ever. She looked up from her work of stocking the pillowcase wall and saw the back of a man talking to her manager. He was a million feet tall, with hair that, under the fluorescent lights, looked like the inside of a down comforter.

"Esme?" her manager asked.

"Yes," the man said. His voice was deep, smooth, and not from around here. "Short, slender, biggest brown eyes you've ever seen."

"Oh, you mean Hannah Jane up in Juniors."

The man sighed. "Why would I shop in Juniors? No, she works in Housewares, and her name is Esme. It's on the receipt."

She dusted her hands off on the apron and put the box cutter in her pocket. Slowly, she made her way around to the back of the register, careful to keep behind the display of AS SEEN ON TV products until she got a look at him.

It only took one glimpse of him running his fingers

through his hair before she recognized who it was. Black damask sheets. Seven-hundred-count. Credit card. His hand had trembled as he handed her the card.

As she rounded the display, her manager sighed. "Thank God. Do you know someone named Esme?"

"I'm Esme."

Her manager sighed and walked away, which left her in the very keen sight of the man with the black sheets.

"What can I do for you?" The words didn't feel natural coming out of her mouth. She rarely had to speak at work, let alone help a customer. It's why she worked in Housewares, the only department without a monthly sales quota for its workers.

His broad shoulders relaxed, but he didn't smile. "I was in here a couple of days ago, and you helped me pick out a sheet set."

"Seven-hundred-count Egyptian cotton in black with a damask stripe."

There was a twinge at his mouth. "You've got a great memory."

"It was my only sale this month." She finally saw a white plastic bag hanging around his wrist. "Did you need to return them?"

"No. Actually, I'd like another."

"Oh. Um. This way."

She walked him over to the exact same spot they had stood last week. She felt stalked, like a dark cloud just before a storm was following her. It only intensified when she turned to him at the display and found that the storm was in his dark blue eyes.

She really wasn't sure what happened next. She didn't really do the customer thing, except at Christmastime when everyone was looking for the electric blankets, and that was mostly pointing like a game-show host, like she was doing now. "Ta-da."

God, she had actually said that out loud. She was pathetic. She tucked her hair behind her ear and waited, staring down at his unusually shiny black shoes. Come to notice it, he was a little dressed up for sheet shopping.

"Thank you," he said as he took another set, exactly the same.

In his smooth movement, she was flooded with the smell of him, a musky cologne with undernotes of Downy, but there was a darker twang to it. Something familiar tickled her nose.

As he inspected the plastic package, she looked up at him. His tired blue eyes, his pale skin. But even her caramel skin looked peaked under these lights. It was probably nothing.

"Did you need the matching comforter? It's on sale." Wow, maybe she *was* cut out for this sales thing.

"Sure." He chuckled. "Lead the way."

She walked him over to the wall of comforters. "The store brand is pretty nice. Comes with a bed skirt."

"Never really understood the need for a bed skirt."

"My abuelita believes it keeps the dust bunnies from nesting."

He laughed. It was a deep laugh, short but honest. "Good to know."

"We have pillows, too."

"I think I'm good on pillows. I have to walk home."

"Walk? No one walks in Dallas."

"I enjoy the exercise."

And it showed. Even under his black trench, she could see the broad expanse of his chest and how his buttons strained when he'd reached for the sheets. Given the wrinkled shirt under her dusty apron, she looked like she didn't shower. But then again, until him, no one had noticed her. Ever.

"Can I help you find anything else?"

He opened his mouth but closed it again and shook his head.

"Then the cash register is this way."

As she walked him back to the register, she felt it, that pressure in the back of her head. She wondered if all girls got this when they were being followed, like she could feel him looking at her, watching her messy ponytail bob back and forth.

And he just kept looking at her, and she just kept smiling like an idiot as she rang up the bed set. "Total is seventy-three ninety six."

"That is a good sale." He handed her the credit card again, and again, his hand trembled. This time she paid attention to the name. Val Lance. Very knightly.

She ran the card and handed it back to him. Their fingers brushed for a second, and his fingers were cold, like touching an ice cube. She snapped her hand back.

"Sorry about that," he apologized as he put his card back in his wallet and his wallet in his coat pocket, not in the back pocket like most boys these days. "I really should start wearing gloves."

"We have gloves in men's wear." She blushed when she realized that she hadn't talked so much in ages. She was like a babbling brook under his intense gaze.

Esme pulled her hair behind her ear and slipped his purchases into the handled paper bag.

"I came to get your number." The statement spilled out of his mouth like a gangly kid in a foot race.

Her jaw dropped as her brain contemplated the possible answers to "Why?"

His blond brow furrowed. "To ask you out for coffee?"

Excited goose bumps trickled down her arm. "Why do you need my number to do that? Just do it now."

He laughed that one short laugh and let out a long breath. "Would you do me the honor of having coffee with me?"

She looked up at him and into those tired blue eyes. They were old. Older than her abuelita's, but she felt seen. For the first time in a long time, she felt like she was a normal girl. That should be something, right? Even if it was just a cup of coffee before he realized how completely boring she was, and he forgot her like everyone else did. "Yeah. Yes."

He smiled, and something glowed within him. It was a wide smile that completely changed the dynamic of his features. It lit up his eyes and chased away the storm clouds. "Wonderful. May I have your number so we can set up a time?"

"Actually, I don't have a phone."

"Why not?"

"No one remembers to call me."

She wanted to giggle but fought the light, fluttering feelings in her stomach. She knew exactly where to meet. One of her favorite places in Dallas, where the baristas never forgot her order. "There's this coffee shop off Oaklawn. Big black cat in the window?"

She watched as what little blood colored his cheeks faded, and his Adam's apple bobbed slowly.

"Do you know it?"

He licked his lips. "I sort of know the owner."

"Really? I love that place." She let one excited smile slip.

"Thursday night?"

She nodded.

"So Thursday. Coffee shop. Eight?"

"Sounds good. I'm Esme, by the way." She stuck out her hand.

"Val," he said.

As his cool hand slipped into hers, she shivered again, this time with excitement as the hair prickled on the back of her neck.

He squeezed gently, then pulled away. "See you on Thursday, Esme."

She stayed behind the counter for at least fifteen minutes after watching him walk away. What had gotten into her? Did someone seriously just ask her out on a date? And not just *a* someone. A tall, Viking-looking thing who should be wielding a sword and not sipping coffee.

Esme smiled. Her first date. Her abuelita was going to be so proud. And she might just go upstairs and visit Hannah Jane in Juniors to find something to wear.

Chapter Two

UP UNTIL THAT moment, Valiance was convinced vampires didn't sweat. One hundred and sixty-seven years old, and he was as nervous as a long-tailed cat. It made him smile. Violet would appreciate that. Violet wound be proud of this whole endeavor, no matter how badly it ended. He wiped his palms on the legs of his jeans before he took a deep breath and pulled open the door.

The smell of humans hit him hard in the gut. He should have fed. He'd thought about it, but there was an echo within him whispering he shouldn't pulse with someone else's blood, someone else's life, on his date with Esme. Some very old-fashioned part of him wanted him to be pure for this.

Like he could ever be pure again. He had the lives of a thousand people running through his veins. One more shouldn't have mattered. But it did tonight.

His nose twitched with the soft scent of baby powder

and flowers. His gaze was drawn to the front window, where Esme was sitting in the window seat, watching him with doe-like eyes.

She stood and smoothed her green skirt over her dark leggings and pulled at her jacket. Her rose sweater reminded him of just that, a flower, with her soft scent and delicate features.

Esme met him halfway to the register. "Hi." Her eyes fluttered somewhere around his elbow as she pulled her dark hair behind her ear.

"Hello." He led her over to the register. "What's your usual?"

"The Mexican Mocha. It's got this kick like Abuelita makes."

Valiance turned to the manager. Bastian was one of the few humans in Dallas who knew of the Wanderer community and happily served them coffees and cookies. It struck Valiance that this might be the first time he'd ordered anything here. "Two Mexican Mochas."

Bastian raised his eyebrow at the order. "Really?"

Valiance pressed his lips together in a tight smile. "Please?"

The manager shrugged and rang up their coffees. "It will be a moment. I'm a little behind on orders."

"Are you hiring?" Esme asked.

Bastian laughed as he went to make their drinks. "Don't I wish."

Valiance saw an instant of sadness cross her eyes, and a metal hook pierced his heart. He needed to change the subject quickly. "You talk about your grandmother a lot."

"I live with her." Esme dropped her face into her hands, and the flower scent around her increased as she blushed. "I wasn't going to tell you that. Now I look pathetic. A twenty-two-year-old still living at home."

Valiance chuckled. "Families should live together."

She peeked out from between two fingers. "Really?"

FROM THAT MOMENT on, he was sunk. She was adorable. And nervous. And honest. She spun the porcelain cup in its saucer as she talked about her college literature courses and how the poetry class she was taking now was her last before she graduated though she didn't know what she could do with her degree. She talked about her incredibly large family and how she had to live with her grandmother to get any peace because everyone in her family was loud and in each other's business. She talked about how he was the first customer who ever asked for her again.

"Oh God. I shouldn't have said that. You're going to think I'm even more pathetic."

"I'm not going to think you're pathetic."

She scrunched her nose. "Can you tell I don't talk to people much?"

"Probably more than I do."

She raised an eyebrow. "So now we're going to play who's more pathetic?"

"I'd win. I work in a storefront alone, selling things online. The only person I talked to this week was the mailman. And you."

She smiled up at him, her sparkling brown eyes, her rosy lips, her sharp chin. The only thing that could have pulled him away from that moment was the spike of icy energy that rammed down his spine and made him jerk.

The café was suddenly less illuminated than it had been a moment earlier, a grim shadow quickly cast over his evening. His hand moved to his neck and inside the collar of his jacket. He brushed the familiar hilt just to make sure. He'd tried to leave the house without his sword, but it had been his only companion through all this. And, frankly, he felt naked without it.

"Something wrong?" Esme asked. "Something's wrong. You went all stony."

He was honest. "I don't know."

"Did it get cold in here?" She rubbed her hands up and down the arms of her jacket.

"More than just cold," he said as he scanned the front windows of the shop. It was never cold here, part of the spell the Prima had put on the place. "It's time to go."

"Oh. Um. Okay."

"Where's your car?"

"In the lot out back."

"Let's go."

She didn't question him. She just grabbed her bag and put it across her chest, taking one last drag of the mocha before he escorted toward the rear of the café.

"Are we allowed back here?" she whispered as he ushered her through the storage room.

"I know the owner, remember?"

He guided her through the dark and toward the glow

of moonlight from the back door window. His senses heightened by the fear creeping down his back, he was completely lost in the smell of her hair, the flowers, and her warmth as it pushed against him in the darkness.

He knew right then that she was too good for him. Too sweet. Too pure. What was he thinking even talking to her?

Valiance reached around her to push open the back door, and they broke out into the cold night.

"Which one is yours?" he asked as he reached into his front pocket to get his cell phone.

"The . . ."

Esme sucked the words back in with a gasp as a dark figure swooped down and skittered in the gravel before them. Valiance pulled her behind him. He inhaled sharply as she buried her face between his shoulder blades, pressing the long, hard edge of iron against his spine.

The darkness faded around the figure, and his Clade Brother Mondrian's violently blue eyes smiled at him. "Nice to see you again, Valiance."

Six months of loneliness hit Valiance like a load of bricks in the pit of his stomach. "What do you want?"

Mondrian ran his fingers through his long brown hair, then pulled at the cuffs of his black leather jacket. "A little hospitality, for starters."

"What do you want, Mondrian?" Valiance repeated.

Mondrian spread his hands out. "Just to talk, older brother."

Slowly, Valiance pressed his cell phone into Esme's leg. Her hand wrapped around the phone, catching his fingers in hers for a moment. The thrill of it jumped up his arm and made him stand straighter. "Now is not a good time."

Mondrian's rage twisted his usually perfect face. "You think you're too good for your Clade now? That shifter bitch tell you that?"

This wasn't right. Mondrian's first emotion wasn't anger. His brother would have tried charm first, seduction. Swung around to flattery before resorting to anger. This wasn't a hospitality visit, and the knowledge grated on Valiance's nerves, setting everything on edge.

Valiance's power spiked around him, and the magic enhanced him. His muscles readied, his vision focused, and his fangs pressed down on his lower lip. "You do not talk about the Prima like that."

"You can't tell me you've actually gone native?"

"And if I have?"

"Going to make this harder than planned."

A shadow swooped down and plowed into Valiance. He slammed against the pavement, the wind knocked from his lungs. The figure was gone as quickly as it attacked.

Valiance's only thought was that Esme was exposed and defenseless against them as she stood frozen.

He sat up too quickly, and black spots swarmed in his vision. "Run."

His hoarse voice must have made something click within her, because she ran off into the night.

When Mondrian didn't blink, Valiance scoured the darkness around the parking lot, looking for others, waiting for the next attack. He didn't have to wait long. The shadow swooped again, but this time he was ready. His hand reached behind his head and pulled out his sword. When the figure hit him, he rolled and grabbed the material on the man's chest. He slammed him down to the gravel and had his sword to his throat in less than a breath.

"Finnegan?"

Valiance dropped the man's shirt, and both were on their feet in the blink of an eye. His muscles rejoiced at the feeling of his sword in his hand, at the use of his speed again, but his heart sank at seeing another one of his brethren on what now had to be a mission from Andrin, the leader of his former Clade.

"Brothers don't attack brothers in the darkness."

Mondrian just smiled, and Valiance remembered everything the two of them had done together. Every war. Every city. Every woman. His stomach churned as he remembered the carousing, the drinking, and, most of all, the camaraderie he had desperately missed in the past six months.

Valiance's gaze bounced between the men. Three. There were three ways out of this. None left him unscathed, but Esme would be safe. "You left me here, Mondrian. That's not a very brotherly thing to do."

"Andrin ordered us to leave. It wasn't our fight."

"Prima Jordan was fighting for all of us. Fighting to make sure we could still have something to fight for."

Finnegan snickered. "He really did drink the Kool-Aid."

Valiance heard the rumble of an engine, and Mondrian began to turn his head. Valiance flicked the tip of his sword and pressed it to Mondrian's chest. "Andrin was a coward, running from the fight. I will not align with cowards or those who follow them."

Mondrian looked down at the blade against his jacket and shook his head. "You shouldn't have said that."

"Why? You're in the compromised position here."

A yellow Volkswagen Bug revved its engine and flew out of the parking lot. A weight lifted off Valiance's shoulders as he saw Esme's features in the window, her knuckles glowing white on the steering wheel. But he also knew he was watching his last chance for any sort of normal relationship drive terrified into the night.

Mondrian brushed away the tip of Valiance's sword and continued with his speech. "Andrin wants you back. He's gotten us into trouble, and he needs his warrior prince."

"Why aren't you good enough?" Valiance tested the weight of his sword in his hand. She was perfect, had always been perfect.

He could hear Mondrian's teeth grind across the space between them. "He wants you."

"I've pledged my allegiance to Dallas and to the Prima. I will not break my word for a coward."

"You sound like you're still in the eighteen hundreds, Val. Back when you were still Thomas Valmont, son of an aristocrat. Your perspective needs to change. It's not about honor and codes now. It's about survival and us against them."

"You never had honor and codes, Mondrian. You wouldn't understand."

Mondrian had always been faster. At least that part of him remained the same. Mondrian slammed Valiance against the brick wall so hard he was sure they'd shaken the foundation of the coffee shop. Mondrian's breath was fresh with blood, but there was something else beneath the metallic scent.

"Are you drinking from Andrin?" The words themselves left a sour taste in Valiance's mouth.

"He shares his power with us."

Valiance strengthened his jaw against the fresh pain in his head. "It's a way to control you. You know that, Mon. We've seen this frantic power grab before. Next, he'll start trying to bond new vampires to the Clade."

Mondrian's face didn't betray him, but his teal eyes did. The look told Valiance that his former leader had already started hunting for purebloods with the vampire potential. Once Andrin bit them, and their power had been solidified, they'd be his Clade Brothers forever. Like Emilio had bitten Valiance, and Valiance had bitten Mondrian.

Valiance dropped to the ground and swept Mondrian's legs out from under him. The boy never could predict a leg sweep. The younger vampire bounced against the concrete like a child's play ball and came at Valiance again, but Val's sword was faster.

The iron blade pressed into the hollow of Mondrian's throat. "I will not go."

Something happened to Mondrian. He shivered, from top to toe.

"You will rejoin your Clade." It wasn't Mondrian's voice. Mondrian had been born in the Americas, like Valiance. This voice was deeper and had the lilt of an Irishman in it. Full possession. It was worse than Valiance thought. Andrin's energy coursed through Mondrian.

Valiance couldn't believe what he saw. His best friend reduced to the point that another could possess him. It both fueled him and disgusted him.

"I will not live under the tyranny of a coward."

"Then you will die under one."

WHEN ESME REALIZED she could barely see where she was driving, she pulled into the parking lot of a brightly lit convenient store and tried to get her brain to stop yelling at her.

Of course, he's a monster, and you were just about to be one of those girls in the movies who gets eaten. You are nothing. Why would a guy like him even notice you in the first place unless it was for dinner? How stupid could you be? Maybe there is a reason your parents gave up on you.

Her brain went a little numb after the last thought. The following tears were hot and thick, and she sobbed for a good ten minutes before her tear ducts ran dry.

But he saw her. She shuddered through a deep breath. He saw her, and he had told her to run when those other things showed up.

Esme looked over at the cell phone in her passenger seat. Why'd he given her the phone? Because he knew she didn't have one. What kind of a monster gives you a phone so you can call for help?

Her hand still shaking, she reached out to take the phone. The simple flip model jumped to life when she opened it. Did she call 9-1-1? What could they do? These things moved faster than she could see. What were the cops supposed to do about that?

Did she call his family? She'd heard them say brothers. Maybe they were looking for his brother?

Not used to the phone's buttons, she pressed a few and ended up opening his contacts list.

His extremely short contacts list. One. Jordan. She'd heard that name before. The coffee shop, as a whisper in the air. He'd said he knew the owner. Was that his only contact?

Taking in another breath, she made a decision. Call this person. Let them know Val was in trouble, then race home and never leave her abuelita's couch ever again. That was all she owed him for the coffee.

The phone rang a few times before a woman answered. "Hey, Val. How'd the date go?"

Esme didn't exactly know what to say, so she was honest. "Not good."

"Who is this? Is this Esme?"

Her skin prickled. How did this woman know who she was? "Val was attacked at the coffee shop. He needs help."

"My coffee shop. Nothing can get into the coffee shop."

"Behind it. Look. I don't know what those guys were, but he's in trouble."

"How many?"

"Two, that I saw. I hightailed it out of there pretty fast."

The woman actually laughed. "Thank you, Esme. You may have just saved his life."

Esme closed the phone. Did she want to save his life? Would he try to eat her now?

She didn't know, but she started up her car and wished she'd just stayed hidden down in Housewares.

Chapter Three

MONDRIAN SLAMMED VALIANCE'S face against the car door and Val heard his jaw crack. That was going to hurt in the morning. If there was a morning.

Mondrian turned him around and buried his nose into Val's shirt and inhaled deeply. "You've got a girl on you."

"Leave her out of this."

"Why you chasing dames the old-fashioned way?" Finnegan asked as he swung Valiance's sword around. "Just sway them. It's easier."

Valiance ground his teeth together, and his vision was lost for a moment in the spinning pain of his broken jaw and his concussed brain.

"Oh, I think he likes this one." Mondrian dropped Valiance's shirt, and Val slid down the car, landing hard on his ass. He felt a rib shift like it really shouldn't have shifted, and his sword arm, ripped from its socket, dangled loosely at his side.

"Is that why you won't come back with us?" Mondrian asked. "Some girl. We can find her, you know. See if she's right for the bleeding."

"Never," Valiance growled as he pushed himself up to his feet.

Mondrian let him. Valiance knew he was being played with. After the possession had faded, Mondrian was just enjoying kicking Valiance's ass on principle for all the times he had had to rein Mondrian in, keep him from crossing a line Valiance knew didn't even exist for him anymore.

"Is she pretty, at least? Tall, dark, and exotic. Like that Jolie woman?"

"She's totally one of us," Finnegan pitched in as he spun Valiance's sword around like a parade rifle.

Valiance looked from one to the other. They didn't see Esme. She'd been right there, and they hadn't seen her. *How could they not have seen her?*

The sudden realization ripped a gasp from him. It wasn't just her quaint manner. She might actually be invisible to some people.

Valiance chuckled at the sheer cosmic joke of it all. That he could see invisible girls. Next thing he would discover was that she was a ghost who had died in a tragic pillow avalanche. Sounded about par for this year.

"Going to share the joke?" Mondrian asked.

Finnegan was at his throat in a blink, the sharp edge of Val's own blade pressed into his sensitive skin. "Yeah, Brother. We like a good joke."

The smell of burnt magnolias filled the parking lot. "Then you're going to think that I'm hilarious."

Valiance had never been more relieved to smell Prima Jordan. He swore in that moment he would never make a long-tailed cat joke for the rest of his long life.

She sauntered through the parking lot. When she was within striking distance, she studied both men. "These those Clade Brothers you keep talking about?"

"Every family has its fights," Mondrian said, leaving Valiance for a moment. "Stay out of this one."

Violet shrugged. "Not impressed, Val."

Mondrian was fast as he charged her, but Violet's reactions were faster. Something like pride swelled within Valiance as he watched Violet throw Mondrian across the parking lot. Maybe he had taught her something in their sparring sessions.

She took a moment to recover Valiance from the ground. "So, night going well?"

Valiance took her offered hand and got to his feet. His ears were ringing courtesy of the last slam into the car. "I don't think your phrase *friggin' peachy* has ever really made sense until now."

"Are you good?"

"No."

Finnegan and Mondrian didn't give them time to organize a proper strategy. Mondrian went for Valiance's throat, teeth out and ready for blood.

Valiance was ready for him. He knew every move Mondrian would throw at him, every just-off-center punch and the way he favored his left claw to his right. Even after a harsh blow to the ribs, Val felt a smile cross his lips.

"Please share the joke, Brother."

Mondrian landed a fast backhand across Valiance's jaw but couldn't shake the smile.

"You're too predictable. Always have been."

"Predictable?"

"Even down to your taste in clothes. Must everything be black?"

"Brings out my—"

Valiance landed a hard right hook on Mondrian's jaw, reveling in the sound of the contact that echoed off the brick building.

Blood trickled out of the corner of Mondrian's mouth, and he wiped it with the back of his hand. "So you're really not going to consider coming back to us?"

"No."

There was a shimmer in the air, and Violet's panther made a black streak across the parking lot after Finnegan. The young vampire ran in panic, dropping Valiance's sword as he fled.

The two vampires saw the sword at the same time, but Valiance was faster this time. They slid across the parking lot, but Valiance felt the familiar thrum in his fingertips as touched the metal.

He curled his fingers around his sword, and she felt amazing in his hand. *Good girl.*

"Are you forgetting I have one of those, too?" Mondrian pulled his own blade out from its sheath.

"Mine's bigger." Valiance winked before he swung the sword in the first of a dozen attacks. He wasn't as strong with his left arm, but Mondrian hadn't trained any more than what Valiance had put him through the past seventy years. Valiance had never stopped practicing. Even Violet had taken up swordplay and had the speed to be a challenge for Valiance. She had made him better.

Mondrian had only slowed him down, made him wait for his younger brother to play catch-up.

Valiance was tired of waiting. He wanted this done. He hated waiting. He hated that he'd been in limbo for six months, and the one night he decided to try to get back on the horse, they showed up.

With every angry thought, Valiance's blade lashed out. For every word he couldn't say, his iron spoke for him.

Until Mondrian was pressed against the wall, unarmed, bleeding, and smelling of fear. Valiance took in a deep breath of his scent though he didn't need a reminder of Mondrian's smell.

Iron sliced through flesh with a sickening sucking sound that made Valiance turn away from his brother just in time to see Finnegan's head roll under a parked car.

Violet, in human form, stood over the body, weapon hanging at her side.

Valiance was frozen by the feeling of his Clade Brother as he died. A cold chill ran over his skin despite his battle-charged heat. It was like spiderwebs drawn across his chest as Finnegan's energy was released back into the earth.

Mondrian obviously didn't have the same reaction. He grabbed Valiance's wrist and wrenched his injured arm outward and spun under it.

The tendons in Valiance's shoulder ripped around the dislocated shoulder. The pain numbed his hand and screeched into his ear. Mondrian rammed his knee into Valiance's torso, then was gone, like the air in Valiance's lungs.

"Crap," Violet said as she dropped the sword and went to help Valiance up.

The power of her panther still ebbed around her, and the heat of her pressed against his injured body. As they shuffled over to the dead body, he might have held on to her shoulder longer than he needed just to have her soothing power close to him.

"I didn't mean to . . ." Violet said as she stood over the headless vampire. "I think you taught me a little too well."

"Right. You didn't mean to chop his head off." Valiance shook his head. Pain flared from his right knee to his left ribs to his right shoulder to his left jaw. He was a zigzag of pain. Thinking in a straight line was nearly impossible.

"Well . . ." Violet turned to him. "Want me to fix that arm?"

"You a medic now, too?"

"No, just accident-prone. I've had to do it enough times that I'm an expert. Take off your jacket."

There really was no saying "no" to her, so he slipped off his jacket carefully. His new dress shirt was shredded, blood drying in long lines across his chest. He had the thought that more blood was on the outside than on the in.

He could feel the heat of her hands through his shirt, She walked her fingers down his shoulder blade. Carefully, she took his wrist and brought his arm up to a right angle. "We probably need to talk about something happy because this usually hurts."

"Andrin's using his blood to possess the Clade."

"That's your idea of happy?"

She carefully rotated his arm outward, and every inch she moved it made his head swim in pain. She could relocate it, but the ligaments would still need time to mend. She kept moving his arm, her fingers at his back to gauge the process.

"It's not like it is in the movies, you know. That dramatic pop as the hero slams his shoulder back into place. You need to relax. This isn't going to work if you're tense."

He knew she was talking to keep his mind occupied, keep it from focusing on the pain, on the betrayal of his Clade. His failure to his brothers. She was kind of great like that.

Violet kept cranking his arm back and forth, but he couldn't relax with her touching him. It hadn't been that long since he'd been with a woman, but he was definitely affected by the heat of panther power against his side. It reminded him of Esme, her soft warmth that smelled like flowers.

The thought of her relaxed him for a moment, and Violet hit him like linebacker in the shoulder. A pop echoed through the parking lot, and Valiance grabbed his shoulder as he jerked away from Violet.

"Finally got you to relax enough."

Valiance bent over and let the pain consume him for a second before it settled into a dull throb. He stood and slowly rotated his arm. He'd be better by morning, providing he got something to eat.

"Your girl called me. Told me you needed help." She pulled out her phone and began texting.

"She's not my . . ." Valiance stood quickly as the pain cleared his head, and his thoughts resumed in a straighter line than before. "Mondrian said he'd go after her, and she might be special."

Violet looked up from her glowing phone with a raised eyebrow. "Like Wandering special?"

"I don't know. But I wouldn't put it past Mondrian to go after her just to get me to come with him. He never could disobey an order."

"Sounds like there's a story."

Valiance looked across the dark and empty parking lot. "We went through three wars together, and we got the job done. Mondrian was . . . overzealous on occasion."

"And you?"

"When the cause was right. Never dull a good blade on an evil purpose. The purpose and the sword will betray you."

"Sound advice."

Violet's phone buzzed in her hands. "The Cleaners are on their way to get rid of the body."

"Tell them to box and burn the head."

"Afraid he'll come back? 'Cause I don't think he's coming back."

Valiance sighed but still relinquished a small smile at

her ability to bring levity to every situation. "It is a show of respect," he explained. "Now you need to find Esme. Make sure she's safe."

"Me. No. This, this is all you, honey." Violet started toward the back of the coffee shop. "I got you out of the trouble that came to you. You have to get out of the trouble that you caused yourself."

She threw open the back door, and Valiance had to lengthen his stride to follow her. "What are you talking about? There's a potential innocent about to get attacked by a vampire."

They hit the bright lights of the coffee shop, and Valiance flinched and blinked away his enhanced vision. The light hurt his eyes, and the scent of blood on the both of them overwhelmed him. He probably looked like death, yet the few customers just looked at him, then went back to their reading. Maybe this is what Esme felt like all the time?

"And what are you going to do about it?"

Valiance's feet stopped as Violet leaned against the counter casually, like a waiting customer.

He studied her. Six months wasn't enough to completely decode her. He had no sympathy for her husband. "Is this one of those tests? You're forcing me to grow up somehow. Listen, I'm a full century older than you. I'm grown. You need to stop being childish and go help a Wanderer."

"How? I know her name, and that's about it. I don't know what she looks like, what she smells like. How am I supposed to help her?"

Bastian slid a hot cup of coffee across the pickup area, and Violet sipped it. There was a shimmer in her energy as the hot liquid touched her lips and a glimmer in her eye as she looked back at Valiance, waiting.

He needed a drink.

ESME THREW OPEN the door of the little house, and the walls shook.

"My goodness, child, no need for—"

Esme threw her arms around her grandmother's neck and knocked the words from her as Esme began to sob. Again. She took in a deep, safe breath of her grandmother's baby-powder scent and tried to focus on that one thing instead of the fifty-seven other things running through her head.

Her grandmother stroked her hair and cooed in Spanish. "It's okay, little bird. It's okay, palomita. You're safe here. You're safe now."

Esme let herself be led to the couch and dropped down into the well-worn cushions. The flight response had left her body tired and her bones aching.

Her grandmother locked the door and kicked down the ash branch that always rested in front of it. Within minutes, Esme's hands were wrapped around a cup of hot chocolate with a bit of her grandmother's special spice. One sip, and she immediately calmed down, her mind seemed to focus, and the fear of monsters' chasing her subsided.

Her grandmother sat next to her, her knees creaking all the way down. "What happened, little bird?"

The words flew out of her mouth so fast Esme didn't have time to filter out any of the crazy. "This guy asked me for coffee and I met him at the same place I always go, and then he got this stony look and said we had to go and I thought he was just ending the date early because I'm not the most interesting person in the world. When he walked me to my car, this guy, like, attacked him, but it was like he couldn't see me and then he gave me his phone and then this shadow thing knocked him down and he told me to run. So I did and then I called his sister or something and she knew who I was and then I drove home because I got the distinct feeling they wanted to eat me."

Esme watched her grandmother process the information, too calm for Esme's liking. Her grandmother stirred her cocoa. "You had a date?"

"That's the part of the story you're paying attention to? These things were monsters. They moved too fast. *He* moved too fast, and he had a freaking sword down his back."

"Iron or silver."

"What?"

"Was the blade shiny silver or a dull gray?"

Fear crept across Esme's skin despite the hot drink in her hands. She didn't need to think about it. The image of his pulling the blade out of his coat like a sinister magic trick was burned into her retinas. "Dull. Not like the ones in the movies."

Her grandmother let out a long breath and muttered something in Spanish Esme didn't catch. "What?"

"Drink your cocoa, palomita."

Esme did as she was told. She relaxed again, swirling the spicy flavor around in her mouth before swallowing.

Her grandmother's eyes focused sharply on Esme. "The others didn't see you?"

"Looked right past me, like I wasn't even there. But everyone looks past me. Except Val." That thought kept dancing around her brain. He had seen her. But saying it out loud made the thought even more real and even more frightening.

"Good to know the magic is still there. I was afraid the spell had worn off."

Esme realized she was about to freak out and took the precaution of putting her hot cocoa on the coffee table. "Spell? Abuelita, what are you talking about?"

"It's all real, my little bird. All the fairy tales I told you. All real."

Esme's thoughts stopped. She just stared into her grandmother's brown eyes, which had always held all the answers before. "What?"

"The chupacabra, la llorona, the skin-walkers, all real. And all alive and well in Dallas."

The flight response was back and in double force. Esme leapt off the couch and started to pace. Her Mary Janes echoed off the wood floors. "Why are you telling me this?"

"Our blood is very faint. The magic only surfaces once a generation. Skipped your mother entirely. "

"Magic?" Esme stopped before her grandmother. "Are you trying to tell me you're a witch? I'm a witch?"

"Fairy actually."

Esme laughed. "Seriously?"

A furrow formed between her grandmother's brow, nestled between her other wrinkles there, and she rose from the couch. "I would never lie about this, palomita. Not now. Not that you've been seen by one."

"Seen?" Esme's entire life flashed before her eyes. Everyone ignored her; she slipped by in every class because the teacher never called on her. She was ignored in movie lines. She'd started wearing steel-toed boots at work because people stepped on her feet so often. Everything clicked in her head. "I'm invisible."

"No, my little dove. You burn too brightly. The magic keeps you hidden from those who would take your light. Take another sip of your cocoa."

Esme looked down at the table. That clicked, too. "The spice. Have you been drugging me all these years?"

"Don't be ridiculous, Esme. It's just nutmeg, cayenne, and maybe some ground poppy seed." He grandmother didn't meet her eyes, suddenly very interested in the rug beneath them.

"Oh God. You've been using magic on me."

"It's nothing, just a bit of garden magic, palomita. It's part of our heritage."

"You're insane."

Her grandmother grabbed her shoulders and poked a stubby fingernail into Esme's chest. "You need to listen to me if you've got vampires after you."

"Vampires?" Esme's knees gave, and her grandmother pushed her toward the chair, where she landed with a jarring bounce. "He's a vampire?"

"Iron blade. If it were silver, I would have said shifter."

"I just went on a date with a vampire." Even when she said the words out loud, they didn't feel real. Didn't jibe with what she knew of vampires. He'd been kind, and opened the door for her, paid for coffee.

But he didn't drink it. He'd just spun it as they talked, as he watched her talk. And he'd probably just opened the door for her to see the long line of her neck in the moonlight. See what his next meal was going to look like.

"But he saw you," her grandmother said.

"Yeah, probably as dinner." Esme pinched the flesh of her pinky, the pain focusing her thoughts as the tip turned bright pink with blood.

"No," her grandmother said. "He saw you. He saw through the magic. You said the others didn't." Her grandmother smiled. "His intentions are good, Esme."

Esme huffed. "Well, his intentions can stay on his side of town."

She rose and brushed past her grandmother as she grabbed her bag and went back to her room and made a spectacular show of slamming her door. She was going to have to find a new place to work, a new coffee shop, and maybe a new life altogether.

Chapter Four

"HE'S HERE."

Valiance could smell his blood on the wind. Mondrian had always been good at tracking, but Valiance had never fully appreciated his brother's skills until his scent stopped right outside a house with a magical border around it a mile thick. The white stones around Esme's house glowed in the moonlight, creating a boundary around the property Valiance was sure he couldn't even get through.

Violet crouched beside him. "Think we just confirmed your girl is family."

"She's not my . . ." Valiance dropped it. Violet wasn't going to stop, and he didn't have the breath to waste.

"What's the plan?" she asked.

Valiance had to shift his weight to accommodate the fire burning down his injured leg. "Wait him out. And then you can see if she's okay tomorrow morning."

"That's not the Valiance I saw stand up against his Clade Source."

Valiance clenched his jaw, and the entire back of his head lit up like a lightning storm, all bright lights and pain. His jaw was still throbbing though he'd set it himself on the way over here. The blood from the crack on the back of his head was dried now and made the leather of his sheath itchy.

Violet winced for him. "You need to feed, don't you? It's why you're not healing. Not enough of your own power to heal yourself. Isn't that how it works?"

"You volunteering?"

Violet finally shut up for two seconds, so he could think. Mondrian wouldn't be able to get through that border, especially if his intentions were to hurt Esme. But even if Valiance was right and Mondrian couldn't see Esme, he might be able to see her grandmother.

Valiance might be able to make it through the border. Make sure they were okay. But if Esme had seen three seconds of what happened in the parking lot, she was never going speak to him again, let alone invite him in to wait out the night against another vampire.

His head dropped down to his chest. His true colors had shown through, and she'd seen them and ran.

"I smell pity," Violet said.

"You smell a man realizing he should have stayed in the shop."

"Yep. Self-pity. Smells a little like rotten milk."

"Were you always so campy?" He looked over at his Prima.

She nodded. "Yes, actually. But I'm right."

Violet jumped and reached for the glowing cell phone in her back pocket. "Just when things were getting good." She sighed as sat down on the cold ground. "Hello. What? Now? I'm kinda in the middle of something, Nash. Oh, well talk about burying the lead. Of course. I'll meet you there."

Violet hung up the phone, and her energy danced around her. "I have to go."

"What?" Valiance snapped.

"Kandice just went into labor a month early. I have to go."

"You've got a hostile vampire hunting innocents in the city."

Violet patted him on the back. "And I've got my best Riko on the case."

"Riko? That's a shifter title."

Violet ran her fingers through her long hair as she pulled it back into a ponytail. She slipped off her tennis shoes and shoved them in her messenger bag. "I'm a shifter. The words are pretty. Do you accept?"

"Accept what?"

"The rules and responsibilities of being the warrior and the protector of the pack?" She zipped up her jacket against the cold wind. She dropped her personal borders, and her power sizzled around them. "Do you accept?"

Valiance knew you didn't say "no" to Violet, and even if you did, it didn't stay a "no." "Yes?"

"Wonderful. From what I've heard, there's a vampire

going around and attacking innocents. Take care of it. Call Tucker if you can't handle it."

Violet winked. In a blur of black and a whirl of energy, her panther form streaked down the street in the direction of downtown before Valiance could even manage a protest.

He clenched his jaw, and the pain flared again. "I don't have my cell phone," he finally said to the wind.

"Told you she wasn't worth it." Mondrian appeared in the street before Valiance, his hands casually in his pockets.

Valiance rose. The slick red over Mondrian's lips was unmistakable, even in the dim glow from the streetlights. He'd gotten a chance to feed. It was like hitting a reset button on the evening. He'd be faster now, stronger than Valiance who barely had anything, power or blood, left.

"The Prima trusts us to clean up our own messes."

Anger made the angles along Mondrian's face sharper, uglier. "Is that what I am? A mess to clean up?"

Valiance walked out onto the street, hiding the wince of every step. "Destroyed my evening."

Mondrian looked at the small house. "So your girl is special?"

"Yes."

"And you're going to kill me, your own brother, to protect her?"

"Yes." The honesty rang through Valiance and made the sword on his back hum with anticipation.

Valiance saw another figure in the darkness. Female. Older. And completely under the sway. He recognized the glassy eyes of the woman as she stumbled this way and that. Like a marionette on strings, she danced how Mondrian wanted her to dance.

Valiance didn't have time to get her before she fell to her knees beside the white stone periphery of the house, her teeth snapping against each other as she dropped. Where a vampire couldn't touch the protective border, an innocent human would have no problem pulling a stone out of place to break the spell.

He ran for her, but Mondrian met him in the middle of the street. His brother slammed against him with the force of a semitruck, and they flew down the street. Valiance landed hard on the pavement, with his brother on top of him, and they rolled, both struggling for the upper hand.

There was a distinct clap of flesh meeting something solid, but it didn't come from him.

Valiance looked over from his position beneath Mondrian to see an old woman with a baseball bat standing over the limp body of the puppet woman. It had to be Esme's grandmother, the abuelita she spoke so lovingly about, wielding the bat like Babe Ruth himself.

The older woman's courage gave Valiance the kick he needed. He threw Mondrian over his head and jumped to his feet. He used the last of his energy to enhance himself, heal his leg, and give his muscles the strength they needed to wield his sword.

"Keep the circle," he called out to the old woman.

The woman yelled something back at him. But he missed it when his eyes landed on Esme standing in the doorway of their small house. The entire world stopped for a moment, and he was caught up in the sight of her. Her dark hair unbound, her cheeks flushed, she glowed in the doorway of her home with her tear-filled eyes.

He heard Mondrian's sword sing as it cut through the air behind him. Valiance ducked and felt the wind of the attack against his hair.

Valiance swung his arm back hard, and Mondrian's ribs cracked under his blow. He turned around sharply and swept Mondrian's legs out from underneath him. The other vampire bounced against the concrete like a rubber ball. Valiance caught his shirt in his fist and threw him at the protective spell.

Mondrian slammed against the magical border and sizzled and seized within the white energy before being thrown across the street into a car. There was no alarm, just Mondrian's long groan.

Valiance tried not to smile, but it was the first break he'd gotten all evening.

He turned back to the house, where Esme and her grandmother were together on the porch. He walked over to the edge of the white stones but didn't dare step across. He looked at Esme. "Are you okay?"

"No problem here," her grandmother said, her grip still tight on the bat.

"Stay inside. I'll be right—"

Mondrian's boot landed square between Valiance's shoulders, and he flew forward through the white-stone protective spell and landed hard on the frozen ground of her front yard.

Mondrian's hand clamped down on Valiance's ankle and raked him back along the ground. As Valiance struggled to stop, he felt the protection spell break around him as he pulled a white stone from its place, like the pop of an electrical transformer.

Mondrian ripped him from the ground and threw Valiance into the same car that had broken his own fall. Valiance let gravity take him and slid down to the pavement. He couldn't feel his legs for a moment and fell forward to his knees, seeing nothing but stars.

He leaned back against the car and shook the celestial array from his vision. He had to blink a few times for his sight to focus.

Mondrian was already on the porch. He grabbed Esme's grandmother and locked an arm around her neck, swinging her petite frame around like a rag doll.

He was less than a foot away from Esme, who had plastered herself against the outside wall next to the door.

His brother didn't need to yell; the wind carried his threats fine enough. "Bet she never goes out with you again if you let her grandmother die."

Mondrian cloaked him and her grandmother in darkness and blurred away into the night.

Valiance tried to push himself up against the car, but the power was gone. He fell to the concrete. He couldn't breathe. Everything hurt, but it wasn't over. He might not have his unnatural strength, but he was still breathing. He wouldn't stop fighting until he stopped breathing.

Slowly, he pushed himself up to his feet and stumbled

to the edge of the yard. He carefully put the stone he'd dragged out of alignment back into place.

He looked up to see Esme still standing on the porch, like a frightened statue, only her wide eyes following him across the yard.

"Do you know where the locking stone is?" he asked. He started to walk the periphery. He didn't know much about this kind of magic, but he knew the locking stone needed to be recharged if the border was going to go up.

Esme didn't answer, just watched him.

He kept walking. Fairy magic wasn't foreign to him; he was one, for Christ's sake. The glamour, the seeing of the unseen. The taking and giving of natural magic. Granted, he was the darker distant cousin of what normal people thought as fey, but the same principles applied. Too bad he'd never dabbled too much in garden magic.

It could have been his raw state, but as he passed the corner stone in the yard, a power sort of tickled at his ankle. He knelt. Well, it was supposed to be a kneel, but really he fell forward, landing next to a larger than average white stone half-buried in the yard.

He put his hand on the stone, and it was warm. A normal fae could probably just push power into the stone, but he was a vampire. It had to be blood with him.

He looked down at his hand to find a small trickle seeping from a wound on his knuckles. He smeared it against the stone. The periphery jumped back to life, like plugging back in a line of Christmas lights. What did you know? He did have it in him.

He had to take a deep breath before he pushed himself to his feet. When he did, Esme was standing right next to him. The spell between them didn't prevent him from smelling the flowers in her hair or seeing the bright sparkle in her eyes from the fearful tears that stayed wavering on the edge.

"Where did he take her?" she asked.

"I do not know. But I will get her back."

Esme looked him over from head to toe. "She didn't tell me much except that you're a . . ."

Valiance cringed. He didn't want her to say the word; it would kill everything within him to hear the disdain in her voice.

"That you can see me because you're a good guy."

Valiance felt like he could breathe again.

"You'd better come inside. You don't look so good. And someone's going to notice that car."

He shook his head. "We need to find your grandmother."

"Abuelita is strong, apparently stronger than I ever gave her credit for. You need help before you go and get yourself flattened. Again."

SHE TOOK HIM into the kitchen, but when she flipped on the light, he flipped it off right behind her. It left the only light in the small room the glow from the stove top and the moonlight that filtered in from the small window.

Fear sizzled down her spine as she went to the far side of the room to get the first-aid kit. However, all the fear turned to a kind of strange excitement as she watched him gingerly take off his jacket and his shredded dress shirt, exposing the sword running down the length of his back. His shoulders were broader than any man's she'd ever seen, and the handle of the sword seemed to wink at her in the moonlight streaming in from the windows.

He slowly walked across the kitchen to the sink and began to wash his hands.

She grabbed a few towels for him and quickly set them beside him before scurrying back to her place at the end of the counter.

She could see pain in his eyes as he moved. He slowly dried his hands. He wetted the towel and held it to his face, wiping off some of the dried blood and sweat.

He drew in a tired breath before he spoke, his voice low, soft. "Do you still have my phone? I think I need to call for help."

Esme had to think. The encounter already seemed like a lifetime ago. "It's in my purse." She scooted around him quickly and dashed into her room to find it.

The foreign phone was easy to find in her familiar purse, and she slipped back into the kitchen swiftly, setting the phone between them on the counter.

Valiance took it and popped it open. He hit a few buttons and growled as he put the phone to his ear. At least, it sounded like a growl. "No answer."

Esme gulped. "So no backup?"

Valiance turned around and leaned against the kitchen counter. "I don't know."

"You've said that too many times."

Valiance turned his blue eyes to hers. "I am sorry, Esme. I never meant to . . ."

Her spine stiffened, and the words that came out of her were hers but from someplace within her she wasn't familiar with yet, someplace jarred loose from this evening's activities. "It's too early in the evening for apologies. What do you need to get her back?"

Valiance sighed. He walked over to the table and sat down, looking much smaller than he had just moments ago as he put his bruised face into his hands.

He was less than two feet away, and she swore that every cell within her pulled toward him, pulled toward the fragility draped across his shoulders.

The decision solidified within her as she spoke words that were hers but not hers. "I'm willing." Her voice was barely a whisper across the kitchen.

His steel blue eyes were grayer now, as if the color had drained out of them, along with his blood, as he looked up at her. "You don't know . . ."

"I do." Her voice was stronger as she reached for the unused first-aid kit. She cut an appropriate-sized piece of gauze. "I mean I think I know what you need. Abuelita told me stories about people like you. You need blood to heal, and I can't find my abuelita without you."

She ripped off four pieces of tape and dangled them over the edge of the kitchen counter. Then she rolled up the sleeve of her jacket and held out her arm. "I trust her, and the only thing she said to me tonight that made any sense was that you wouldn't be able to see me if you really wanted to hurt me."

His cool fingers reached out and slid around the inside of her wrist, just holding it gently. Goose bumps shot up her arm, and she gulped.

"I made a promise to myself that I . . ." He was so exhausted, he couldn't finish the sentence.

"I've never had to make promises to myself. I've never had anything this horrible ever happen before."

He looked down at her pale wrist as he stroked it with his finger. "You think I'm horrible."

She took in a deep breath, trying to calm the stammering of her heart. Her words might be brave, but her body was still catching on to the idea. "No. But as far as first dates go, I'm sure this is up there with the worst ever."

"It was selfish of me. I just wanted to have a pleasant evening with a pretty girl."

His words caused a flutter in her stomach. She tried to convince herself he would say anything right now to get blood, but she couldn't believe it. Especially after he looked up at her, his skin paper white in the dim light. The heavy look in his eyes made her forget about the press of sharp white on his lower lip.

"Esme, I . . ."

She cut him off. "I did nothing, Valiance." The name those men had called him fit better as she said it out loud. It was more him than the abbreviation. Even more regal than the name on his credit card.

Esme went on. "He was three feet away from me, and I froze. I couldn't even move until after he'd already taken her. I need to do this. I failed in my first attempt at bravery. I will not fail in my second. I will not fail her."

His hand tightened on her wrist, and he pulled her down the edge of the counter until she stood before him. Her pulse raced in her ears as he leaned forward, his forehead almost resting against her breasts as he pulled something off the counter behind her. He pressed that something into her right hand as he pulled away.

She looked down at the silver knife. "Will this really do any damage?"

"It's sharp enough to ensure I stop."

Esme curled her fingers around the handle though she wasn't sure she could use it on him.

His eyes trailed down to her tender wrist, still in his hand, as he sat back down on the chair before her. "I promise this will not hurt much."

When his lips touched her arm, heat flew up her wrist and burned into her core. She barely felt the slice of his teeth against her skin. She was more focused on the other hand he slid around her waist, pulling her closer to him, keeping her still.

His tongue began to coax out the blood, undulating slowly against her skin. Not that he needed to work much, her stammering heart was rushing blood to all her extremities and warming every part of her.

She leaned back against the cabinets, and her eyes fluttered shut. Immediately, her thoughts traveled to what else he could do with that tongue, where else it might have the same flushing effect.

He gripped her waist tighter, and the pressure on her arm increased. She gasped as she felt a stronger pull of blood out of her veins.

"Val," she said softly.

When his fingers began to dig into her arm, she gasped, and cool fear fought the intense heat that had spread throughout her.

"Val," she repeated. She tried to pull her arm back, but his grip was too strong.

"Valiance," she cried out.

He was standing above her in less than a blink. His eyes were livid blue with blown pupils, and his mouth was stained red. His body pressed her against the counter, and she was awash in the smell of blood and sweat. The monster was here, and still hungry.

But just as fast as he had risen, Esme had the knife to his throat. The flash of the silver blade dug into the pale skin, and her eyes steadily gazed into his dark pools. Her heartbeat steadied, and she let out a long breath. That other part, that braver part, saved her and settled in for the evening.

"Sit," she ordered.

Valiance did as he was told, and the moment he was in the chair, he looked away.

Esme looked down at her wrist to see nothing more than an inch-long slice on her lower forearm. It wasn't like the movies at all, probably wouldn't even scar, but then again, she didn't need anything to remind her of what happened tonight. She grabbed the bandage and taped up the small wound, keeping her fist to her chest to stop any bleeding.

He was looking down, away, his neck exposed.

She watched the fair flesh come back together at his

cheek, mend itself until it was a bruised reminder of what had happened earlier. Esme couldn't believe the magic before her eyes. That a little bit of her blood could do all that wonder. Maybe she really was something special.

"Valiance?" She kept her voice soft as she reached out to his shoulder.

"Are you okay?" he asked, still looking away from her.

"You were the one pulverized."

"Please, Esme." When he looked up at her, she'd never felt so seen. His blue eyes glowed with power, and everything about him was perfect. The bruises on his cheeks were gone. He looked rested, flushed even. His cheekbones could cut leather, and his lips were the most perfect shade of rose.

He still wasn't as beautiful as when he had smiled at her in the coffee shop the first time.

"I'm fine," she finally managed.

"Please don't look at me like that." He stood and strode across the kitchen to a darker corner.

"What?"

"It's part of the blood, part of the glamour. It attracts, and I feed. Do you understand?"

"The power makes you pretty?"

"It makes me attractive, so I can feed." He licked his lips of any red still left there. "And you're fey, right? I wasn't really sure."

Esme grew colder as she thought about the why of his perfection and that he was tasting the magic in her blood. She shivered. "But you're faster, stronger, too. I mean, I saw you fight that other vampire, and you were—"

"Some days, the other perks aren't worth it."

She tried to lighten the mood, get the conversation going again because the guilt that shaded his eyes struck a pain through her heart, and the last thing she needed right now was a sullen vampire on her hands. "Did you know that to her family and friends, Emily Dickinson was more known for her gardening than her writing, and she would send bouquets to her friends with poems attached?"

Valiance frowned, but his expression slowly turned into a smile. "You really do like that poetry class you're taking."

She smiled, relieved, and started packing up the first-aid kit. "I just relate to them. All the great ones looked in from the outside. We loners have to stick together." She thought she heard him chuckle from the other side of the kitchen. "What do we do now?"

Valiance looked down at his hands, his long fingers, and turned them over to inspect them. He rubbed his chin and tested it. "I should be able to track him down now. He's not a strategist, so he'll go where he feels safe."

"What will he do with my abuelita?"

"Nothing. He's still trying to get me to go with him."

"What about kidnapping my abuelita will convince you to go with him?"

"I have no idea. Just managed to piss me off really. You don't touch grandmothers. They are universally off-limits in the rules of engagement."

"Rules of engagement? You sound like one of those old generals in a Civil War movie."

"I was one of those generals in the Civil War."

"Oh." That meant he was old. Like really old. She let the fear wash over her again before she took a deep breath and just integrated it with what she knew about him. He opened doors, he drank blood, he fought to protect her, and he was older than her grandmother.

It was more interesting than her list of traits: inviso-girl.

Esme put away the first-aid kit and rolled down her sleeve. "So what do we need to do?"

"We?"

"She's my grandmother. I'm going after her. Don't exactly know what I can do as the invisible girl, but I'm going with you."

Valiance stepped out of the darkness and into the light from the stove. Gold fell across his perfect features, and her breath caught in her throat as he continued toward her.

Even his voice was smoother now, deeper, softer. "I want you to be sure about this, Esme. Once you've seen violence, seen evil, it changes you, and I don't want to be the reason you see the world a little darker."

Esme's skin flushed with his words and with his scent as it beat around them both. "What's your real name?"

"What?"

"That thing called you Valiance, but it's not the name on your credit card. What's your real name?"

Valiance licked his lower lip.

"Why?"

She was honest. "Valiance sounds made up."

"It was."

Esme looked up and tried to fight a smile. "What?"

"My Clade Source Emilio, the one who made me, renamed us into our new life. One word to describe us."

"And yours was Valiance?"

"Warrior prince, he used to call me."

Esme knew that no other name could suit him. "Like the fairy tale?"

"I'm not a fairy tale."

"I'm not saying you are," she said quickly. "I'm simply saying that it's like a fairy tale. Like everything else that's come true tonight. And if vampires and fairies can be real, then I think we have a good chance of getting my abuelita back."

Valiance watched her for a long moment, then went to get his jacket from the kitchen chair. His movements were fluid, smooth, not the jerky pain from before. "There are three places he might go. The apartment, the shop, or this warehouse off Industrial."

"Great. Let's go find him."

"We need more of a plan than just knocking on the door."

"What if I knock?" she asked. Her stomach tightened. Where would an insane plan like that come from?

"What?"

Esme licked her lips. "What if I knock, he doesn't see me, and I sneak in? Distract him somehow?"

Valiance thought. It took him a long time, and Esme was suddenly nervous. What did she know about covert ops and rescue missions? It was probably a ridiculous idea that might lead straight to her death. Or worse, her grandmother's.

Slowly, a smile spread across his lips. "I don't think you're the same girl I asked out for coffee."

"I've been through a lot this evening. I'm not the same girl I was five minutes ago. I woke up this morning a normal human girl with low self-esteem, and now I'm some fairy who's invisible to bad guys. Who knows what I might be by dawn?"

He laughed. That one deep laugh as he looked at her. "We need to get going. Can you drive?"

"Is that why you walk everywhere? You can't drive a car."

"Over a hundred and fifty years old, and I still can't get the hang of it."

"But you have a cell phone?"

"I like texting."

Chapter Five

VALIANCE WAS HAVING a hard time sitting still in the front seat of her car. The power, the energy that flowed through him, was like nothing he'd ever had before. The little bit of blood that he had taken had given him more power than he'd had in a decade. Everything smelled sweeter, everything felt softer. His muscles tingled anxiously, waiting for action again. Not only was she a fairy, but she was powerful one.

When his cell phone rang, he jumped in the passenger seat, and Esme swerved.

"You all right?"

"Fine." Valiance looked at the caller ID and put it on speakerphone. "Talk quick. Phone's almost dead."

"You guys okay?"

"He took Esme's grandmother. We're hunting him down."

"I'd volunteer to send Chaz, but there's a swarm of ghouls tearing up some butcher shop in Oak Cliff."

"So your night is going well?"

"Never a dull moment. How's your girl holding up?"

Valiance looked over at the driver's seat. He wanted to say Esme was the most luminous thing he had ever seen. But it was only a first date. Maybe all first dates were like this, minus the kidnapping and bloodletting.

Esme beat him to it. "We are going to get my grandmother back, then you and I are going to discuss getting me a job at the coffee shop."

The phone line was quiet for a moment. "Well, Bastian is really the manager there."

"I'm tired of folding towels, and I'm sure the owner could put in a good word for me."

"Val, take me off speaker."

Valiance did as he was told, prepared to get an earful.

Instead, Violet only said. "Keep her, please. You don't meet a girl every day who can just fall into violence and still be confident enough to backtalk the Prima of a city."

"She doesn't know—"

"Keep her. Sounds like you've got some pretty good backup. But if you really need help, send up a flare, and I'll be there."

"Yes, ma'am."

Valiance hung up but looked down at the phone in his hand.

"What didn't I know?" Esme asked.

Valiance licked his lips as he prepared his words. "Violet's not just a coffee-shop owner. She's the most powerful Wanderer in the region. Possibly in the country."

"And?"

"You just told her she needed to get you a job."

"And?"

Valiance smiled. "You're just nothing that I've seen before."

"I'm nothing anyone has ever seen before apparently." Esme flashed him a smile as she continued down the highway.

ESME PARKED ALONG the curb. It was an older neighborhood she had never been to before. Just another example of her universe expanding this evening.

"Welcome to my second home," Valiance said as he pointed to the shop across the street. Emilio's Antiques was a restored home in a long line of restored homes turned into shopfronts. If this looked like a normal shop, she wondered how many other places her grandmother had dragged her to were also run by things that went bump in the night.

Suddenly, Valiance turned to stone in the passenger seat next to her.

"He's here, isn't he?" she whispered, as if Mondrian could hear them.

"Yes," Valiance said. "I wasn't able to feel him like this before. Forgot how much of an effect we have on each other."

"Which means he knows we're here, too. So much for the element of surprise." She sighed. "What about me? Can you feel me in your head since I'm supposed to be magical or something?"

He looked over at her. "I don't know," he whispered. "My head's a little funny around you anyway."

Esme bit her lower lip and suddenly found the edge of her jacket very interesting. This was now officially the worst best date ever.

Valiance turned to her in the car. It was a bit comical, his long legs twisted up in the front of her VW, as he reached down by his boot to unlace a bowie knife from his calf. "When we get in there, your only goal needs to be getting your abuelita out of there."

The skin tightened along her shoulders as his perfect accent caressed the familiar word.

"Do you understand?"

"Yes, but how?"

"You're going to knock on the door."

Esme laughed. "You can't be serious."

"Completely. You knock on the front door, and I'll go in through the back door."

"And if he's got both covered somehow?"

"You hide. I'll fight. Now take this." He shoved the leather-sheathed knife at her. "He will get violent. Ultimately, he wants me to come back with him—"

"Which means he doesn't care about me and abuelita."

"Exactly." Valiance sighed.

"So we protect ourselves and leave you to the wolf?"

Valiance looked into her eyes. "I'll survive."

"I don't want you to survive. I want you to live with all your parts in place. I'm not leaving you in there like a coward. If I've discovered anything about myself in the past four hours, it's that I am not a coward."

Valiance blurred before her, and his lips were upon hers before she could finish her thought. His lips were warm but hesitant. He slid his hand up to hold her jaw but didn't deepen the embrace.

Her body hummed like a fluorescent bulb. Energy danced along her skin with the novelty of being kissed in the front seat of her car like a high schooler, something she hadn't actually had done as a high schooler.

She kissed him back, taking in more of his soft lips, tasting the slight copper of him. She burned the taste of him into her brain, the warmth that pulsed against her. *Their warmth*, she thought again. Her bravery had brought him back to life.

He was the one who pulled away, and when he did, she knew he was different, changed from the moment before to the moment after. Everything she'd ever read about warriors flashed through her mind, and she had half a notion to give him a token as he went off to war.

Valiance licked his lips, leaving them shiny in the moonlight and completely distracting. "You knock on the front door. I'll go in through the back, and we'll meet in the middle."

Esme looked ahead and tried to focus on the plan. Knock on the door and sneak in. But as she shifted in the seat again, his arm brushed against hers, and all she could think of was his lips on hers and how she wanted to do that again.

"Esme?"

She could feel his breath on her neck. "Yes?" She gulped as she stared at the steering wheel.

"I think you're glowing."

She looked down at her hands, held out before her. They looked like her hands, all normal and small. "I think you might be seeing things."

"I don't think so." He turned the rearview mirror toward her, and she could see what he had seen. Like someone had sprinkled her with candlelight, there was a slight illumination to her skin. And there was a sparkle in her eyes that wasn't normally there.

Her gaze snapped over to Valiance. "What does that mean?"

Valiance shrugged and put the rearview back where it had been. "I only know one fairy."

"And does she glow?"

"Only when she's happy."

Esme looked away but fought the urge to bury her hands in her face. "So much for being dark and exotic and not pathetic at all."

"Dark and exotic has nothing on you."

Esme tried to bite back the smile that accompanied the butterflies in her stomach. She didn't think that one human could feel so much in one moment. Fear for her grandmother, embarrassed that he could see right through her, and complete admiration for the man in the seat next to her.

But then again, she wasn't all human, so maybe this was just par for the course.

"We'd better get going."

He hurried out of the car and swooped around to the driver's side to open her door for her. He offered his hand to help her out. She knew that she shouldn't be smiling, but she did as she slid her hand into his. It was warm, soft, and gave her just enough support as she exited.

It was a horribly outdated gesture, but effective. It gave Esme the distinct feeling that this was still a date. There might still be some hope, providing they survived the night.

Chapter Six

VALIANCE STILLED HIMSELF at the back of the building and drew the darkness around him. It was an old talent he hadn't used in a while and the power, the glamour, was hard to hold.

He locked his eyes on Esme. She'd taken a position at the front of the building and was leaning against the wall, her head against the brickwork as she prayed. He watched her cross herself and close her eyes. Her rose lips muttered a prayer.

For the first time in a century, Valiance prayed, too. It wasn't to God or anything. It was just to the wind and the dirt. He didn't know any blessings or anything. He kept it simple. *Keep Esme safe. If you gave her this power, then keep her safe so she can learn how to use it.*

The wind carried Esme's floral scent to him, and for a moment, he thought maybe the wind had heard him.

Maybe the wind was at their back. Maybe the earth was a fan of grandmothers as well.

Esme let out a long breath and fluttered her eyes open to look back at him. Despite his cloak of darkness, Esme waved and gave him a thumbs-up. With a soft smile, she slipped around the front of the building.

She was going to be something amazing, and every ounce of him wanted to be there when it happened.

Valiance squared his shoulders and turned the hilt of his sword over in his hand before finding a grip. He walked softly up to the back door and surveyed it. Carefully, he reached out and touched the door handle. No electrical charge. Not iron. No precautions.

Did Mondrian want to get caught? Was a part of him asking Valiance to kill him to get it over with? There was only one way this was going to play out. One.

He closed his eyes and listened, with a capital "L," for Esme to knock on the front door.

The sharp rap on the door echoed through the building. Valiance counted to ten before he turned the knob and pulled open the door.

The explosion lifted him up and off the ground. The flames burned his jacket, and his fair eyebrows were forfeit.

The chain-link fence at the back of the property cradled him like a wiry catcher's mitt, and he rolled forward onto the ground. He landed on his knees, and his lungs smoldered as he tried to catch his breath.

Mondrian wasn't going to give Valiance those brief seconds to recoup. He charged toward Valiance, his sword slashing out before him. Valiance had moments to flatten himself against the ground to avoid the edge of the blade.

Valiance grabbed Mondrian's leg and jerked him to the ground. Mondrian crashed, and his sword was knocked out of his hand.

Valiance shook the ringing from his ears before he went on the offensive. He jumped to his feet and darted to where his own sword rested in the long grass. The sword vibrated in his hand as if agreeing to his purpose.

It took Valiance one thought, one flash of a second to let his power consume him, let his energy enhance everything about him, heal his burns, and adjust his eyes to the dim lighting in the yard. The thought that this energy was Esme's fueled him further; that he was doing this for her made him stronger

Mondrian still searched for his sword. "Didn't peg you to come alone. Thought you'd have that pussy Prima of yours."

Valiance waited. His brother might have taken the wrong path, but he still deserved an honorable death. "You're stalling. You always get mean when you stall."

"I'm not stalling. I've got 'til dawn to convince you to come home."

"My home is here."

"Our place in Atlanta is amazing. The old family seat, Valiance. It really would be Thomas Valmont coming home."

Atlanta. The memories were so far gone that Valiance's mind fogged trying to recall them. For a moment, he saw himself happy. He saw himself with his family, with his grandmere on the porch, her soft sweet smile as she hummed into her needlepoint.

Valiance shook the memory from his head. His grandmere was dead. The house had been burned in one bout of violence or another. There was no home for him there anymore because there was no family there anymore. He wasn't Thomas Valmont anymore.

Just as Valiance was about to say that, Mondrian slammed into him. Valiance doubled over the man's shoulder and rammed the hilt of his sword into Mondrian's spine. The man cried out and crumpled beneath him.

Valiance kept hold of his sword as the fight became a twisted mesh of swinging arms and wrestling legs. Once they regained their footing, Valiance always had the upper hand; his sword did not fail him. Mondrian's grunts punctuated the heavy staccato of metal on metal.

Valiance spun Mondrian's sword off into the darkness, only adding fire to his fury. As Mondrian set up for another attack, Valiance watched as his friend, his brother, disappeared and was replaced by a monster. Valiance would mourn later, only after he'd put him out of his misery.

Valiance cried out into the darkness as he ran at the man. There was another exchange of blows. This demon was fast, but Valiance was smart. He tasted blood, smelled blood, but his energy, her power, was a fire that ran through him.

The sound of a car door distracted Valiance for a moment, and in that one moment, Mondrian pinned him to the ground. His lips were pulled away from his sharpened teeth, and his eyes burned with a dark fire. A kind of dark Valiance hadn't seen since, well, since the demon he and Violet had taken out six months ago.

Until Violet, he had never known true darkness.

Until Esme, he'd never known true light.

"I will never go back."

Mondrian's Master spoke. "What have you got that's worth dying for?"

For the first time, he was honest with his brother, and the wind and the stars that shone down on him. "Hope." Hope in her. Hope in his city. Hope that someday he could be that man.

"Pfft," the Master said. "Hope is a city in Arkansas."

"Hope is a thing with feathers."

Mondrian's blade flashed above them. The sword made a sickening thud as it sank into the back of Mondrian's neck.

The man reared up and spun on his invisible attacker.

Esme screamed and ran.

Valiance jumped to his feet. He grabbed the handle of the sword and pulled it out of Mondrian's neck. The force pushed Mondrian off balance, but he still stumbled in Esme's general direction, his claws lashing out into the night, his head dangling by his windpipe.

Using gravity and the sheer need for this to be over, Valiance swung the blade over his head to deliver the last strong blow to Mondrian's neck.

Blood sprayed the small yard as Mondrian's body fell lifeless to the ground. His head rolled but found a resting place in a soft patch of weeds.

Valiance's chest heaved as his heart raced. His arm dangled at his side as he looked at the still body. For the second time that night, he found himself praying. *Keep him. Take his energy back into the earth and remember him, remember what he was.*

That's when Esme started screaming.

Valiance dropped his sword and rushed to her. "Are you okay? Are you hurt?"

Esme burrowed her face into his chest and shook. He wrapped his arms around her and felt every ounce of his fight response seep away, replaced by a warm pulse, her pulse. It was only when he realized he'd synced to her heartbeat that he let her go. Her fingers were wound tightly in his cotton shirt, so he couldn't go far.

"Please, Esme. Are you okay?"

Her wide brown eyes were not filled with tears, but her body still shook. "I just killed someone."

"Technically, you just injured him really bad."

A strand of her dark hair fell across her forehead and caught in her lashes. "But he's dead. I did that."

Valiance reached up and pushed the errant strand of hair behind her ear. He'd been wanting to do that all night.

Esme frowned slightly. "And I did it to protect you."

He nodded. "You did. Thank you."

Esme smiled, then her entire body shook.

"Where is your abuelita?"

"In the car with the bowie knife. She told me I needed to rescue you."

"It seems you have."

Esme closed her eyes and took in a long breath as she rested her head on his chest. Valiance's eyes closed as he reveled in the heat of her, the pulse of her, so close and so unafraid of him. This was a quiet he could get used to.

Slowly, the shaking stopped. "It's grass."

"I was just rolling around in it."

"No, the deeper smell. I thought it was just a cologne or something, but that's the real you. The underneath you. A vampire that smells like fresh-cut grass."

Valiance couldn't stop smiling; his cheeks were beginning to ache with it. "I guess I don't notice it."

"What do I smell like? My deeper smell."

He knew part of this was the trauma talking. He took the opportunity to run his arm around her shoulders and begin to nudge her slowly toward the front of the house.

"Wildflowers. Sun-warmed wildflowers."

They cleared the backyard, and Esme's fingers finally unfurled from his shirt.

"I guess for a fairy, smelling like flowers isn't very original." Esme pulled away from him and seemed steady enough to walk on her own.

"I can with all honesty say that I've never heard someone quote Emily Dickinson before delivering a deathblow."

Esme stopped and put her face in her hands.

Valiance's stomach tied up in knots. "I'm sorry," he said quickly.

Esme started to softly chuckle. "No," she said as she dropped her hands from her face and shrugged. "I guess that's what I do in times of action. Something else I learned about myself today."

"So what's the grand total?"

They stopped by Esme's car. Valiance gave a small wave to her grandmother, who sat in the front seat with the knife clearly displayed.

Esme counted the newly learned facts on her fingers. "I'm invisible to bad guys. I'm a fairy. I'm not a coward. And I quote poetry when I fight. What have you learned today?"

Valiance took in a deep breath. There was a dead body in the backyard that the Cleaners would need to dispose of, and he was pretty sure he should call their contact in the police force because an explosion would catch someone's attention, even in this neighborhood. But none of that seemed to matter. "This was probably the worst best date ever. Or the best worst date ever."

A blush spread across Esme's cheeks, and her floral scent filled the air around him and seemed to seep into him. "It was a first date. I've been told all first dates are hell."

Valiance found his hands shaking as he asked the question, so he jammed them in his pockets. "Is it too early to ask for a second?"

Esme looked down at her hands. He saw the blood crusted in her fingernails, the crimson spray across her shirt. The moonlight caught the white bandage at her wrist, and again, he felt his palms begin to itch with nerves.

But when she looked up, and those wide brown eyes caught his, the hope that he had spoken about earlier seemed to flutter through him.

"Sure beats folding towels on a Saturday night."

Blood and Water

Kim Falconer

Chapter One

STELLAN SHOT TOWARD the ferry, his naked body gliding through the water just under the waves. He swam over sharks and knobble-backed sturgeons, while above, the setting sun turned everything to gold. Brilliant clouds were mirrored on the glassy surface. Beautiful . . . but worrisome. There would be dozens of passengers on the observation deck tonight. Dozens of deaths.

The more the merrier, Salila said, her voice rippling through his mind. She wasn't too far behind him.

He swam harder. The ferry was heading southwest and coming up on Goat Island, a rock in the middle of the bay. *Listen to me, Salila. You don't have to do this!*

Oh, but I do!

The paddle wheel churned through the waves. It rose over the hum of the steam engine and the distant siren sounds of whales traveling slowly along the coast. Stellan was tempted to break the surface when he reached the Bay City ferry, but the sun, and better judgment, kept him beneath the waves. He dove, skimmed the hull, and came up on the port side, sticking to the shadows. In a leap, Stellan grabbed the lifesaver netting and climbed until he could see the main deck.

People were chatting in small groups, gazing at the horizon, taking in the last rays of the sun. Stellan counted them, sweeping his eye across the deck, up to the wheelhouse, and down the other side before stopping short. The fine hairs on the back of his neck stood on end.

A woman walked toward the starboard railing, her breathtaking figure radiant in the light. The wind danced in her floor-length skirt, revealing the outline of long, slender legs. Fine lace pulled tight across her lower back, accentuating the curve from hips to breasts. Stellan felt a pounding in his chest. Impossible, he thought. Everything else was falling away, his vision a vignette with only the center, only her, in bright clarity. She was like living fire, or was that the sunset? Magnificent! What are you playing with, my lady? She seemed inordinately preoccupied with a small wooden box mounted on stilts. He watched, fascinated. Ah, a camera . . .

Isn't she lovely? Salila cut into his mind.

He growled deep and twisted around, his dark hair trailing over his shoulders and down his broad back as he tried to spot the Mar woman in the water. *This has to stop!*

That's not what Teern says. She surfaced and disappeared again. Taunting.

Stellan's eyes went back to the deck. The object of his attention was sliding a glass plate into the camera. Quickly, she ducked under a black hood, and the whole thing flashed like a shooting star. A photographer! The thought would have made him smile if he weren't so busy working out how to save her life.

The sun dropped into the sea, and the belated fog began to rise. A Mar fog. It was Salila's shroud against detection. Stellan tore his eyes away from the woman long enough to dive back in and swim to the prow. The ferry chugged on, but the sound of the whales vanished. They tended toward silence when the Mar were hunting. The waves beat against his back as he clung directly underneath the main deck. He couldn't see her anymore, but he could hear.

"There's enough light for one more shot."

She's optimistic.

"Put your cape on and come inside, Miss Ralston! It's gone quite cold and will be pitch-dark before we dock. You'll catch your death . . ."

He hoped she would heed the warning. It would be the death of all those left chatting under the stars if Salila and the others had their way.

"Angelina Ralston!" The well-dressed matron beside her continued. "You're not listening."

Angelina . . . Stellan licked salt water off his lips. An angel . . . Her hair was auburn red and reminded him of autumn trees along the Atlantic Coast. Her eyes were dark like Egyptian onyx, and her lips full, inviting. She wore a long-sleeved ivory dress with pearl buttons that ran from her slender waist, between her round breasts to her high, lace collar. On her head was a matching hat, cocked up on one side. Stellan's throat went completely dry when she spoke.

"Mrs. Blackwell, I am comforted by your concern." She donned a forest green cape that hung to her black leather boots. "I assure you, though, I'm not the slightest bit cold." She lowered her sweet voice. "The sea is mesmerizing, and the vista like warm embers. Look how the pale evening light dances across the rising mist. It's so beautiful. If only I had a camera that could make sense of these subtleties . . . this other world."

"VERY POETIC, I'M sure . . ." Mrs. Blackwell huffed.

"Ah, but light is poetry," Angelina said to herself. Then louder, over the chatter of the other passengers, "There's too much to experience on deck, Mrs. Blackwell. I can't bear to walk away from the sensations."

"Miss Ralston! Now I must insist you retreat to the safety of the cabin. Your father wouldn't have you lingering in 'sensations' of any kind, I am sure."

"Fortunately, Father is not here," Angelina whispered.

"What did you say?"

She cleared her throat. "I'm a hunter of light, Mrs. Blackwell. I put my consciousness upon its reflection, watching, waiting to capture what I can."

Stellan's eyes widened as he listened.

"Life isn't all about photographs, Miss Ralston."

"It is this evening. Father's instructed me to record the seascape."

"Yes, for the bridge . . ."

"Bridges." Angelina emphasized the plural. "One along this ferry route, from Oakland Mole to Market Street Landing, and the other . . ."

"Across the Golden Gate, I know!" Mrs. Blackwell sighed. "The esteemed Mr. Ralston, and my son, your fiancé"—she exaggerated each syllable of that last word—"speak of nothing else."

"Then perhaps you'll appreciate . . ."

"I appreciate nothing in this damp, cold fog and endless sloshing of water all around. It's unnatural."

"Not to me." Her voice was wistful.

"Yes, I've heard about your proclivity toward swimming." The older woman fussed with her coat buttons, doing them up to her chin. "I'm going inside, and you are to follow directly. Gather your things. I'll not have you out here unattended."

"Of course, Mrs. Blackwell." Angelina kept her eyes on the sea, making no move to leave.

The matron turned to a man who stood a small distance away with his hands clasped behind his back. "Assist her, Gerald."

"I can manage myself, thank you," Angelina said. She turned to the man. "Could you please see Mrs. Blackwell safely inside."

"What will my son think if I allow his fiancée to catch

a chill?" Mrs. Blackwell said over her shoulder while being escorted to the doors.

"I'm sure he will think nothing unkind of you, Mrs. Blackwell."

The woman snorted at that and disappeared into the cabin.

Stellan struggled with conflicting desires as he watched Angelina lean against the railing. There were other people still on the deck. He had to be ready. Salila would act soon.

You should be helping us!

I think you do fine without me.

We are Mar, Stellan. Have your forgotten your own nature in all these centuries?

No! He frowned. *But your way is . . .*

That of the Ancients!

We don't even know who they were! A master race from the sunken continent? Remnants of children sacrificed to the sea? We've lost our history, Salila.

But not our traditions! Her voice stung. *We need human blood to rise from the tombs. We need it to walk on land.*

We don't need so much that they die! I've found . . .

A better way? So I've heard. What's Teern think of your big idea?

Stellan didn't have an answer for that. He'd yet to discuss it with their leader.

You might want to move away from the bow, brother. Salila's warning shot into his mind. *There's going to be a little spill.*

The Bay City ferry had two ballast tanks with a thirty-ton capacity each. If one malfunctioned, the nose of the vessel would momentarily dip, and any passengers on deck would slip right down into the sea. Salila was very good at making things malfunction.

Don't do it!

Too late.

The ferry lurched, and Mar began to tear up the side of the vessel, splintering the hull in their race to the top. The prow smashed nose first into the swell, and the main deck, moments ago a stately, horizontal surface, upended. People lost their footing, all but Angelina. She gripped the railing with both hands and held fast. Salila made to jump at her, but Stellan caught the Mar woman by the ankle, a bone-crushing hold.

She spun and snarled. *What's wrong with you!* With a disgusted look, she kicked free and dove, hitting the water, where people were splashing and waving.

Angelina screamed, her grip nearly gone. Stellan threw himself into motion, ripping apart the railing in his vertical ascent. As he launched toward her, the bow of the ferry bounced back up, tossing passengers into the sky, Angelina among them. Stellan's collision course ended with a resounding thud, his chest slamming into the woman as his arms encircled her.

Thousands of sparkling water drops sprayed out from their impact. Streams arced from his long hair, reaching toward her face. The sounds of the paddle wheel and engine, the screams of drowning humans, and the clang of bells faded into the background. But suddenly there was only this young woman, this angel, in his arms. The scent of her filled his nostrils, her warmth turning his head light as air. Angelina's heart pounded hard against his bare chest as she clung to him. Her eyes were shut tight, and she was still screaming as they began to fall.

"Angelina!" he shouted.

Her lids flew open, and she stared straight at him.

Stellan couldn't breathe. Seeing her, holding her . . . it felt like sunshine, open fields, and a fullness of heart he'd never known. She pierced him with her beautiful, dark gaze, a weapon more potent than anything imaginable. They held each other tight, speechless, until, like a stone, they plunged into the sea.

A CACOPHONY OF sound rushed by, punctuated by the snap and flare of misshapen voices. Comprehension was futile. When she managed to grasp hold of anything, it disintegrated into blind, meaningless noise. Then darkness settled, calm until a whoosh of air inflated her chest. Heat rolled over her skin. Pain registered, then a heartbeat, pounding, earsplitting. She sucked in the air, hungry for more. Pins and needles shot down every nerve. Pressure built, and Angelina's eyes flew open.

Who are you? The question echoed off luminous walls.

A figure hovered close by. His hair was long, and water dripped from the ends onto her exposed neck. For a moment, she could see the contours of his face. Then they blurred into memory, a strong jaw, full lips. A man planting his mouth over her own, breathing life back into her body. His shoulders, beautifully curved as he leaned in, were marble white . . . Then the shouting started.

"What in the dead bone's deep did you bring her here for? Have you lost your mind?"

"She would have drowned otherwise!"

"Who cares?"

"I do!"

The words tumbled together, mixing with the incessant ring of high-pitched water drops and rolling waves that surged up and down the walls of her reasoning. A shadow streaked into view and was immediately banished. Angelina licked the salty tang of the sea from her lips. It tasted like blood.

"Fine. Protect her if you want. But Teern will never let her live, now that she's seen you."

"She won't remember!"

"Are you sure about that?"

Angelina's head throbbed. Water splashed over her face, and a deep, commanding energy slammed her.

"You have interfered with the hunt, again!"

"Teern, forget what Salila says. The girl can be useful."

"How?"

"She knows about the bridge."

Bridges, Angelina thought. She managed to lift herself up on her elbows.

A hand pressed ever so gently on her bosom. It replaced the swirling void with warmth. Peace. She closed her eyes and drifted away.

"I can take the human girl back. Learn more of their plans."

A single word taunted her. *Human?* Angelina fought against the confusion as she was swept up in strong arms. The rush of cold air forced her eyes wide open. Into them stared two jewels, gray-green like the sea. She stared back. "Who are you?"

Chapter Two

04:12 P.M.
Monday, April 16, 1906

SOMETHING TERRIBLE HAD happened, Angelina was sure of it, but for the life of her she couldn't recall what. Sun shone onto her face, and she could hear waves pounding the sand. Buoys clanged, or was that the sound of cable cars? Her fingers traced across the sand. "Where am I?"

"You're safe, Miss."

She opened her eyes to find a gentleman bending over her. He reminded her of someone, and she wondered at herself for imagining smooth marble skin beneath his white, high-collared shirt. He wore ferndale striped trousers, a gray-green vest that matched his eyes, black silk puff tie, black riding boots, and a tweed frock coat. His face was . . . beautiful, and his long, wavy hair was secured at the nape of his neck. She studied him until the sun's glare made her look down. He must have been wading in the surf, for his trouser cuffs and boots were soaked. With his help, she sat up. Her clothes were wet and utterly disheveled. She touched the top of her head. "My hair's come down," she said, her mouth feeling like it was stuffed with cotton.

"What do you remember?"

Angelina frowned. "I was returning from Oakland with Mrs. Blackwell, taking photographs for my father." She rubbed the back of her neck.

"On the Bay City ferry?"

"Yes!" Her hands went to her mouth "There was an accident! People went overboard!" She raised her voice. "My fiancé's mother, Mrs. Blackwell! Gerald, our manservant! Did they survive?"

"The event was in the papers this morning, Miss. No mention of names, but seven people were still unaccounted for."

"And I must be one of them." She buried her face in her hands and exhaled long and slow. "This is terrible!" With another deep breath, she looked up. "But you saved me? Pulled me from the sea?"

"From the surf," he said. His voice was warm and rich. "You washed up on a raft of driftwood. I spotted you from the wharf." He pointed to the pilings near the water channel.

She took in the industrial waterfront, with its warehouses and longshoremen working the docks. Facing west was a sign reading PIER 42. "China Basin?"

"Indeed."

She stared at him, her mouth open. Angelina didn't remember hitting the water or swimming to the driftwood, or anything else past hanging on to the railing for dear life when her tripod went over. "My camera!" She looked about as if it might appear beside her.

"No sign of that, I'm afraid." He helped her to stand. "Please let me introduce myself. I'm Stellan Fletcher." He shrugged off his coat and draped it over her shoulders. "Is your home far away?"

"Pacific Heights." Her mind was in a whirl. Stellan. She turned the name over with her tongue. Where was he from? She couldn't detect an accent. "Mr. Fletcher," she offered her hand. "I'm Angelina Ralston and deeply in your debt."

"You mustn't mention it."

Their eyes met, and chills went down her spine. For a moment, she thought her knees would give way. "This is a most peculiar event, Mr. Fletcher, but I do think you've saved my life. That is worth more than a passing mention."

He gave a small bow. "I'm at your service."

Angelina smiled and brought her hand to her neck. It was wet even though her lace collar was beginning to dry in the breeze. Her fingers came away bloody. "I must get home." She lowered her voice. "And avoid the press if at all possible."

"I will find a cabdriver and escort you." He pointed toward the docks. "It's not far to King Street if you can manage."

"I can." Angelina allowed him to take her elbow and lead her up the sandy dune to the pier and on toward the bustle of the city. She sat on a bench while he hailed a taxi. It didn't take long. Inside, she sat for a moment with her eyes closed.

"Directions?" he asked.

"Fillmore and Washington Street."

Stellan repeated the location to the driver and climbed in the other side. With a chug and backfire, they were off, swerving through the traffic. The cab was a Model A Ford that had seen heavy use. It moved at a snail's pace, which was fortunate considering the reckless driving on Market Street. Stages, hack carts, donkey traps, and cable cars vied for right of way along with what Angelina thought were far too many pedestrians. They bumped over the tracks, veering out of the way of oncoming cable cars just in time. The noise jarred her mind. Out the dusty window, the angle of the light was severe.

"What time is it?" She stuck her head out from under the canopy before Stellan could answer. Captivated by the light, she watched it cross the tall buildings, glinting off windows, forcing shadows to lengthen.

"Nearly sunset," he said.

"It's been twenty-four hours?"

"Since the accident? I believe so."

Angelina pulled her head in, suddenly thinking of her hatless appearance and her wild hair blowing in the breeze. "I suppose it's a miracle I survived." The smell of city refuse, horse manure, engine oil, and bricks wafted in. It jolted her back to the present, reminding her there was a strange man, her rescuer, sitting quite close. Automatic manners took over. "Do you live in the city?" she asked.

Before he could answer, the driver slammed on the brakes and pounded the horn. A man on a wheel, one of those bicycles she'd been wanting to try, much to her family's vexation, had nearly plowed into them.

Stellan stared after the contraption. "I'm a visitor."

The way he looked at the world going by, she was sure he was glad of that. "Where then?"

He hesitated. "Europe."

"That hardly pinpoints it, Mr. Fletcher," she said, and pressed her forehead into her hand. It was getting more and more difficult to keep up the social niceties.

He noticed. "I'll tell you my full life story if you like, but perhaps for now you'd rather rest."

Angelina closed her eyes. "I think I will. Please rouse me when we reach Fillmore and Washington."

NOTHING'S CHANGED, STELLAN thought. He didn't want to breathe. The air was foul, the land dust dry, and the crowds of humans, more visible than ever in daylight, smelled acrid. San Francisco had no order, no symmetry. There certainly had been no improvement to the system of traffic since his last visit. People crossed at any and every point, as did riders trotting into view from behind wagons or blind corners. He'd witnessed three near calamities since they started and it had only been a matter of minutes. At that point, Stellan wondered if his whole plan seem mad. Maybe it is. But when he looked over at Angelina, resting quietly, with her hands in her lap and her eyes closed, her long hair falling in tangles over her shoulders to brush the seat of the car, he knew he'd made the only possible choice. He drank her in until the driver dropped speed and shifted into low gear. They were moving away from the business district, driving nearly straight uphill. Upon reaching the top, they turned again and descended a short way, pulling over to the curb. Stellan placed his hand lightly on Angelina's shoulder. "Miss Ralston?"

She straightened and attempted to put her clothes in better order. "Hello." She gave him a soft smile. "Come. You must see the view."

Stellan got out to get her door, but she was already climbing out. She pointed toward the sea.

The homes lining the hilly street were grand, but the vista took his breath away. He could see all the way to the marina. Beyond that was the Golden Gate Channel, turning red with the sinking sun. And beneath it . . . ah, beneath it lay the sheltering tombs. "The light is extraordinary."

Angelina tilted her head. "Are you an artist?"

"Not like you."

She raised her brows but didn't reply. For a few moments they stood side by side, watching the sun go down. It was a rare sight for Stellan, considering what it took for his kind to tolerate the day. He glanced at her neck and frowned. Hopefully, no harm would come of his choice.

The driver stepped up, dusting off his cap and clearing his throat. Stellan pulled a fine leather wallet from his breast pocket and paid.

"Mr. Fletcher, I will not be any more of an inconvenience."

"It is no trouble, I assure you."

She curtsied. "Shall we face the family then?"

He offered to support her, but she kept a slight distance between them.

"I'm rattled, Mr. Fletcher, I'll admit, but I'm not an invalid. I only hope the news is that all have been as lucky as I to survive." Angelina led the way up wide steps that began at the sidewalk. They were lined with an ivory, wrought-iron fence. Wandering roses grew over the metal, their vines following the contours of every loop and curlicue, dotting them with apricot and yellow blossoms.

"This is your home?" he asked as he tilted his head to take in the three-story mansion.

"It's my father's." Her back straightened. "He designed it when he and my mother first married."

"Your father is an architect?"

"In more ways than one."

Stellan looked at her sidewise. "Controlling?"

"He's planned my life from birth to grave." She shook her head. "But it is a lovely house."

Stellan felt obliged to make some show of actually looking at the building and not her. "Marvelous rooftops. Copper cupolas?"

"Yes, capping the turrets and oriels, too."

"Wonderful bay windows."

"My favorite is on the south wall. The stained glass is from Italy. I will show you."

He smiled. His face actually hurt from how much he'd been doing that today. "I anticipate viewing it with pleasure, Miss Ralston."

Angelina laughed, and he felt heat rush through his body. "I think you really are an artist, Mr. Fletcher, a quite famous one perhaps, who is keeping his identity a secret."

He wanted to say he had no secrets, but instead, he winked at her. In moments, they reached the entrance-way, where pillars and arches supported the high ceiling. From the beams, hanging baskets overflowed with ferns and colorful flowers. "Your home is extraordinary, Miss Ralston."

She leaned toward him. "I must warn you about my family . . ."

For a moment she was close enough for him to catch the pulse of her heart. It was so distracting, he didn't immediately register the front door's opening and the voices' exclaiming in surprise. Soon shouts and a rush of people crowded the entrance, all talking at once. Angelina was whisked inside, and Stellan followed, for the moment forgotten.

"Gerald! Call for the physician!" a booming voice commanded. "And send word to the Blackwells this instant!" He pointed his finger at Angelina. "Twenty-four hours, young woman! That's how long you've been gone without a word! Nearly ruined our new connections. Your fiancé was ready to cut all ties. He thought you were dead!"

She went red in the face. "My sincere apologies, Father."

The family closed in, assaulting Angelina with questions.

"What were you thinking, not doing as Mrs. Blackwell asked?"

"Have you no concern for your own future?"

"How did you survive?

"You look like something the tide washed in!"

"I feel like something the tide washed in," she managed to say. "But I'm alive and well, and it's a relief to know that Mrs. Blackwell and Gerald are, too." Her eyes went to the servant.

"Of course they are," her father yelled. "They went inside the cabin, where passengers ought to be." He glared at her. "How did you manage to get home?"

She pursed her lips slightly. "We have Mr. Fletcher to thank for that."

Stellan felt the entire gathering turn to him. "It was no trouble," he said, his eyes still on Angelina.

She returned his gaze and mouthed the words "thank you," as several women led her up the stairs. "He pulled me from the surf," she said before disappearing into a room.

Stellan sagged for a moment as if released from a spell.

One of the women, her mother, he guessed, from her age, called down the stairs. "Don't just stand there, Mr. Ralston. See to this man who's found our daughter." She called to a maid. "Hot water for the bath! Quickly! Where is that physician?"

Mr. Ralston stepped forward and extended his hand as he introduced himself. "The ferry situation is appalling! What we need is a bridge."

"My thought exactly," Stellan lied.

The older man smiled. "You'll dine with us, at the least. Are you visiting the city?"

"For a few days . . ."

"You'll stay here! I insist."

"Thank you, Mr. Ralston. That will be a pleasure."

ANGELINA WAS IN her own bed, freshly bathed, with the comforter pulled up to her chin. The elderly physician, Dr. Medleys, had poked and prodded her from toe to tonsils while he mumbled questions to himself, supplying his own, unintelligible answers. Eventually, he gave her a clean bill of health, dressed her neck wound, an injury she could have received when falling over the broken railing, and told her mother to feed her a simple meal and let her sleep. Angelina got the meal, a small portion of fish broth and a piece of sourdough bread, no butter. She also took a few moments to dash off notes to several friends who would be frantic by the news of her disappearance, but even with that accomplished, her mother seemed reluctant to let her rest.

"You did well, Angelina, keeping your counsel in front of Dr. Medleys. He's competent, of course, but he doesn't need to hear the details. You know how word gets around."

"I wasn't keeping my counsel, Mother. I truly can't

remember what happened." Until I opened my eyes and saw Mr. Fletcher standing on the shore . . . She sighed into her pillow.

Mrs. Ralston proceeded to test her memory by asking her everything she could think of, from "When did you know you would fall" and "Aren't we blessed you're such a strong swimmer" to "Who would have thought that a useful skill?" She wasn't quite through scolding her, though. "Mrs. Blackwell assured me you'd been asked several times to vacate the deck . . ."

"And she suffered no injury?" Angelina cut in, hoping to change the topic.

"A nasty bruise on the arm and an attack on her nervous system are all. She was seated inside."

"Yes, Mother. And did all survive?"

Mrs. Ralston shook her head. "Sadly, no," she said, then started talking about the tea she'd had to cancel on Angelina's account.

Angelina closed her eyes to feign sleep, deepening her breathing until she heard footsteps brushing over the rug. There was a pause at the door, then it clicked shut. She peeked to make sure a maid wasn't stationed in her bedside rocker. Finally alone, Angelina felt free to contemplate recent events. Her mind went out to those lost though she couldn't picture any of the others who'd stayed on deck. Then slowly she felt pulled toward the young man who had found her, Stellan Fletcher. What incredible happenstance to put him in her path at just such a moment. Or put me in his path is more likely. With that thought, her lids closed softly, and Angelina drifted away.

THE HOUSE WAS deadly silent, but Angelina felt another presence in her room. The door hadn't opened, and there were no footsteps approaching the bed. Still, something had roused her, like a warm mist rising between the cracks in the floorboards. She opened her eyes and startled. *Stellan?*

Pleased don't be alarmed, Angelina.

What are you doing here?

If you can forgive the intrusion, I was only hoping to see that you were recovered from the ordeal.

Part of her thought it was beyond forward to be making such a private inquiry. And at this hour! Another part thought the gesture was both sincere and endearing. While she tried to focus on the outlines of his face, he took her hand and lifted it to his lips.

My beautiful Angelina.

The kiss on her hand lingered, causing sensations to spread throughout her body. The next thing she knew, he was embracing her, his mouth kissing her lips once, very tenderly, then moving to her neck. A pleasurable sound escaped before she could contain it.

Just a few drops . . . he whispered.

Her lids became heavy, and she had the distinct sense of falling into the sea.

Chapter Three

6:00 A.M.
Tuesday, April 17, 1906

ANGELINA SAT BOLT upright, gasping for air. She checked the scream about to escape her lips and took in the room. She was alone, the dawnlight tinting the bay windows rosy red. Slowly, her hand went to her throat. The dressing was in place, but her satin gown had slipped off one shoulder. Her hair had escaped its braid and was damp with sweat. She sat there, in the middle of the bed, trying to make sense of it all.

What happened last night? Her face was flushed, but the images in her mind were fading fast. Whatever it was, it had made her feel good . . . to the core. She got up and filled her washbasin with water from the pitcher. After a wash, Jeanie came in to help her dress. Breakfast was served early at the Ralstons', and no doubt Mason Blackwell would call to see that she had indeed survived. And discuss the latest engineering developments with her father. She frowned. Mason . . .

The engagement had not been her idea. Mr. Ralston simply announced one day that it was time for her to do her duty to the family.

"I wasn't aware of such obligations," she'd said.

"Then I'm glad to have enlightened you, daughter," he'd answered back.

Mason Blackwell was a young architect in the Ralston firm, and not without independent means.

"It's a logical choice," her father had insisted.

"Hardly the best motivation for marriage!"

He'd dismissed that outright. "What else would you base your choice on?"

Shortly after that conversation, Mr. Blackwell came to call. Angelina thought him too much like her father, but both families were congratulating them before she got the first protest out.

"Think it through," her mother had said in private. "You're twenty-seven and have yet to accept any prospects. Enough is enough!"

"I haven't accepted any because none have shown the least interest in my art, or my philosophies."

"My dear! Why on earth would you want them to?"

Angelina thought of her photographs hanging in New York galleries and being purchased for publication in the *Yellow Ribbon,* a statewide suffrage newspaper. How could she wed someone who didn't recognize her creative goals or respect her politics? What am I going to do? The families were pressuring them to set a date, her mother hoping for June! It didn't give her much time to figure a way out. I must make a stand!

Angelina held on to the thought, as well as the back of a chair, while Jeanie laced up her corset. It was yellow satin with white ribbing, made from the latest pattern out of Paris, *La Mode Illustrée.* Thank you, cousin Emily. Yesterday, her corset strings had come completely loosened in the accident, and the freedom of that sensation was hard not to long for. Jeanie helped her slip on a pale rose tea dress and buttoned it up the back. Her hair was untangled, put up, then on went the matching hat, with its trail of paper roses on one side.

"Lovely," Jeanie said, as Mrs. Ralston pushed into the room.

"A great improvement over yesterday's appearance!" her mother confirmed.

"Thank you." Angelina cleared her throat. "Is Mr. Fletcher at the table?"

"Of course. Where else would a young man be? Though his appetite for conversation seems bigger than his stomach."

"Mother?"

"He's as obsessed with the Golden Gate as Misters Ralston and Blackwell. I suspect he's an architect or an engineer. How many men of such persuasion can fit into my house?"

"Three at least, it seems." Angelina turned from the mirror. "I'm ready."

Her mother narrowed her eyes. "You're positively glowing, child. Are you sure you're not fevered? How's your appetite?

"I could eat a horse," she said, making Jeanie smile and her mother gasp. Angelina headed downstairs, leaving them to follow.

STELLAN GLANCED NOW and then at Mason Blackwell. The human was unimpressive, as far as he was concerned. Stocky build but leaning toward portly, a weak jaw, and hairline receding like a full-moon tide. None of this would matter if he had heart. Strength of spirit. Reverence for Angelina. So far, these attributes had not been displayed. Blackwell had barely asked after her, making Stellan's opinion of the man fall even lower. Utterly unworthy.

Stellan . . .

He startled, turning his gaze to the dining-room entrance. It was empty. *Now I'm imagining her voice in my head?*

Moments later, Angelina appeared in the doorway, her eyes going to Stellan's and resting there.

"Miss Ralston," he said, and stood. "And, Mrs. Ralston," he added, as her mother came straight in and sat down.

The other men finally rose as well. Mr. Ralston gave his daughter a cursory look. "I trust you're fully recovered and have written formal apologies to Mrs. Blackwell and her son?" He indicated Mason, who stood next to him.

Angelina seemed unable to respond.

Mr. Ralston sat back down, leaving Stellan to pull her chair out, seating her next to him. It put her directly across from Mason, who was still standing. When the other man spoke, Stellan had to contain the low growl threatening to escape his lips.

"Dear Angelina." Blackwell spoke as if reciting a passage. "It was such a relief to hear of your safe return. Mother is still recovering from the shock of it all, of course." Somehow, he managed to make it sound as if it were Angelina's fault. "A harrowing experience, I am sure, but all's well that ends well." He smiled briefly, then sat back down to his morning paper.

"Thank you, Mr. Blackwell, for your, and Mrs. Blackwell's concern for my welfare." She kept her hands in her lap as her breakfast was served: two fried eggs, bacon, and toast with blueberry jam. Along with it came a silver tray with a mountain of envelopes. "I can see my recovery is an utter relief to some. Thank heavens."

The paper rustled. "Yes, thank heavens."

She didn't reply, but Stellan thought the *San Francisco Call* might ignite from her look alone. He turned to her slightly. "Do you feel completely yourself today?"

She blushed. "I feel more myself than I ever have in my life. I might go so far as to say a new self is emerging." She focused on her breakfast, attacking it with knife and fork, taking large bites of egg followed by the toast. After washing it down with tea, she said to the table, "I seem to be ravenous."

I, too . . .

Her head jerked up, eyes on Stellan's. "Pardon?"

"It's . . . a beautiful day." He tried to cover his shock. "Sunny again. I'd always thought your city was filled with fog."

"Not always, sir," she said softly.

Blackwell, ignorant of the small exchange, interrupted by reading aloud from the morning paper. "Dockworker found in the early hours of the morning, drowned."

"A careless man, no doubt," Mrs. Ralston said. "Falling down on the job."

"Quite careless, I agree. He also managed to have his throat torn out." Blackwell read on. "Second man found in such a state in as many days . . ."

"Sharks?" Stellan asked in a level voice.

"Don't they usually take the whole torso?" Mr. Ralston asked, his paper lowering as he took a sip of tea.

"Mr. Ralston, please. How morbid," Angelina's mother said.

"It's a scientific fact. Sharks feed in a kind of frenzy, dismembering . . ."

"Enough!" Mrs. Ralston snapped. "Our daughter was only just fished from the very same bay. Please don't conjure such frightful images."

"I can't imagine Miss Ralston being too distraught," Blackwell said from behind his paper. "Knowing her, she'd want to photograph the scene." He laughed.

Mrs. Ralston didn't approve of that statement either.

"Only if the light was good," Angelina said. But her hand went to her neck. Stellan watched as a drop of blood escaped the confines of the dressing and trickled toward her collarbone. Quickly, Stellan handed her his napkin. She blotted up the drops and secured the dressing tighter. It took her a moment to recover, but when she did, she squared her shoulders and addressed Mr. Ralston's paper. "Father, I must prevail on your generosity. My camera was lost . . ."

"Negligent of you," he said. "I hope you learned from the experience."

"Yes, Father. But if I am to photograph the shores . . ."

"I see." He dismissed her with a wave. "Procure the camera. I need those images by next week."

"Thank you, Father. I shall be about it today."

"Today?" Mrs. Ralston said. "Isn't that a little soon to be traipsing about the Emporium?"

"I'm fine, Mother."

"You'll not go out alone."

"I am perfectly capable of . . ."

"I will escort her," Stellan said. "If that suits you, Miss Ralston."

She smiled. "Thank you, Mr. Fletcher. I know you have an interest in the arts. Your presence would be helpful." Her voice was even, but she was blushing.

"If there are no objections?" Stellan said to the other men in the room.

Slowly Mason put the paper down and folded it in thirds. "None from me." He turned to Mr. Ralston. "We're going over the designs with the steelmaker today, aren't we?"

In moments, Ralston and Blackwell were in deep conversation, Angelina's shopping expedition forgotten.

"It's settled then," Angelina said. She dabbed the corners of her mouth and stole a look at Stellan.

Mrs. Ralston didn't miss it. "You'll not go out with this young gentleman unattended, Angelina," she said. "Mr. Blackwell may condone it, but I do not. Think of the press . . ."

"Gerald will drive us," Angelina cut in. "But really, Mother, it's the twentieth century. Women are . . ."

"As capable as men, yes, I know. Emancipated whatnot. Take Gerald to chaperone. That would suffice." Mrs. Ralston knit her brows. "Be back by dinner. Six o'clock sharp."

ANGELINA WAS BEAMING. The Emporium on the corner of Market and Fifth, two blocks down from the Call Building, was one of her favorite stores. It had everything from garden tools to lingerie, hot coffee, books and sheet music, furniture, horse harnesses, and china teacups. Most important, it catered to the arts, with a section of brushes, paints, and canvases, stage props, costumes, and the latest in photographic equipment. She smiled as she led the way up to the second floor and toward the back corner, where the scent of linseed oil, fine leather, and boar bristles was welcoming. As soon as the shopkeeper spotted her party, he gave a frantic wave. "Miss Ralston! What a comforting sight. I read all about it in the papers! Are you quite alright?"

"Mr. Higgins, thank you. I'm fine, but my camera was lost. I must replace everything."

"Such a relief to see you alive and well," he said. "Gave us all a shock." He hefted a thick catalog and opened to a bookmarked section. "I can order in exactly what you had before, but you might like to consider some new innovations. "A plastigmat lens, for example . . ."

Angelina was lost for some time in the catalog. The Plate Series D was an improvement, indeed, and it sported a price tag to match. "Ninety-seven dollars and fifty cents?"

"Plus shipping, but you get what you pay for, as I am sure Mr. Ralston knows. It's superior quality. Aluminum body, nickel frame, mahogany inserts, and fine leather cover. Two tripod sockets." He tapped the picture. "Nothing surpasses Eastman Kodak, and a woman of your talent deserves the best."

A woman of my means can afford the best, I'm sure you mean to say.

Stellan, who was studying the photographs along the far wall, chuckled.

"I'll take it." Angelina smiled. "How soon will it arrive?"

"The tripod is in stock. The rest will be sent as soon as I telegraph the order through. Call back late next week. We should have it by then."

She sighed. "That long?"

"I'm afraid so, unless you'd like to rent in the interim? A similar setup for, say one dollar a day, with your tripod and plates?"

"Done!" She signed the various documents Mr. Higgins pushed in front of her and nearly jumped out of her skin when Stellan appeared at her side as if from nowhere.

"You've found what you were looking for?"

She lifted her eyes to his. "I believe I have, but you must see something over here." She stopped herself from taking his hand. "This way." Angelina went to the visual arts display and looked on as he studied the range of oil paints, tube upon tube, mounted in fans of colors on the wall.

"Extraordinary!" He leaned in very close and motioned her to do the same. "Look at the subtle shifts. From yellow ochre to sienna to gold. Like the sun."

She quivered, wondering if he could hear her heart pound. "I love the names," she whispered. "Terra Rosa, Prussian Green, Quinacridone Magenta . . ."

"These are the colors of daylight, but your photographs are of the night, the shades of gray."

"I capture the truth of light," she said. "What is seen in the absence of color."

You would love my world then . . .

"Pardon?"

He stared at her blankly, and in her nervousness, she reached out to touch the indigo tube at the exact same moment he did. Their hands collided and seemed to entwine of their own accord. She pulled back. "Pardon me . . ."

Gerald cleared his throat behind them, and they both straightened. "Are you ready to proceed, Miss Ralston?"

"Quite." She looked to Stellan. "Join me for late lunch? The clam chowder on Fisherman's Wharf is beyond superb."

"It would be a pleasure."

Gerald frowned but hoisted the camera gear and followed them out of the Emporium.

Fisherman's Wharf was across town, across being a misnomer. They drove up steep inclines, streets rattling with cable cars and all manner of traffic, and down such severe slopes that if the brakes failed, there would be no saving them. Angelina let it all rush by as she sat in the backseat, chatting with Stellan. "Do you want to stop in Chinatown?" she said, her face lighting up. "It would make an exotic background for a portrait of you, Mr. Fletcher. I shall try the camera today."

"Is Chinatown wise, Miss Ralston?" Gerald said from the driver's seat. He made no apology for eavesdropping. "The quarantine has only just been lifted."

She shrugged. "I suspect that affair was motivated more by politics than good medical practice, a heinously racist move by Governor Gage."

"As you say, Miss Ralston."

She glared at the back of Gerald's head.

Stellan spoke before she could say more. "I agree he's not taking his custodianship seriously, at least not in favor of American-Chinese civil rights."

"Thank you." She nodded to Stellan. "Far from helping, it appears Gage is thwarting all advancements."

"Still, is it wise?" Gerald let his protest hang.

As they crested Telegraph Hill, she gazed out at the East Bay. "Very well. The fog's rolling in anyway."

"It will be a cloud sea about us," Stellan said.

She smiled. "We'll take photos here then." She gestured out the window. "While we still have the sunlight." Her eyes danced. "I will capture you yet, Mr. Fletcher."

"Perhaps." Stellan smiled.

"Are you shy of being photographed?" she asked.

"Not by you."

Gerald parked the Ford, and he and Stellan made to unload the newly rented camera gear. Angelina elbowed in before they could get very far. "I've got it," she said to both men. "I need no assistance, thank you."

STELLAN WAS CAPTIVATED as Angelina moved here and there, testing the light, feeling the wind. She chose a gnarled old oak as the backdrop and had him stand beside it, his hand resting on the trunk. The light dappled through the branches like ripples in a tide pool. The touch of the wood was solid as reef.

"You like trees?" Angelina approached him to straighten the fall of his coat.

"I like all living things."

She paused. "What a splendid and unusual response. Are you a humanitarian?"

"You could say so, yes." He was lost in her dark eyes and the gentle floral scent that rose from her body. He memorized her every movement, comment, and instruction, letting her fill his mind completely.

"With the coat over your shoulder, I think."

He obliged her.

"Perfect. Can you hold that?"

He didn't answer but instead studied the tree with

its twisting branches that reached for the sky, dark arms against the glimpse of blue.

"You're a very good subject," she said, sliding in a glass plate. She had him strike different poses until Gerald pulled out his pocket watch and cleared his throat, a practice that was beginning to make Stellan's upper lip twitch.

"One more," Angelina said, and she turned to Gerald. "It's all set. Just shoot when I give the word."

Gerald's face became even more dour as Angelina stood on the other side of the trunk and placed her hand on it as well. The sensation, through the tree, jolted him. He could hear her heartbeat through the living wood.

"Now, Gerald," she said.

They were meant to be looking at the camera, but somehow their eyes found each other's and remained engaged until Gerald, having taken the shot, asked them if that would be quite enough.

"To the wharf?" he whispered before she could move away. "For lunch?" If he didn't get a full breath of sea air in his lungs and fog on his face soon, he didn't know how he would continue.

Angelina touched her neck, feeling the edges of the dressing. "Yes, to the wharf!" she replied, and gathered her camera gear. He carried the tripod back to the car while she speculated on how the shots would turn out. Best not think about that . . . They jumped in the backseat laughing, while Gerald's posture became even more rigid than usual.

Chapter Four

5:30 P.M.
Tuesday, April 17, 1906

THE WHARF REVIVED him. Angelina revived him, and relief flooded his body. The fog formed droplets on his lashes, and the lull of the waves below made it possible to relax though he longed to strip off and dive headfirst into the sea. They sat across from each other at a small table outside the fishmongers'. The aromas were heavenly, a mixture of salt air, whitecaps, and fresh fish. Colored lanterns hung on strings overhead. They radiated bright, glowing auras that turned Angelina's hair red as starfish. Stellan took full mouthfuls of the chowder. "Delicious!"

"Not too salty for you, Mr. Fletcher?" Angelina looked up from her bowl.

"I enjoy the salt, Miss Ralston. You can be sure of that." His left hand rested on the red checkered tablecloth.

Angelina laid her gloved fingers on top of his. "I'm so glad you do." She pulled back immediately, as if she'd touched a hot stove.

Heat rushed through his body from the contact. "I don't think there's anything I wouldn't enjoy in your presence."

She laughed, a light sound. "I'm sure you exaggerate, sir."

For moments uncounted, he basked in her presence. The distraction and bustle of the wharf receded until all he could hear was her, the rhythmic flow of her breath, and, unfortunately, Gerald's incessant throat clearing. The man stood over them, his look admonishing.

Angelina turned to the valet, her eyebrows raised.

"I believe we must leave at once, Miss Ralston, if we are to arrive on time for dinner." Stellan watched her response. It was a shrug at best even though Gerald made it sound as if they were breaking universal laws with their impromptu repast. The man was actually getting his watch out, again, and throwing them both accusatory looks.

"Shall I bring the car around?" he asked in a flat voice.

Angelina dabbed at the corners of her mouth. "We'll walk, thank you."

"It would be more expedient if I . . ."

"We'll walk fast." She cut in. "If you go start the car, we'll not lose a moment. You know how long it takes to crank over in the cold."

Gerald's frown lines creased. "Very well." He left at a clip, apparently wanting to set an example.

Stellan rose, as Angelina did, but instead of heading for the car, she went to the edge of the wharf. He joined her, and they stood side by side, listening to the water slosh against the pilings.

The lanternlight made extraordinary patterns on the surface.

"How beautiful," she whispered, and her whole body shivered.

"You're cold." Stellan took off his coat and draped it over her shoulders. "Shall we go?"

Yes, do hurry, Stellan. You're missing all the fun.

Stellan's blood froze. *Salila? Where are you?*

I am having quite a time entertaining the Ralstons and that delectable Mr. Blackwell.

"No!"

"Pardon me?" Angelina turned toward him.

"Gerald is right. It's best we return home with all haste."

ANGELINA DIDN'T HAVE time to ponder the change that had come over Stellan. Their easy intimacy and the pleasure of the day had suddenly evaporated, and he seemed preoccupied with his own thoughts. She inquired again to no avail and decided to let it drop. Whatever had assailed him on the wharf would come out, or not. A person was due his privacy. She knew she needed her own. And why would he want to discuss his personal feelings in front of the enormous ears of Gerald anyway? She clasped her hands in her lap and stared straight ahead. *I've been too forward.*

Never . . .

She stared at him, but he didn't acknowledge her until they were home.

"My apologies, Miss Ralston," he whispered, when they reached her front door.

It flew open before she could respond. "Dinner is already served, Miss," Jeanie said behind the butler. "Shall I help you get ready?" They were ushered into the foyer.

"I'm sure my tea dress will do tonight, Jeanie. Better that than arriving any later." The look on her maid's face told her something was quite out of the ordinary, but she stuck to her decision. "Shall we, Mr. Fletcher?" Angelina offered him her arm, and they headed for the formal dining hall. Nothing could have prepared her for the scene they walked in on.

The room was a din of conversation, laughter mostly, and much of it coming from Mason and her father. Mrs. Blackwell and her mother seemed quite stiff, if anything, and it didn't take her long to discover why. Between her fiancé and the esteemed Mr. Ralston was a woman in a provocative evening gown, a gold-and-black affair that plunged far lower in front and back than even the latest fashion from Paris demanded. She had shimmering hair done up high on her head with a few curling strands falling down her flawless white cheeks. Her face was extraordinary, with full lips and feline eyes. The air around her positively zapped and crackled.

Both men were intoxicated, displaying manners far less than formal. Their guest, this Aphrodite, was telling a story about a voyage in the Mediterranean. Stellan and Angelina stood in the doorway, staring, until all conversation stopped.

"Stellan! There you are!" The shimmering goddess put her hand on Mason's forearm while leaning in to Mr. Ralston to whisper none too quietly, "You have no idea how long I've been looking for him." The men laughed and swigged down their wine. Then she stared at Angelina, and said, "Whatever have you done to my brother?"

"Salila." Stellan's voice was icy.

Heat rushed to Angelina's face. "Your brother?" Somewhere in the shock of it all she felt relief, until noticing Mason again. Mason, my fiancé. She'd had no right to entertain thoughts of Stellan, not when she was spoken for. Angelina, pull yourself together. She stepped forward. "How delightful to meet you. Miss Fletcher is it?"

Mason and Mr. Ralston got to their feet, dropping their napkins and scraping their chairs. "Allow me to introduce you to Mrs. Fisher, of late from the Mediterranean." Her fiancé slurred his words and smiled stupidly.

"Pleased, I'm sure." Angelina gave a very small curtsy.

Stellan mumbled something under his breath. She couldn't catch the words. There was much fuss settling everyone back at the table, but once they were seated, the story of the voyage, to Crete, it turned out, continued. Angelina didn't think her mother's face could get any tighter, but Mrs. Blackwell appeared to be surrendering to the fiasco. She started guzzling down wine as fast as the servant could refill her goblet. Stellan didn't say a word as Mrs. Fisher carried on though his jaw clenched tight, and his eyes stared daggers. Angelina would not have wanted that gaze turned her way under any circumstances. No sooner did she think this, he looked at her, but his expression had changed. Instead of frightening her, it brought a rush of heat and excitement. Angelina fanned her face and took a sip of wine.

As the food was served, the whole table became even more animated. Salila devoured an entire salmon, then downed a whole bottle of Napa Valley white herself, alternately enveloping Mason and Mr. Ralston, whispering in their ears and hanging off their broad shoulders. During one prolonged intimacy, Mrs. Ralston stood, tossed down her napkin, and said she would oversee the coffee. She turned to Mrs. Blackwell, but the woman was sound asleep in her chair. That seemed to disgust her mother even more, and she left abruptly.

STELLAN GLARED AT Salila. *What in the dark tomb's mercy are you doing here?* He gripped his goblet tight enough to turn his knuckles white.

I could ask you the same thing! She wrapped herself around Mr. Ralston and whispered into his ear. The man bellowed with laughter.

"Why have you come, dear sister? What news?" Stellan spoke aloud.

"Brother! You'll be thrilled. I've a message from our

father!" Salila said, as the servant took her plate, with its entire fish skeleton.

"Do tell." He tried to keep his voice even.

"He wonders when you're coming home."

I said I would be back in due course!

True, but nobody thought "due course" would involve sightseeing trips through the city with your little angel. You were to get in, get the information, and get back.

I've done my part! Studied the plans for the Golden Gate Bridge. Discussed them . . .

And?

They're preposterous. Enormous cantilevers to counter the span. The cost of materials alone is prohibitive. More importantly, even if they could build it, such a monstrosity won't touch us.

How can you be sure?

It's a suspension bridge. The pilings are nowhere near our tombs. He was aware of Angelina, her face pale as she stared at him. "I'll be home soon enough, Mrs. Fisher."

"Really? Father will be so pleased." Salila batted her eyelashes. "You must come back with me then." *What I mean to say, Stellan, is I'm not leaving until you do, and you know what that means . . .*

You're not to touch these people!

But my fun on the dock has already made the papers, twice. I shouldn't risk a third.

Then go back to the sea! Angelina isn't food, nor is her family!

Really? What keeps you in the daylight then?

His grip tightened, and the glass shattered in his hand. The contents spilled over the white tablecloth.

Angelina startled and immediately reached out to him. She blotted his hand with her napkin as servants came to clean up the mess. "Are you hurt?"

His eyes softened. "I'm sorry I alarmed you." He lowered his voice. "I'm fine."

Salila burst out laughing. *I see. Love?*

You see nothing at all!

Salila went on as if he hadn't spoken. *But your little angel is engaged. Silly human tradition. Anyway, it's not like you could offer her your hand. Is that how they say it?* "*Your hand?*" *So quaint. She looked over at Mason. Though he's hardly interested, is he? Not with me here anyway. How fickle . . .*

"Salila, stop!" Stellan shouted aloud, bringing all eyes to him.

Mrs. Blackwell roused for a moment, snorted, then went back to sleep, her chin dropping toward her bosom.

I think you best call me Mrs. Fisher, while we're guests, don't you? It already appears we are overly familiar. She winked. Just as Mason leaned in to whisper something in her ear, she turned to him and planted her lips on his mouth.

I will not witness this! Angelina clenched her fists.

Angelina? Stellan pressed his temples and turned to her. *Did you say that?*

What are you talking about, Stellan? The girl hasn't opened her mouth all night. Salila caught the look on his face. *Unless . . .* She leaned back in her chair and slowly clapped her hands. *My dear Stellan, I do think you have created a blood bond. How utterly inconvenient.*

Don't be ridiculous. Blood blonds can only be formed between two Mar who are . . .

Yes, I know. Deeply in love. For an instant, Salila's eyes softened, and she touched the hollow of her neck. *Or of the same family line,* she went on briskly. *Unless she's our lost sibling, or secretly Mar, I believe we have something rather unique!* Salila cackled as she applauded them both. *Wait until Teern hears of this! Another Mar-human coupling. It will kill him!*

Another?

Never mind! This is priceless.

Mr. Fletcher? What did you say? Angelina looked at him with round eyes.

Stellan stared back, unable to respond. Finally, he cleared his throat and spoke aloud. "Your neck. It's bleeding."

Gerald appeared in the doorway, interrupting them all. "After-dinner drinks are served in the reception room."

"Wonderful!" Salila smiled. *Shall we? No point in raising their suspicions, is there. Not if we want to stay on? Though I don't know how you're going to explain this all to the angel. Did you drink from the girl nonstop?*

Twice! Only twice! And, you're not staying on, Stellan said with a mental growl.

Oh but I am. They've offered me a room on your floor. Isn't that sweet? Shall we visit her together tonight?

Touch her, and I will destroy you.

She laughed. *I'd like to see you try.*

ANGELINA PRESSED A clean cloth against her neck. The wound wasn't healing, and the evening's madness hadn't helped.

"Angelina, are you alright?" Stellan rose, and they all made a move toward the reception room.

"Of course she is," Mrs. Fisher answered. She stood tall and elegant, making Mason look like a red-faced garden gnome clinging to her side. "Fresh and . . ."

Shut up!

Angelina flinched.

"I am well, Mr. Fletcher, Mrs. Fisher, though somewhat confused." Angelina took a moment to glare at Mason, who didn't register her presence. "I might forgo drinks and retire . . ."

"Nonsense! We haven't even had a chat." Mrs. Fisher dropped Mason's arm and offered it to Angelina. "Shall we?"

Stellan pulled his sister back. "If you don't mind, dearest, I would like a moment with Miss Ralston." *And you keep away from her before I stake you with the first shard of wood I find!*

Angelina startled. "Excuse me?"

Mrs. Fisher chuckled into her hands. "Definitely a problem, brother."

Stellan whispered something to his sister, and the woman literally bared her teeth at him before taking Mason's waiting arm and walking away. He turned to Angelina. "Miss Ralston, let me explain."

Angelina composed herself. "Please do."

They stood in the hallway and allowed the others

to precede them, all but Mrs. Blackwell, who remained snoring in the dining room.

Stellan let out a long slow sigh. "I have to return."

"To . . . ?"

"My father's realm."

"Realm?" she whispered. "Is he a king?"

"Not precisely, but my presence is urgently needed."

"I see." She waited for more, and when nothing came, her brows knit. "That's the sum of your explanation?"

Stellan took a step closer. *There is so much to tell you.* "My family is . . . eccentric."

"I see that," she said. Her uncertainty melted as their eyes met. Stellan took her hand, and warmth washed over her like a tide. She breathed deeply. "Mr. Fletcher, will you be coming back?"

He stopped outside the reception room, and they faced each other. "It's . . . not as simple as that, but I will, if I can."

Her smile slowly faded. "There is much mystery about you, Mr. Fletcher. I fear . . ."

The reception-room door burst open, and Mason Blackwell, arm in arm with Mrs. Fisher, waltzed right past them.

"Where are they going?" Angelina asked

Salila!

Angelina pressed her temples. She was hearing voices in her head more and more. "Stellan? Did you just say . . ."

"I believe your fiancé is showing Mrs. Fisher to her room."

"How considerate." The man she was engaged to

couldn't care less about her, and the one who turned her world upside down was leaving, with no foreseeable return. "If you'll excuse me, Mr. Fletcher, I really must retire."

Before he could reply, her father threw open the reception-room door. "Mr. Fletcher, there you are! Come! I must show you those alternate designs, as promised."

Angelina and Stellan exchanged a lingering look until she whispered good night and headed up the stairs. It was beyond her ability to resist glancing into the guest room as she passed. Mason lay facedown on the bed, apparently unconscious, boots being pulled off by his valet. She shook her head and entered the comfort of her own room. Jeanie was fluffing pillows and turning down her bed.

"Whatever was I thinking," Angelina said, and flopped into the overstuffed chair by the window.

"About what, Miss?"

"Either of them!" But in her mind, she felt Stellan's warm touch and caught the faint scent of the sea. As the sensations engulfed her, she let the tears fall silently down her cheeks.

Chapter Five

3:00 A.M.
Tuesday, April 17, 1906

A KNOCK ON the door jolted her awake. Before she could say a word, it creaked open, then closed with a soft snick. Angelina held her breath, feeling the presence in her room. The hairs on her arms lifted, and chills zipped down her spine. His presence engulfed her. *Stellan . . .* She knew it was he.

I wanted to make sure you were alright. He came to the edge of her bed and stood there, looking down at her, just as he had when she'd washed up on the beach. The window shade must have been left up because she could see him clearly. He was luminous in the moonlight, his eyes deep and penetrating.

You're so thoughtful. Angelina sat up, letting the

covers slide down. She wore a sky blue satin nightgown, one sent to her by a cousin in Paris. Her mother thought it completely improper, so Angelina wore it often.

I can think of nothing but you, Angelina. He had taken off his vest and tie, letting them fall to the floor. When she looked up again, his shirt was gone, and there in the moonlight, for a brief moment, her mind went to another vision, in which a beautiful naked body was leaning over her. *Is this a dream?*

It's whatever you want it to be, Angelina.

The thought made her smile for the impropriety, Stellan in her bedroom in the wee hours of the night, shirtless . . . She looked again. Naked! It was both shocking and thrilling. Something nagged in the back of her mind, but for the life of her, she couldn't figure out what it was.

Angelina . . . His voice caressed her, and she shivered.

I was hoping you would come. She opened her arms, and a moment later, he was wrapped in them. The warmth of his body embraced her as heat rushed to her limbs. He pulled her into his lap and tilted her chin. Angelina's lips parted in a smile. He smelled like a fresh sea breeze.

What is it about you that has captured me so completely? His lips closed over hers in the softest of kisses. She twined her legs around his back, wanting to get closer, wanting nothing to come between them. As the kiss deepened, she felt sweat prickle down her spine. For long moments, they shared the intimacy, barely able to stop for breath. She drank him in, astonished by her building hunger. Stellan answered her need, kissing her more fiercely. He slipped the satin straps off her shoulders, exposing her round, ample breasts. She called out when he suckled her, one breast, then the other. Dampness spread between her legs. In that moment, the world fell away, and Angelina couldn't imagine a place where her body ended and his began.

Stellan held her tight, lifting her up as he lay back, his head at the foot of the bed. Angelina straddled him, kissing his neck, his checks, his hard abs. He groaned as she grasped his shaft, rock hard, with skin soft as silk. *Angelina . . .* His voice was deep and husky.

She laughed and covered his mouth with her hand to smother the moans.

He sat up, kissing her smile. *Two can play that game!* Before she could answer, he flipped her onto her back, pushed her hands over her head, and, excruciatingly slowly, kissed and sucked and licked his way to her mound. When his tongue found the folds between her now-parted legs and the hot moisture there, they both cried out. She grabbed his long hair as he thrilled her, again and again.

Stellan! she called like a wolf to the moon. *Stellan, Stellan Stellan!*

He ran his tongue up over her mound, her belly, her breasts. He kissed her face, her eyelids, her earlobes, and as his lips touched the fullness of her wet mouth, he pushed slowly into the heat between her legs. She called out again, hands digging into his back.

Open your eyes, he said.

Angelina looked up at him and for moments, like years passing, they stared into each other's depths. She began to rock beneath him, and he matched her rhythm, plunging deeper with every thrust. His eyes never left hers as he bellowed his pleasure into the night, his whole body shuddering.

Angelina tucked damp strands of hair behind his ears and traced the contours of his face. *Stellan . . . Don't leave me. Ever.*

I won't. He hesitated a moment, opened his mouth, and sank his fangs into her neck.

4:45 A.M.
Wednesday, April 18, 1906

STELLAN LEFT ANGELINA'S room and closed the door behind him. The house was asleep, his footfalls dead quiet. He thought of her lying there, wrapped in a black-and-red-embroidered silk dressing gown, her body glowing from their passion as she drifted off to sleep. It was almost impossible to walk away. How could he leave her? How could he stay? For her to join him was to ask the unthinkable. But the blood bond. It would never be broken, at least it never could be between Mar. He wondered at his sister. Had it happened to her all those centuries ago? It might explain a few things, but if it was any indication of the outcome for a Mar-human coupling, it didn't bode well. Salila had lost her man, and it had left her more than a little jaded. No! It can't be like that for me and Angelina. Stellan went down the hall, each thought wrestling with the other. He'd said his good-byes; he only wished she would remember them when she woke.

The smell of fresh blood halted his thoughts. He sniffed the air, the aroma rushing through his nostrils and tickling the back of his throat. It led him farther down the hall to Mason Blackwell's door. Salila? He tried the handle, but it was locked. She wouldn't . . . A loud thump sounded, and he shouldered in. It took him a moment to register the scene.

The room pulsed in the glow of soft candlelight. The bed was rumpled, the covers thrown back. On the floor was Salila's evening gown. The Mar woman hunched naked over a dazed, and equally naked, Blackwell.

In a blink, Stellan was there. He pulled her up and slammed her against the closet. *Salila! Stop!*

She flung hair out of her face and snarled. Faster than humanly possible he flipped her to the ground and pinned her down, his teeth grating against her ear. "Listen to me, sister, and listen carefully. You're going to get up, gather your things, and leave. In that order and nothing else."

"What is the problem with you?" She ground out the words into the carpet. "He was willing!"

"He was extremely drunk!"

She sighed, relaxing. "You do know how to ruin a good night, don't you."

"I'm not joking, Salila! You have to leave."

Let me up. She growled. *Someone's coming.*

Damn . . . As Stellan released her, there was a knock at the door. It squeaked open, and Angelina appeared. Her face was momentarily soft in the candlelight until she took in the scene. "Mr. Fletcher, what is going on here?"

"Shall I show you?" Salila sprang at Angelina. Stellan

grabbed the Mar woman and hurled her to the other side of the room. By then, Jeanie and Mrs. Ralston were at the door, gasping, then screaming.

Get out of here! Now! Stellan roared into Salila's mind. *And put some clothes on!* He threw the top sheet over Mason as the man tried to sit up. His hand clutched his neck.

Footsteps thundered down the hall. "Nobody move!" Mr. Ralston's voice boomed as a rifle was cocked. He burst in on them, let out an oath, and leveled his rifle at Stellan. Salila got behind him.

"Don't shoot," Angelina cried out. She moved directly in front of the gun.

"Get out of my way!" he shouted at her.

Mrs. Ralston grabbed her daughter and handed her off to Gerald, who stood near the door, eyes wide, his usual reserve abandoned. Mrs. Blackwell pushed past him into the room, and the screams began again.

"We're so sorry to have caused a disturbance," Stellan said, as he and Salila backed toward the window.

Mr. Ralston looked from the bed, to the floor, to Salila. At that moment, Mason slumped, the bite wounds obvious as his head lolled to the side. "Don't move, or I'll shoot!" Ralston said.

Salila broke for the door, and Mr. Ralston squeezed the trigger.

"No, Father!" Angelina yelled.

Faster than the human eye could follow, Stellan dove for Salila. He rolled with her and flung them both backward out the window, ahead of the bullet. They slammed hard into the ground, glass shattering around them like ice. Stellan released her, jumped to his feet, and ran toward the sea.

5:00 A.M.
Wednesday, April 18, 1906

ANGELINA'S HANDS SHOOK as she sipped her tea. Jeanie tried to pour more, but she nearly dropped the pot.

"It's alright, Jeanie. Sit down."

"I mustn't, Miss."

"This is not the time for propriety. Sit down. I insist."

"Thank you, Miss." The young maid sat on the edge of the parlor chair and looked at her hands.

Angelina got Jeanie a cup and filled it for her. "You've a right to be as distraught as the rest of us."

Her maid took a deep breath. "I agree it was no small horror. What a scene! The gunshot was earsplitting. I was sure Mr. Fletcher and Mrs. Fisher would be splattered on the pavement, but . . ."

"They were nowhere to be found."

"I've never seen a man altogether nude. Quite startling." She glanced at Angelina. "Does this mean the engagement is off?" Jeanie asked.

Angelina pushed her long hair back from her face. "Let's not speculate on that topic right now, shall we, Jeanie."

"Sorry, Miss." Her maid blushed.

Angelina nodded and sipped her tea.

The police had arrived and questioned everyone. They were upstairs now with her father and Dr. Medleys, and a very confused Mason Blackwell, who seemed to remember nothing but a knock at his door in the wee hours of the night. She frowned. Stellan was in the room. He and his sister ran . . .

But Stellan couldn't have been involved, she argued with herself.

Then what was he doing there in the first place?

He must have heard a noise, same as I . . .

Are you sure? Images of Stellan falling backward out the window flashed again into her mind. How could he survive and run away. Her most troubling question was, When will I see him again.

"I can't stand this!" Angelina stood up.

Jeanie jumped as if prodded. "Miss?"

"There's too much whirling in my head. I'm going to my darkroom if anyone needs me."

"To develop photographs, Miss?"

"I have to do something, or I'll go mad," she whispered.

"Do you need help, Miss?"

"No, thank you." Angelina gave Jeanie a quick hug. "Get to the kitchen with the others. They will all have their appetites back soon enough."

Jeanie curtsied and left. Angelina headed for the one place she could be alone with her feelings and put some kind of meaning to the night's crazed events.

Chapter Six

5:00 A.M.
Wednesday, April 18, 1906

STELLAN DIDN'T STOP running until he reached the end of the pier. Salila was ahead of him, and she dove from the edge, disappearing beneath the black swell. Stellan shucked his coat. There was no turning back, thanks to Salila. He could only hope Angelina would understand his sudden disappearance. But how? He stared at the water, dark and lapping against the pilings. Minutes passed as he watched the gray light of predawn give form to the city. I can't leave you, Angelina.

Salila surfaced beneath him. "What's taking you so long? Get out of those ridiculous clothes and dive in."

"Something's wrong."

"Of course something's wrong. You're not in the water.'

"No, I'm serious. Listen."

"To what?"

"That's just it. Nothing. It's dawn, and the gulls aren't screeching at the fishing boats. No sea lions barking . . ."

Salila sprang from the water and stood dripping beside him. She grabbed his arm and made to drag him off the edge. "You need to stop worrying. I got us out of there in time, and now all we have to do is swim for it."

He pulled back. "What aren't you telling me?"

"Teern's set things in motion."

The color drained from his face. "No! He doesn't have to! The bridge isn't going forward, not for decades by the looks of it, and when it does . . ."

"That's just it, Stellan. When it does . . . Teern's making sure that 'when' isn't going to happen."

The air grew still, as if the city held its breath. Before Stellan could say another word, the ground began to rumble. Whitecaps appeared on the water, and the whole length of the wharf undulated like a serpent. A thunderous roar welled up. Waves splashed high, soaking his clothes. It sounded as if the city would tear apart.

"Earthquake?"

"Yes, Stellan, a large one, and it's arrived, so be smart, jump into the water, and swim to the tombs!" She let him go and dove back into the choppy waves.

Stellan! A voice rippled through his mind.

Angelina! He turned toward Pacific Heights in the distance.

5:10 A.M.
Wednesday, April 18, 1906

ANGELINA IMMERSED THE photographic paper in the developing tray. The soft red light made it look as if it rippled in a bath of blood and water. As she moved it to the fixer, her frown lines deepened. Give it a minute, she told herself, but a minute made no difference. A photograph didn't lie, and this image of her and Stellan was missing one essential component: Mr. Fletcher himself. "Impossible."

The camera had captured Angelina, one hand on the gnarled old oak tree and the other resting softly against the folds of her skirt. Her eyes were supposed to be on Stellan, if memory served, but instead they stared across time and space into . . . nothing. Not even a fog or blur. There was simply nothing where his body should have been. Where his body was! She dropped the picture back into the fixer and released the tongs as if they'd caught fire. Who is this man? Her hand went to her neck, and she shivered.

The fixer settled over the image and went still, but as she watched, it began to ripple on its own. Soon, the liquid in all three trays became agitated and sloshed onto the table. The red light overhead swung violently, and upstairs, someone yelled "Earthquake!" Footfalls sounded above. Shouts and confusion. Someone called her name. The floor seemed to rise, and she buckled to her knees.

"I'm down here!" She tried to climb the stairs, but the floor tipped, and she fell, rolling toward the back wall, along with bottles of developer, tools, bags of flour, and boxes. When she struggled to her feet, the light winked out. "I'm down here!" she screamed again. As the walls cracked and caved, she had one thought and one only. *Stellan! Where are you?*

5:12 A.M.
Wednesday, April 18, 1906

STELLAN BOLTED ALONG the wharf, past the ferry building, and up California Street. The buildings rushed by in a blur, his speed as fast as light. The paving warped under his feet. Whole sections of street dropped away. Others shot up as if punched by an underground giant. *Teern! Stop this madness!* But the only thing he heard was Angelina's voice in his mind.

He ran on. People were pouring out into the street, carrying their belongings, running for their lives. He tore past, only a rush of wind to them. Stellan reached the house and leapt the wrought-iron gate. It was still standing though the fence was gone, the bricks scattered into the street. The Ralstons' Queen Anne home looked as if it had been uprooted and slammed back into the lot askew. It listed downhill, shutters and doors dangling open. The entrance wall had fallen, and a turret lay in the garden. Inside was worse. Dust rose, thick and gritty. Mr. Ralston climbed over the rubble.

"Where's Angelina?"

"I don't know." Screams came from upstairs, and Mr.

Ralston ran toward them. "I have to get them out. Gas fire's started in the kitchen!"

"Angelina!" Stellan shouted.

"I'm in the basement!"

He was at the door in seconds, heaving aside timbers and bricks. Flames shot up from the adjacent kitchen. Faster than human sight could follow, he pulled the rest of the rubble and beams aside, stormed down the stairs, and jumped the last few feet to land in front of Angelina. Light from above flooded in, and black smoke billowed. Suddenly, the tremor stopped, and they fell into each other's arms. For a moment, the horrors of the world faded. The flames and falling ceiling, the broken ground and the devastation disappeared as he held her tight. He looked into her eyes, fire turning them golden. "We have to get out."

She took a step back. "The wound on Mason? Did you do that?"

"Of course not. Let's go!"

"Not until you tell me who you are."

He frowned. "What are you talking about?"

"The photographs I took. You're not in them!"

"Angelina . . ."

"You're a demon, aren't you."

"No." He took her hands. "We must go!"

"What then?" She pulled out of his grip. "How can we hear each other's thoughts?"

"Angelina, there's no time. I promise you, I will not harm you."

"Just say it, Stellan. Ghost? Apparition? Angel?"

"Nothing like that!"

"Then tell me the truth!"

He clenched his fists. "Mar!" he shouted. "I'm Mar!"

"I don't know what that means!" she yelled back.

He looked around as if seeking an answer in the devastation. "Mar are what you would call sirens, or mer--people."

She knit her brow. "You saved me from the ferry accident?"

"I did, but it's complicated. I . . ."

"How do you live?"

"In the sea, we are deathless. But blood sustains us on land."

"Blood?"

"Human blood. And, somehow, sharing yours has given us . . ."

She touched her neck and stared at him. "Given us what, Stellan?"

He took her face tenderly in his hands. *It was only a few drops, but for us it seems it was enough to create a blood bond.*

The far wall collapsed as a shock wave ripped through the basement. No more time! Stellan bundled her into his arms and took off.

Wait! The others! We have to help them. She struggled to get free.

He held her fiercely until they were out of the house. Gerald was in the street with Jeanie and the rest of the staff. He deposited Angelina there and turned to Gerald.

"Where are Mr. and Mrs. Ralston? The Blackwells?"

"I couldn't see them. We'll have to wait for the fire department."

"That will be too late!" He ran back to the front door as the entire entranceway collapsed. Flames lashed out at him, forcing a retreat. Fire was not his element, and, like the sun, it could consume a Mar's life force. He leapt to the side of the house and grabbed the base of the large bay window, tearing it from the framework with a single heave. He jumped through the gaping hole in the wall, calling for Mr. Blackwell.

The house was thick with smoke and falling plaster. It made it impossible to see farther than his hand. Heat seared him, and he fought every instinct to get away, get back to the sea. Above the crackle and roar of flames, his sensitive hearing caught screams. He followed the sound to the base of the stairs. Mr. Ralston was there, trying to lift a beam that blocked the way. He was nearly done in by the smoke. Stellan stepped up and wrenched it away, tossing the hardwood support beam as if it were a matchstick. Mr. Ralston collapsed in a fit of coughing, and Stellan, with one arm over his shoulder, raced him out the bay window and down the steps, depositing him in front of Gerald. Instantly, he ran back into the burning house.

Stellan!

Help your father. I'm getting the others.

He dashed up the stairs. The floor gave way underneath his last step, and he slipped, grabbing hold of the step as he swung in midair. Stellan dragged himself up to the hallway and ran to the doors, throwing each open until he reached Mason's. Too hot to touch, he kicked it in. Black smoke spewed out as the fire sucked back. "Stay low! Crawl toward my voice!" he shouted.

Mason appeared, red-faced and panting, dragging himself along the carpet.

"Who else is in there?"

"No one!"

Cries rose up from the room behind him. Without another word, he threw Mason over his shoulder, raced to the stairway, and jumped to the ground floor. In a few strides, he was close enough to stand Mason up and propel him out the gaping bay window. Pausing only long enough to see that the man could walk, Stellan tore back for the two women.

They were both nearly unconscious when he found them, huddled together in the middle of the last room. The fire had traveled up the walls and across the ceiling. It creaked, and the light fixtures fell, exploding the gas lines. Using curtains to beat a path to Mrs. Ralston and Mrs. Blackwell, Stellan hauled both women up, one on each shoulder and smashed out the window as the entire floor collapsed. Coughing and choking, he staggered toward the street.

Chapter Seven

6:00 A.M.
Wednesday, April 18, 1906

ANGELINA STARED AT the gap in the wall where the bay window had been. Her hands clenched, fingers twisting into knots. An icy chill gripped her as she strained to see through the haze. When Stellan didn't appear, tears welled.

"Look there!" Gerald shouted.

She wiped her face in time to see a figure slowly emerge from the smoke. "Stellan!" In one arm, he held up her mother. Over his shoulder was draped Mrs. Blackwell. Angelina stumbled toward him. His clothes were smoldering, his hands burnt. Gerald and the cook appeared behind her, ready to help with the injured women. For once, Mrs. Ralston had nothing to say and could only concentrate on catching her breath. Mrs. Blackwell remained unconscious, and Gerald carried her out. Angelina supported Stellan as they made their way to the curb. "You're injured," she said, breathless.

"I'll be fine."

Both women were settled into the Ralstons' car. The window rolled down, and Angelina was barely aware of her father speaking from inside.

"Car's full," he said. "Traffic bottlenecked. You and the staff will make better time on foot. Get going! The whole street's ablaze."

"Pardon?" She turned from Stellan toward her father.

"I'll keep her safe." Stellan pointed toward the bay. "We should all head for the eastern ferry terminal. The city's going up in flames."

Mr. Ralston held his hand out to Stellan. "I don't know who you are, young man, but when you say you can protect her, I believe you." Angelina's father stared unblinking as they locked hands. "Your strength . . . Your speed . . . It's uncanny." He shook his head to clear it. "If you can't find us on the ferry terminal, head for Sausalito." Just then, the family home's roof dropped into the maw of flames. Her father cursed and rolled the window up. Gerald revved the engine, pulling out into the street.

Angelina watched them go, then encircled Stellan with her arms. "You saved everyone!" She looked up at him through fresh tears. "I was so afraid you wouldn't come out."

He sagged against her, his legs almost giving way.

"What's wrong?"

"Nothing. We must get to the ferry." He straightened, but could only stagger forward a few steps.

"Stellan!"

"I need . . ." He coughed uncontrollably.

"Tell me what I can do!"

He leaned heavily into her. "Angelina, I need blood."

Her eyes widened, and she touched her neck. "This will save you?"

He nodded once.

Of their own accord her fingers started to loosen the wrap. "I . . . trust you." Slowly, she turned her neck toward him. As the dressing fell to the ground, her eyes drifted across his chest. There was a gash that ran deep into the muscle.

"Angelina," he whispered, and held her tight.

First she felt a tender kiss along the hollow of her throat, and then a fleeting stab of pain. "Oh," she exclaimed. It was followed by soft, longing moans from the rush of euphoria. She leaned against him, watching the wound on his chest heal without leaving a trace. "My blood can do that?"

"Yes," Stellan said into her ear. "Are you alright?"

She stumbled back a step. "Light-headed. Nothing more." A sudden memory crossed her mind. There was a cave, a young man . . . a kiss. She touched her lips, noticing how his face glowed from the warmth of her blood. "Stellan, what will we do?" she asked, oblivious of the raging fire around them.

"I'll get you to the ferry. You'll be safe."

"Not that." She buried her face in his chest. "I mean, what about us?"

"Angelina . . ." He stroked her hair. "I am of the sea. You are not. We have to say good-bye. There's no other choice." They stood like a statue, face-to-face, entwined, her long black robe snapping in the wind while, in the background, the city burned.

"Stellan," she whispered, "there is always a choice."

"Then I choose to keep you safe."

The fires flared, and suddenly she was traveling at breakneck speed. Her eyes watered and colors blurred. In strobe-light flashes, she saw cable-car tracks stretched and snapped in two, traffic slammed to a halt, with vehicles skidding on their sides. Drivers were getting out of their cars, arguing, yelling, running. She was propelled past them, knocking into shoulders, tripping up legs, bumping pedestrians out of the way. Building fronts cracked and fell, exposing terrified people inside. Many were caught on fire escapes, dangling from broken rungs. The crowd thickened as they neared the ferry building. Flames blasted out every window and door; smoke blackened the sky. In the distance, fire bells clanged, and the foghorns sounded. Stellan didn't slow down until they reached the pier.

"I'll get you on a ferry," he said, pointing toward the crowded dock. He led the way up the stairs and onto the loading platform. The noise was deafening. "Almost there."

"No!" Angelina planted her feet, forcing him to stop and listen to her. "I don't want to be safe, Stellan." She pulled him to the side, away from the people pushing to get aboard. There, in the echoing clamor of the ferry building, Angelina took hold of his hands and focused on his eyes. Warmth caressed her body, making her heart jump. More images flooded her mind. The longer she held on to him, the clearer it became. "I remember," she whispered. "We were in a cave. You saved me from drowning, and from the other Mar! That was Mrs. Fisher!" She sucked in her breath, remembering the way he had touched her heart, warmed her . . . excited her, loved her. "These nights in my bed! They were real!"

"Angelina . . ."

In the crowded public building, for all to see, she reached up and held his face in her hands. "Look at me, Stellan." Tears spilled down her cheeks as she lost herself in his eyes. "I don't want to be safe," she said again. "I want to be with you." On tiptoe, she lifted her mouth to his, her lips barely touching at first. Heat exploded inside her as he responded. Together, they shared a long, exploring kiss, their bodies merging into one. *Stellan* . . .

He lifted her to him, pressing her hard against his chest. "Angelina," he whispered, breathless. His dark gray eyes devoured her until he came back to himself. "You don't know what you're asking."

"Then explain it to me. Make me understand!" The noise of the burning city dimmed as the wind shifted. Her braided hair streamed wildly, and her body shook. "Tell me there is a way for us to be together."

He shook his head. "I would have to take you to our tombs."

"Where?"

"At the bottom of the Golden Gate Channel."

"How deep?"

"Three hundred feet. More in some places."

"And . . . I'll survive?"

"That's just it, Angelina." He kissed her forehead and relaxed his embrace. "You won't."

"What?" she whispered.

"To become Mar, you must give your life to the sea."

She sucked in her breath. "I have to drown?"

"Yes, and you must remain entombed until the transformation is complete."

She let out the breath she was holding. "But you'll be there. When I wake up?"

"You still don't understand, Angelina. The long sleep can last for decades, maybe centuries, and when you stir, only human blood will give you life. Even then, you may never rise."

"You mean . . . ?"

"The change doesn't always take."

Stellan held her shoulders, his hands trembling. "Angelina! I can't lose you!"

Tears streamed down her face. "Nor I you! There is a way for us to be together, and I choose it!"

"I won't have you give up your life for me."

"And I won't live a life without you!"

Stellan took her hands in his and closed his eyes. The ferry was gone, obscured by smoke. The woman is as strong and stubborn as she is beautiful.

The same could be said of the man. "Stellan, it will

work. I feel it in my soul. You have to trust me. Trust us."

Flames consumed the wharf. The fire moved toward them at an alarming rate. Boards snapped and fell into the sea. Hand in hand they raced to the far end of the ferry terminal. The wall had crumbled, and as he leaned over, he could see the sheer drop to the black water far below. "We'll have to find a way down." As he spoke, an aftershock rolled beneath them, and the platform collapsed. "Jump!"

She fell through the air, holding him tight. The heat from the fire scorched her until she thought she would be consumed. Seconds later, they hit the surface and plunged down into the sea.

Stellan covered her mouth with his own and exhaled. She felt a rush of heat, and, suddenly, the terrifying urge to breathe vanished.

Angelina looked at him, at his face, suddenly serene. Bubbles escaped her lips and sparked as they captured the firelight. *Stellan, it is extraordinary!*

You can't yet imagine . . .

Down they glided, the world slowly draining of noise and color. The water was emerald green with bursts of orange flaring from the burning city. Bricks and charred beams sank with them. They passed a drowned team of pale horses hitched to a black carriage. It was caught against the pilings. Bodies were stuck halfway out the windows, the door crushed shut. Brass harness buckles and iron-shod hooves gleamed in the light while the dead beasts' manes and tails fanned in the current. Stellan turned her toward him, his hand at her back. With the other, he slowly untied her silk robe and slipped it off her shoulders. It floated away like a black medusa, soon disappearing from sight.

Another shock wave jarred the water, followed by a distant explosion. A boiler, twisted and ripped in half, plummeted past them like a comet. It was followed by a rain of bodies. The corpses drifted, floating soundlessly, faces slack, eyes unseeing. Their frock coats and fine dresses pulled away as if to break free of the inevitable descent. Pockets turned out and shiny coins spilled, a shimmering waterfall into the abyss.

I'm disappearing . . . Angelina's face was momentarily stricken.

Stellan placed his hand over her heart, and she relaxed, the corners of her mouth turning up in a smile. *You'll be safe in the tombs.* He slowly turned her back to him and held her close, one arm across her breasts, the other around her waist. Deeper and deeper into the green darkness they went. As they fell, he gently unlaced her camisole, pulling it over her head and upstretched arms until she was finally free, the earthly garments left behind. Lastly, he unbraided her hair, and it streamed about them in the cold current.

Where are we? Angelina asked, her voice fading to a whisper in his mind.

Above the tombs. He laid her naked body down on the ancient slab of jade and felt the living rock mold to her form. His eyes held hers. *Angelina* . . .

Stellan, she whispered as her heart beat for the last time. *I love you* . . . *I love you* . . .

Sunset
Thursday, January 5, 1933

ANGELINA FELT A tingling in her limbs. Warmth infused her as silky water washed back and forth like a tide over her naked skin. Her hair floated and rippled down her body, tickling her belly and thighs. A rich, delicious aroma engulfed her, and she drank it in, the metallic taste searing down her throat, into her spine, and into her limbs. For uncountable moments, she basked in the offering until memory jolted her mind. *Stellan!* she screamed. Her eyes flew open, and she gasped. *Stellan!*

He smiled down at her. *I'm here.*

Can't help but love Kerrelyn Sparks's
Love at Stake series?
Read on for a taste of
WILD ABOUT YOU
Available now!

Chapter One

IN THE DIM light of a cloud-shrouded moon, Shanna Draganesti cast a forlorn look at the flower beds she'd once tended with care. They'd become choked with weeds since her death.

To be honest, gardening had ranked low on her list of priorities for the past three months. She'd had bigger things to fret about, such as adjusting to a steady diet of blood when six years ago she would have fainted at the sight of it, and dealing with an increased amount of psychic power that made it too easy to hear people's thoughts whether she wanted to or not.

Practically overnight, she'd been expected to master all the vampire skills. Levitation? Downright scary to look down and see nothing beneath her feet. With no way to ground herself, she kept tipping over. *Mental note: never wear a skirt to levitation practice.*

And what about teleportation? She was terrified she'd

materialize halfway into a tree or a rock. And why the heck couldn't she materialize ten pounds lighter? Her scientific genius of a husband couldn't answer that one. Roman had laughed, under the impression that she was kidding.

Then there were the fangs. They tended to pop out at inopportune times. Thankfully she couldn't see her scary new canine teeth in a mirror. Unfortunately she couldn't see herself, either. She'd nearly dropped her three-year-old daughter on the floor the first time she'd seen Sofia floating in a mirror, held by an invisible mother.

And that was the most difficult part of being a vampire. She was no longer the same mother she'd been before. Every scraped knee or bruised feeling her children experienced in daylight hours would be soothed away by someone else. Because during the day, she was dead.

She'd never fully appreciated what the other Vamps went through each day at sunrise. Death-sleep was easy enough, since you just lay there like a lump, but getting there was the pits. She had to die. Over and over, as the sun broke over the horizon, she experienced a burst of pain and a terrifying moment of panic. Roman assured her it would get easier in time when she learned to relax, but how could she remain calm when she was dying? What if she never woke again? What if she never saw her children or her husband again?

There was no comforting light in the distance, reaching out to her with the promise of a happy afterlife. There was only a black hole of nothingness. According to Roman, that was the way it was for vampires. As a former medieval monk, he had interpreted the darkness as one more indication that he was cursed and his soul forever lost.

He now believed differently. When he'd fallen in love with her, he'd accepted that as a blessing from above and a sign that he wasn't entirely abandoned. And then dear Father Andrew, may he rest in peace, had convinced the rest of the Vamps that they had not been rejected by their Creator. There was a purpose to everything under heaven, Father Andrew claimed, and that included the good Vamps. They were the only ones with the necessary skills for defeating bad vampires and shifters. The good Vamps protected the innocent, so they served an important purpose in the modern world.

Mental note: remind yourself every night that you're one of the good guys. It should make that glass of synthetic blood easier to swallow.

"Come on, Mom!" Constantine ran ahead of her and charged up the steps to the front porch.

Not to be outdone by her older brother, Sofia clambered up the steps, too.

"I don't have to wait for Mom to unlock the door," Tino boasted. "I could teleport inside."

Sofia scowled at him, then turned to Shanna. "Mom, he's bragging again."

She gave Tino a pointed look. How many times had she warned him to be mindful of his little sister's feelings? So far, Sofia had not displayed the ability to teleport, and she was growing increasingly sensitive about it.

"There, now." Shanna's mother, Darlene, gave Sofia a hug. "Everyone has their own special gifts."

Sofia nodded, smiling sweetly at her grandmother. "I can hear things that Tino can't."

"Mom, she's bragging again," Tino said in a high-pitched voice to mimic his little sister.

With a snort, Shanna carried her children's empty suitcases up the steps to the front door. In spite of the recent upheaval in her personal life, her kids continued to behave normally. Like the weeds, they seemed capable of thriving in any environment.

"Nice porch." Darlene looked around. "It needs to be swept, though. And you'll need to get the yard tidied up before you post a For Sale sign."

"I know." Shanna set the small suitcases down so she could unlock the door. This was the first time her mother was seeing their home in White Plains, New York. And maybe the last.

Since Shanna's transformation, they'd all lived at Dragon Nest Academy, the school she'd started for special children, mostly shifters or hybrids like Tino and Sofia. Roman had claimed she'd sleep easier, knowing their children were well supervised during the day.

He was secretly worried that she wasn't happy, that she wasn't adjusting. And deep inside, he was afraid that she blamed him for transforming her and separating her from her children. He never said it, but she could read it in his thoughts. And sense it whenever they made love. There was a desperation in his kisses and an extra tenderness to his touch, as if he hoped to eradicate her fears and heal her sadness with the sheer force of his passion.

She blinked away tears as she opened the front door.

Poor Roman. She should reassure him that she was fine, even if it was a lie.

She wheeled the two suitcases into the foyer that was already well lit. The porch light and a few lights in the house switched on each evening thanks to an automatic timer so the house would appear inhabited. "Come on in."

"Oh my, Shanna!" Darlene looked around, her eyes sparkling. "What a lovely home."

Shanna smiled sadly. "Thank you." She'd procrastinated for three months before accepting the inevitable. They had to move. No matter how much she loved this house, it no longer worked, not with her and Roman both dead all day.

Thank goodness her mother was back in her life. Only recently had Darlene broken free from the cruel mind control imposed on her by her husband, Sean Whelan. She spent all of her time now with her children and grandchildren, trying to make up for lost time.

"Come on, Grandma!" Sofia clambered up the stairs. "I want to show you my room."

"Don't forget her suitcase." Shanna handed the pink-and-green Tinkerbell suitcase to her mother. "She can bring whatever toys she can fit in there."

"I want my Pretty Ponies!" Sofia shouted, halfway up the stairs.

"And there's another suitcase in her closet," Shanna said. "She needs more clothes."

"No problem." Darlene started up the stairs. "I'll take care of it."

Shanna handed her son his orange Knicks-decorated suitcase. "Here you go."

Constantine regarded her quietly before responding. "Do we really have to move?"

She nodded. "It's for the best. There are more people at the school who can watch over you during the day."

"I don't need a babysitter."

Shanna sighed. Sofia was delighted with the move, since the school now boasted a stable of horses for equestrian classes. But Tino wasn't so easily swayed. "You'll have other kids there to play with, like Coco and Bethany."

He wrinkled his nose. "They're girls. They just want to do silly stuff."

She tousled the blond curls on his head. "Girls are silly now?"

"Yeah. They just want to dress up and pretend they're movie stars. I want to play basketball or backgammon or Battleship."

"Where did you learn those?" She knew her son played basketball with his dad, but she'd never seen him play board games.

"Howard taught me."

"Oh. That was sweet of him." Howard Barr had been the family's daytime bodyguard for several years now. As a bear shifter, he made a fierce protector, but he had such a gentle nature that Shanna had always considered him more of a honey bear than a grizzly.

"Howard loves games," Tino continued. "People always think he's slow 'cause he's so big and eats so many donuts, but he's really fast."

"I'm sure he is."

"He's smart, too." Tino narrowed his eyes, concentrating. "He says winning is a combination of skill, timing, and . . . stragedy."

"Strategy?"

"Yeah. Howard's real good at stragedy. When is he coming back? He's been gone forever!"

She thought back, recalling that he'd gone to Alaska at the end of May, and it was now the end of June. "It's been about a month."

"Yeah! That's almost forever!"

She supposed it was for a five-year-old. "I'll call your uncle Angus and ask him, but for now, I need you to pack whatever stuff you want to take back to school."

"Okay." Instead of heading for the stairs, he positioned himself underneath the second-floor landing.

"Tino, wait—" She was too late. He'd already experienced lift-off and was quickly levitating beyond her reach. "Be careful."

He peered down at her with the frustrated half smile he always gave her when he thought she was being overly protective. "Come on, Mom. It's not like I can fall." He reached the second-floor balcony and tossed his empty suitcase onto the landing.

She gritted her teeth as he swung a leg over the balustrade and straddled the flimsy railing. He could certainly fall now if he lost his balance or the balustrade collapsed. She tensed, prepared to levitate and catch him, but he landed neatly on his feet on the second floor.

She exhaled the breath she'd been holding. "Are you all right?"

"I'm fine. Don't worry so much." He rolled his suitcase toward his bedroom.

Don't worry so much? She was a mom. How could she not worry?

His words echoed in her mind as she wandered into the family room. She *was* worried. She was afraid he'd try something really dangerous. Like teleport into a moving car. Or levitate to the top of a cell phone tower.

She'd heard him ask Angus MacKay how high a Vamp could levitate. And he was always begging Angus and the other guys at MacKay Security and Investigation to talk about the dangerous adventures they'd managed to survive over the centuries.

In the family room, she rested her handbag on the back of an easy chair to retrieve her cell phone. She'd ask Angus about Howard and remind him that the guys needed to be careful what they said around an impressionable five-year-old boy.

Her gaze drifted to the space between the sofa and coffee table where Tino had taken his first baby steps. Why was he in such a hurry to grow up? If he attempted something dangerous during the day, she wouldn't be there to stop him. How could she live with herself if something happened to her children while she was unable to protect them?

The solution was obvious. Howard needed to come back. He could guard her children better than anyone. Tino wouldn't dare disobey when a Kodiak were-bear told him no.

With a twinge of shame, she realized she'd been too fixated lately on her own problems. She should have realized something serious was happening with Howard. It wasn't like him to be gone for so long. In the six years that she'd known him, he'd only taken a day or two off each month so he could go to his cabin in the Adirondacks and shift. Was he having some sort of personal problem? Was he ill again?

She recalled the way he had looked when she'd first met him—a balding, middle-aged man with a broken nose. He'd had a ready smile and a cheerful sense of humor, so she had never guessed that he was ill.

Roman had explained that right after high school, Howard's were-bear clan had banned him from Alaska. He'd spent four years at the University of Alabama on a football scholarship, and then three more years as a linebacker for the Chicago Bears. Separated from his kind, he had no safe place to shift.

In fact, the first time he shifted in Tuscaloosa, news of a grizzly on the loose had quickly spread, and he'd spent a terrifying night dodging bullets and shotgun shells. After that, he was reluctant to risk shifting. He was even forced to play football on nights when his body had desperately needed to shift. It had taken an enormous amount of control and strength to suppress his inner nature, but he'd managed it, knowing he would lose his career and endanger his species if the truth was revealed.

Refusing to shift had caused a chemical imbalance in his system whereby he was slowly poisoning himself. He aged. His hair fell out. The injuries he incurred on the football field wouldn't heal.

It was a chance occurrence that had saved Howard's life. Gregori had dragged Roman and Laszlo to a playoff game at the old Giants stadium, where they'd sensed an ailing shifter on the field. Even in pain, Howard had managed to sack the opposing quarterback three times. Impressed, they sought him out and convinced him he would die if he continued on his current path.

Relieved to find a job where he no longer had to hide his true identity, Howard began working for Angus at MacKay Security and Investigations. He built a cabin in the Adirondacks where he could shift, and slowly, his bones mended, his hair grew back, and he regained the younger, more virile appearance that shifters normally enjoyed for centuries. But he never returned to Alaska where he had been banned. Until now.

Shanna wondered what had changed. She leaned against the back of the easy chair as she scrolled through the list of contacts on her cell phone to call Angus.

"Did you call yet?"

She nearly dropped her phone. Her son had suddenly materialized by the coffee table. "Tino, you startled me. I thought you were upstairs packing."

"I was." He climbed onto the easy chair, kneeling so he was facing her. "Did you call Uncle Angus? Is Howard coming back? Will he live with us at the school?"

"I suppose he will."

"Then why don't we pack some of his stuff?" Tino asked. "We could get a room ready for him."

Shanna glanced toward the hallway that led to Howard's rooms. Since she and Roman shared a large, windowless suite in the basement, they had let Howard use the master bedroom and office on the ground floor. As a were-bear, Howard was very territorial, so they had allowed him to treat that part of the house as his private domain. She'd seen his office a few times, but she'd never ventured into his bedroom.

She shook her head. "He wouldn't like us rummaging around in his room. Besides, he's been on vacation for over a month. He must have plenty of clothes with him."

"But he won't have his games." Tino bounced on the seat cushion. "We can't play without his games."

Shanna bit her lip. Howard might not mind her going into his room to fetch a few games.

"And he'll want his secret DVDs."

She turned toward Tino. "His what?"

"His DVDs. He has a box of them hidden under his bed. He watches them when he's not working."

"They don't sound very secret if you know where they are."

Tino shrugged. "I just call them secret 'cause he won't let me watch them. He said they're for older people."

Adult only? Shanna swallowed hard. Was there a side to Howard no one knew about? No, she couldn't believe it. Sweet Howard, who always had a smile on his face and a donut in hand? Surely he wasn't . . . "Did he say anything else about these DVDs?"

Tino tilted his head, considering. "There's a girl and two guys. The guys are called Big Al and The Hammer—"

"Okay." Shanna tried to keep any alarm from showing on her face. Good Lord, she'd trusted her children with Howard. Forget privacy issues. As a responsible parent, she had to investigate. "I . . . think I could look in his room for a few board games."

"Cool! Can I come with you?"

"No!" Shanna softened her voice to continue. "Why don't you be a sweetie and help Grandma bring your sister's suitcases down?"

Tino frowned. "All right. But remember to get the chess set, too. Howard promised he would teach me."

"I will." She waited for her son to teleport upstairs, then hurried down the hallway.

She glanced inside the office Howard used as his security headquarters. One wall was covered with monitors. A few screens normally showed the outside perimeter of the house in White Plains, while others were linked to surveillance cameras in Roman's townhouse on the Upper East Side. The monitors were all dark now, since no one was living at either place.

Her gaze wandered across the room. A file cabinet topped with a few trophies and awards Howard had earned during his football career, a plain wooden chair, a pair of hand weights on the floor. Fifty pounds each? Good Lord. Howard would be formidable if ever crossed. It was a good thing he was so sweet-natured. Or was he? How well did she really know him? She eyed the handcuffs on his desk.

Howard loves games. Tino's words slipped back into her mind with a new and disturbing meaning. No, this was easily explainable. Howard was their security guard. He needed silver handcuffs to prevent bad vampires from teleporting away. But what about the adult-only DVDs under his bed?

The door to his bedroom was locked, but that didn't present a problem with her new vampire strength. *Mental note: repair the splintered doorframe and broken door-knob before the house goes on sale.*

She flipped on the light as she entered the bedroom, then stopped with a small jolt of surprise. This was how Howard had furnished his room? She'd visited his hunt-ing cabin on several occasions when Connor had hidden the Draganesti family there in dangerous times. The cabin was exactly what you would expect from an Alas-kan were-bear. Lots of wood, leather, Indian blankets in shades of earth and sky, and a few animal heads mounted on the walls.

There was nothing rustic about this bedroom. Sleek, so-phisticated, and modern, it didn't seem to match Howard. Was there a secret side to him that no one knew about?

The king-sized bed was covered with a black-and-white striped comforter and bright red pillows. The bed-side tables were chrome and glass. Across from the bed, a shiny black dresser was topped with a wide-screen TV. A black leather recliner rested in the corner next to a glass and chrome bookcase. She spotted the games Tino wanted on the bottom shelf.

But what about the secret DVDs? As she approached the bed, the unusual headboard drew her attention. Tin ceiling tiles?

She ran her fingers over the embossed tin. How interesting. The tiles were mounted on a piece of plywood to make a headboard. Had Howard made this himself? Apparently, there was a lot about Howard that she didn't know. With an uneasy feeling, she dropped to her knees and peered underneath the bed.

There it was. A black alligator-skin box. She pulled it out, then took a deep breath and opened it.

Homemade DVDs. She rummaged through the stack, reading the labels Howard had written and attached to the plastic cases. *Elsa in London. Elsa in Amsterdam. Elsa in Berlin.* This Elsa certainly got around. *Elsa in Pittsburgh. Elsa in Cincinnati.* Was this like *Debbie Does Dallas*?

Shanna inserted the first disc in the DVD player on Howard's television, then lowered the volume in case she happened across a scene with loud moaning.

A collage of stately old homes rolled across the screen, then the title of the show appeared. *International Home Wreckers.* A map of the U.K. and the Union Jack flashed by, followed by the photo of a well-dressed man. Alastair Whitfield aka Big Al. The outline of Germany and its flag, followed by another photo. Oskar Mannheim aka The Hammer. And finally, the map and flag of Sweden, followed by the photo of a beautiful blond woman, dressed in cut-off jeans, a plaid shirt tied beneath her breasts, a pair of work boots, and a utility belt resting on her hips. Elsa Bjornberg aka Amazon Ellie. A commercial began for the network, HGRS. Home and Garden Renovation Station.

"Oh my gosh," Shanna breathed. "I love this channel." She glanced back at the tin-tiled headboard. Howard was into home décor?

As the show began, the two male stars were gutting a Victorian townhouse in London that had fallen into disrepair. Alastair, dressed in an expensive designer suit, was selecting new wallpaper for the parlor. Oskar, wearing jeans and a T-shirt, was ripping up a hideous orange shag carpet to expose a wooden floor underneath.

"It's extremely important to preserve a site's proper heritage," Alastair explained in a crisp British accent. "But at the same time, we must be sensitive to the needs of the family who will be calling this home. They have their hearts set on a more modern, open concept, so we have agreed to take down part of the wall separating this parlor from the room behind it. Fortunately, we have the perfect person for busting down a wall. Elsa!"

Shanna sucked in a breath as Elsa Bjornberg strode into the room. Good Lord, she had to be over six feet tall. Either that or her costars were a little short. She wore a pair of white overalls splotched with paint and a short-sleeved T-shirt, also white, that contrasted nicely with her golden, tanned skin. Her long blond hair was pulled back into a ponytail, and the upper part of her face was covered with an enormous pair of safety goggles. In her gloved hands she carried a large sledgehammer.

She wasted no time, just hauled off and slammed her hammer right through the wall.

Shanna watched, amazed. No wonder they called her Amazon Ellie. She was a big woman. Big bones, big muscles, and a big smile she flashed at the camera as the last of the wall crumbled to dust.

Returning to the black box, Shanna inspected the contents more thoroughly. A TV guide listed the show as coming on in the afternoon. That explained why she'd never seen it. But why was Howard being so secretive about his interest in house renovation?

Underneath the DVDs she discovered a magazine article with an interview of Oskar, Elsa, and Alastair. And underneath that she spotted a stack of photos that looked like they'd been printed off the Internet. Every one of them showed Elsa. Elsa in her cut-off jeans, which highlighted her long, tanned legs. Elsa in an evening gown showing off her generous curves. A close-up of Elsa's face and her pretty green eyes.

"Oh my gosh," Shanna whispered. This was why Howard was watching the show. He had a crush on Amazon Ellie.

She glanced up at the television just in time to see Elsa rip a bathroom sink off a wall. "Wow."

Her heart pounding, Shanna rose to her feet. Howard had found the perfect woman for a were-bear!

She turned off the television, and with trembling hands, she returned the DVD to the black alligator-skin box. The perfect woman for Howard! She had to make sure he met her. But he was watching the show in secret. At this rate, he'd never meet his dream girl. He needed some help.

Her heart lurched. The old gate house! Just the other night, she and Roman had discussed the possibility of making the old house their new home. Only a few miles from the school, it was part of the estate, so they already owned it. Unfortunately, it was in sad shape. A money pit, her mother called it.

But that made it the perfect project for the International Home Wreckers! It was exactly the sort of historic gem that they specialized in renovating.

She shoved the box back under the bed and jumped to her feet. Did she dare do this? Play matchmaker to a were-bear? Her heart raced, and for the first time in three months, she realized she was grinning.

She grabbed the games off Howard's bookcase and rushed back to the family room. In a few seconds, she had Angus's number ringing on her cell phone.

"Hi, Angus. Can you bring Howard back right away?"

"Is there something wrong, lass?" he asked.

"I'm worried about my children's safety during the day, especially Tino. I'm afraid he'll try something dangerous, and Howard is the only one who can keep him safe for me. I need him back."

There was a moment of silence before Angus replied. "His vacation time ran out over a week ago. There was a mission I wanted to send him on, but he refused to go."

"What?" Her nerves tensed. "He's not quitting, is he?"

"He dinna say he was, but the bugger stopped answering my calls. I sent Dougal and Phil to hunt him down."

Shanna winced. "He's not in any danger, is he?"

"We doona know," Angus said. "That's why we're looking for him. I would have sent more lads, but we have three missions going on right now. We're short on manpower."

"I see." She took a deep breath. Finding a babysitter for her children probably seemed trivial compared to the other issues Angus had to deal with. But that didn't make her worry any less. "If you find Howard, can you tell him that we need him? Tino is asking for him."

"Aye, we'll tell him."

"Thank you." Shanna dropped her cell phone back into her handbag.

It wasn't like Howard to take more vacation days than he was allotted. Or to ignore phone calls from his boss. Angus had sounded annoyed that he'd been forced to track him down.

What on earth was Howard up to?

Want more Vamp City?
A world of perpetual twilight,
A vampire utopia threatened with devastation . . .
Keep reading for a peek into Pamela Palmer's
brand-new Vamp City series with
A BLOOD SEDUCTION
Available now!
And
A KISS OF BLOOD
Available Summer 2013

An Excerpt from
A BLOOD SEDUCTION
by Pamela Palmer

Chapter One

PERCHED ON HER stool in the chilly lab of the Clinical Center of the National Institutes of Health in Bethesda, Maryland, Quinn Lennox studied the lab results on the desk in front of her. Dammit. Just like all the others, this one revealed nothing out of the ordinary. Nothing. She'd run every blood test known to science, and they all claimed that the patient was disgustingly healthy. Utterly normal.

They lied.

The patient wasn't normal and never had been, and she wanted to know why. She wanted to be able to point to some crazy number on one of the myriad blood tests, and say, "There. That's it. That's the reason my life is so screwed up."

Because those lab tests were hers.

"Quinn."

At the sound of her boss's voice in the lab doorway,

Quinn jumped guiltily. If anyone found out that she'd been using the lab's equipment to run blood tests on herself, she'd be fired on the spot. She set the lab report on her desk, resisting the urge to turn the paper over or slip it in her desk, and forced herself to meet Jennifer's gaze with a questioning one of her own.

"Did you have time to run the McCluny tests?" Jennifer was a round woman, over forty, with a big heart and a driving need to save the world.

"Of course," Quinn replied with a smile. "They're on your desk." She might be running tests she shouldn't be, but never, ever at the expense of someone else's.

"Excellent." Jennifer grinned. "I wish I could clone you, Quinn."

Quinn stifled a groan at the thought. "One of me is more than enough." Certainly more than *she* could handle.

"Hey, you two." Clarice, in a T-shirt and shorts, a fleece hoodie tied around her waist, stopped in the doorway beside Jennifer. It was after 6:00 P.M., and most of the techs had already left for the day. Clarice was clearly on her way out since she'd taken off her white lab coat. But she should be, considering she was getting married in two days. A curvy redhead, Clarice had been one of Quinn's best friends in her first couple of years at the NIH. Before everything had started to go wonky, and Quinn had been forced to retreat from virtually all social events.

Clarice clapped her hands together, the excitement radiating from her so palpable that Quinn could feel it halfway across the lab. The woman practically had the words *bride-to-be* dancing in fizzy champagne bubbles over her head. "Are you two going to meet us at my apartment tomorrow night or down in Georgetown? Larry and two of his groomsmen are available to drive anyone who needs a ride home afterward."

The bachelorette party. Bar-hopping in Georgetown. Quinn nearly swallowed her tongue, forcing down the quick denial. No, she would not be going. Absolutely not. "It's easier for me to meet you there," Quinn replied. No excuse was good enough short of sudden illness. And it was too soon for that.

"I'll meet you at your apartment." Jennifer patted the younger woman on the shoulder. "You look radiant and happy, Clarice. Exactly how a bride-to-be should look. Not a bit the stressed-out crazy person so many brides turn into these days."

"Oh, I'm a crazy person, don't worry. I'm just happy-crazy."

"Stay that way. See you ladies tomorrow," Jennifer said with a wave, and disappeared down the hall.

Clarice came into the lab, now empty but for Quinn, and perched on the lab stool beside Quinn's. "I have a *million* things to do. Two million."

Quinn gave her a half-sympathetic, half-disbelieving look. "Then what are you doing here?"

"Procrastinating. The moment I walk out the door, I'll be moving a hundred miles an hour until I go to bed. If I ever get there tonight."

Quinn grabbed Clarice's hand. "I'm happy for you."

"Thanks." Clarice squeezed hers back. "I'm so glad you're going out with us tomorrow night, Quinn."

"Me, too," Quinn replied weakly, hating that she wouldn't be going. It had been so long since she'd enjoyed a night out, and this one promised to be a lot of fun. And she hated to disappoint Clarice. But she didn't dare go. Not to Georgetown. "I wouldn't miss it."

Clarice slipped her hand from Quinn's and hopped off the lab stool. "Enough procrastinating. I've got to get going."

"Get some sleep tonight."

Clarice rolled her eyes. "I'll sleep on the honeymoon."

"Larry might have other ideas."

With a laugh, Clarice disappeared around the corner.

Quinn turned back to her desk, folded the lab report, and stuck it in her purse, then pulled off her lab coat and glanced down at her clothes, her stomach knotting with tension. On the surface, she was dressed normally for the lab—jeans (purple), T-shirt (red), and tennis shoes (bright blue). The problem was, when she'd dressed this morning, the jeans had been blue, the tee yellow, the shoes white. The Shimmer had struck on her way to work this morning, as it did almost every day now. Why? Why did these things keep happening to her and no one else?

Heading out of the building, she began the long trek across the NIH campus to her car, not looking forward to the long slog through D.C. traffic to get home. Traveling to and from work on the Metro had been so much easier. But public transportation of any kind was out of the question now. What if they passed through a Shimmer? How in the hell would she explain such a color transformation to her fellow passengers?

By the time she reached her car, a ten-year-old Ford Taurus, she was sweating in the late August heat. Opening the car door, she stared at the pink interior, which was supposed to be slate gray, the knot in her stomach growing. With a resigned huff, she slid into the hot car and headed back into Washington, D.C., and home.

Her life had always been a little odd. Now it was starting to come unhinged.

Strange things had happened as far back as she could remember, though rarely. Only twice had they been scary-strange rather than silly-strange, like the color changes. And nothing had happened at all after that second bad incident, in high school. Not until a couple of years ago, when the Shimmers had begun playing with her.

A couple of weeks ago, the visions started.

Yes, her life was becoming seriously unhinged.

As she neared the Naval Observatory on Massachusetts Ave., she saw one of the Shimmers up ahead, like a faint sheen in the sunlight, almost like the rainbow that sometimes appeared in water mist. They were always in the same spots, never moving, never wavering—nearly invisible walls in various parts of D.C. that she'd always been able to see, always been able to drive or walk through without incident. Until recently. Now she avoided them like the plague, when she could. But there wasn't a single route to work that didn't pass through one.

Unfortunately, one cut right through the heart of Georgetown, which was why she couldn't possibly meet

Clarice, Jennifer, and the others tomorrow. How drunk would they have to be to not notice her clothes changing color right before their eyes? Too drunk. It was far too great a risk.

As she drove through the Shimmer, the hair rose on her arms, as it always did, her car interior returning to gray, and her clothes and shoes returning to normal.

In some ways, she'd gotten used to the strangeness, but in a bigger way, she was scared. Because the changes were escalating in frequency, and she had a bad feeling that it was just the beginning.

She couldn't help but wonder . . .

What comes next?

QUINN UNLOCKED THE door of her apartment on the edge of the George Washington University campus and pushed it open. The warm smell of pepperoni pizza and the comforting sound of a computer gun battle greeted her.

"Oh, nice kill." Zack's voice carried from the living room, low and even. When had his voice gotten so deep? He was only twenty-two, for heaven's sake. A man, now. A computer geek who'd long ago found his passion in game design and, more than likely, the love of his life in his best friend, if he ever woke up to the fact that he and Lily were meant to be more than programmer buddies.

Quinn locked the front door behind her, set her purse and keys on the hall table, then strode into the living room, a room she'd furnished slowly and carefully, choosing just the right shades of tans and moss greens and splashes of eggplant to please her senses. But it was the room's occupants who pleased her far more. Zack and Lily sat side by side at the long table against the far wall, each in front of a computer. Behind them, the television news flashed on the flatscreen, the volume a low hum in the room. But neither of the kids paid the television any attention. Each fiendishly tapped away at a computer mouse, staring fixedly at his monitor. Beside Lily sat a plate with a single thick slice of greasy pizza. Beside Zack, two large pizza boxes. The kid never quit eating.

Lily glanced over her shoulder. "Hi, Quinn." A sweet smile lit pretty features framed by long, sleek, black hair.

"Hi, Lily."

Without glancing away from the computer screen, Zack grabbed a slice of pizza out of the top box. Overlong curly red hair framed an engaging face as he wolfed down half of it in one bite and appeared to swallow it just as quickly.

"Hey, sis," he greeted absently. Though only half siblings, they resembled one another rather markedly, except for the hair. They'd both inherited their dad's lanky height, green eyes, wide mouth, and straight nose. But while Zack had that mass of curly red hair, her own was as blond and straight as her late mother's. Their personalities, too, were nothing alike, which was probably why they got along so well. Zack personified laid-back serenity, while Quinn couldn't stay still to save her life. Something had to be in motion—her mind, her body— preferably, both.

Only two things truly mattered to her. Zack and her work. In that order. She liked her job, and she was damned good at it. But if Zack gave her the slightest hint that he'd like her to follow him to California after he graduated, she'd move. Just like that.

But he wouldn't. Zack had Lily, now, if he didn't blow it with her. He didn't need his sister. He'd never really needed her. Not the way she needed him.

"Whoa!" he exclaimed around a bite of pizza as some kind of bomb went off in the middle of the game. "Did you see that, Lily? Awesome."

Quinn grabbed a slice of pizza, then turned up the volume on the television and switched the channel to the local news.

"Another person has been reported missing in downtown D.C. in a string of disappearances that has police baffled. This brings the total number reported missing in the past six weeks to twelve. This last incident is believed to have occurred near George Washington University."

"G.W.?" Lily asked.

But when Quinn glanced at her, the girl had already returned to her game, her lack of concern mired in the youthful belief that bad things only ever happen to other people. A view Quinn had never shared. Unlike most young adults, she'd never believed her world to be a safe, secure place. Never.

Quinn finished her pizza, then carried her laptop back to her bedroom and got online. Sometime later, she heard the front door close and glanced at the time. She'd been on the computer nearly two hours. Was Zack going out or coming back? Closing her laptop, she went to find out.

She found her brother in the kitchen, his head in the fridge.

"Did you walk Lily home, Zack?"

"Uhm-hm."

She grabbed a glass and filled it with water from the sink. "Want me to fix you something?"

"No, thanks."

Zack and Lily, both computer science majors at George Washington, had met their freshman year and become instant friends. They'd interned together this summer at a small Silicon Valley gaming company—a company who'd offered them both jobs upon graduation. Zack had mentioned that they might be doing some testing for the company over the school year.

"Were you guys playing or testing tonight?"

"Both."

Zack wasn't the world's greatest conversationalist. Nine times out of ten, she had trouble getting more than one or two words out of him, though every now and then she asked the right question, usually about gaming, and he talked her ear off.

He straightened, holding a small bottle of Gatorade. "Want one?" Her brother's eyes crinkled at the corners, the unspoken love they felt for one another sparkling in his eyes.

She smiled. "No thanks."

With that, he left the kitchen, his mind wholly engaged by whatever thoughts forever zinged around his head. He'd always been that way, seemingly unaware of anything around him. And yet he'd always been there for her. Always. Zack's love was the one constant, the one absolute, in her life. And always had been.

Quinn downed her water, then poured herself a glass of wine and followed him into the living room, curling up on the sofa, utterly content to listen to Zack's tapping at the computer keyboard as she read. She tried to give Zack some privacy when Lily was here, though she was pretty sure he'd never taken advantage of it in any way. As far as she could tell, Zack considered Lily a friend and nothing more. One of these days, he was going to wake up to the fact that his best friend was a beautiful young woman who happened to be in love with him. And when that day . . .

Quinn froze as a familiar chill skated over her skin. Her breath caught, the hair lifting on her arms. Oh, hell. She'd felt this same chill more than half a dozen times over the past few weeks. Only recently had she connected it to the visions.

She set her wineglass down so fast, it splashed onto the lamp table, then she lunged off the chair and crossed to the window with long, quick strides. But as she approached, she slowed, hesitating, her pulse kicking hard and fast. She knew what she *should* see, looking out the window—the dorms across the street, two dozen windows glowing with light and life, cars lining the street below. Her heart thrummed with anticipation and dread at what she *would* see instead.

Dammit, why does this stuff always have to happen to me?

With a quick breath, she stepped forward and lifted

shaking hands to the windowpane, curving her hands around her eyes to close out the light from the room. And, just as she'd feared, she stared at an impossible sight. A line of two-story row houses, decrepit and crumbling, lit only by the moonlight falling from above, stood where the dorms should be. This street, unlike the real one, was unlit, unpaved. Uninhabited?

Three other times over the past weeks, after she'd felt that odd chill, she'd looked out the window to find this exact same scene. *Why?* If it weren't for all the other strangeness in her life, she might think she was hallucinating. Or going insane.

Maybe I am.

The sound of a horse's whinny carried over the sound of the real traffic, for the normal sounds had never died away despite the change in scenery. Her eyes widened. Maybe her imaginary street wasn't quite so uninhabited after all. She pushed up the window and leaned forward, as close to the screen as she could get without actually pressing her nose against it.

"Zack, turn off the light and come here." As soon as the words were out of her mouth, she wanted to pull them back. She'd spoken without thinking. Then again, if he saw it, too . . .

Zack never did anything quickly, but the tone of her voice must have gotten through to him because he doused the light, except for one computer monitor, and joined her a handful of seconds later.

"What?" He folded his long length and peered through the screen beside her.

Quinn swallowed. "I thought I heard a horse. Do you see one?"

His shoulder brushed hers as he turned and looked in one direction, then the other. "Nope. Probably just one of the mounted cops." He straightened and returned to his computer.

Quinn pressed a fist against her chest and her racing heart. Just once, she'd like not to be the only freak on the planet.

The distinctive sound of a horse's clip-clop grew louder, overlaying the true traffic sounds. And then she saw it, pulling a buggy down that empty dirt street, a dark-cloaked figure holding the reins. A moment later, incongruously, a yellow Jeep Wrangler burst onto the scene, swerving around the carriage, causing the horse to sidestep with agitation. The buggy driver shouted with anger. And then the strange sounds and sights were gone, and Quinn once more stared at the dorms and cars that were really there.

"LILY'S MISSING."

At the sound of Zack's frantic voice through the cell phone the next morning, Quinn leaped from her lab bench, her free hand pressing against her head. "Are you sure?" *God.* The disappearances!

"We were going to meet out front and walk to class together like we always do. But she never showed up. And I can't find her."

"She's not picking up her phone?"

"No. She texted me to say she'd be here in five minutes, but that was fifteen minutes ago, and she's not here. She's not anywhere, Quinn. I've been walking around looking for her."

"Zack." She'd never heard him sound so frantic—she'd never heard him sound frantic at all. She scrambled to think of a logical, safe explanation for Lily's disappearance and couldn't come up with a single one that fit Lily's serious, responsible nature. "Have you called her mom?" Lily lived with her parents about six blocks away.

"I don't know her mom's number."

Crap. "Do you know either of her parents' names?"

"Mr. and Mrs. Wang."

"Zack. There have to be hundreds of Wangs in D.C."

"I know."

"Where are you?"

"Starbucks on Penn."

A couple of blocks from their apartment. "Stay there. Inside. I'm on my way."

Thirty minutes later, after handing off her work to a fellow technician, racing to her car, and flying through more nearly red lights than she cared to admit, she found Zack right where he'd said he'd be, his body rigid with tension as he paced. He looked up and saw her, the devastation in his expression lifting with relief. As if she could fix it. *Oh, Zack.* His T-shirt was plastered to his body, his face flushed and soaked with sweat. He loved that girl, she could see it in his eyes, even if he didn't know it, yet. If Lily was really gone, her loss was going to slay him.

And his grief was going to slay Quinn.

She took his hand, squeezing his damp fist. "Where have you looked?"

"Around." His eyes misted, his mouth tightening painfully. "She's not here, Quinn."

"We'll find her."

But he wasn't buying her optimism any more than she was. The cops hadn't found a single one of the missing people, yet. Not one.

"Do you know where she was when you last heard from her?"

"She was close. Within a block or two of our apartment."

Quinn cocked her head at him. "Doesn't she usually buy coffee on her way to class?"

"Yeah."

"Where?"

He blinked. "Here."

"Have you asked if they saw her?"

His face scrunched in embarrassment. "No." He pulled out his cell phone as he walked up to the counter, stepping in front of the line and holding out his phone and, she assumed, Lily's picture, to the barista. "I'm looking for my friend. Did she get coffee here a little while ago?"

The man peered at the picture. "Yeah. Lily, right? She ordered her usual mocha latte no-whip."

Zack turned away, and Quinn fell into step beside him as they pushed through the morning-coffee crowd and left the shop. She squinted against the glare of the summer sun. "She went missing between here and the street in front of our apartment. It's just two blocks, Zack." And the chances they'd find her, after Zack had already looked, were slim to none.

Together, they walked down the busy sidewalk, dodging college kids, locals, and tourists as they searched for any sign of Lily or what might have happened to her. Quinn's chest ached, as much for Lily as it did for Zack. His anguish, thick and palpable, hung in the steamy air.

When that familiar chill rippled over her skin, it startled her. *Oh, hell. Not here. Not now.*

They were nearly to the block their apartment sat on, the street where, just last night, she'd seen an old-fashioned horse and buggy. In the dark. Surely she wouldn't see it in bright daylight.

Her pulse began to race in both anticipation and dread. What if she saw that strange scene again? What if, as always happened when she peered out the window, she suddenly couldn't see the real world? Would she start running into people? Maybe walk in front of a car?

She grabbed Zack, curling her fingers around his upper arm.

His gaze swung to her, hope wreathing his face. "Do you see her?"

"No. I just . . . I don't feel well."

His brows drew down, and he pulled her hand off his arm and engulfed it in his larger one, closing his fingers tightly around hers.

Hand in hand, they crossed the street, pushing through a throng of backpacked college kids, and walked around the construction barricade that was blocking her view of her building. As they cleared the barricade, Quinn swallowed a gasp at the sight that met her gaze. Superimposed upon a small section of her apartment building, to the left of the entrance, was what appeared to be a house of some sort. Or row house. It was set back and partially illuminated as if by a spotlight, surrounded by shadows. A crumbling, haunted-looking house that wasn't really there.

Holy shit. She pulled up short.

"You see something."

Zack's words barely registered, and she answered without thinking. "Yes."

"What?"

His excitement penetrated her focus. "I'm not sure." But she started forward, her gaze remaining glued on that impossible sight. The shadows fully blocked the sidewalk, extending almost to the street, as if the vision were three-dimensional, as if a slice had been cut from another world, a square column, and dropped into the middle of hers. But the house didn't appear to actually stand within that column. In fact, the column didn't appear to quite reach the front of her apartment building at all. It was as if the shadows acted as a window into the world where the house sat, alone and abandoned.

She frowned, trying to make sense of it. Why, when the scene appeared at night, was she able to see what appeared to be the entire landscape of . . . what? Was it another world? Another time? No, it couldn't be another time. Not with a Jeep Wrangler racing across the landscape.

Why could she see it when no one else could? And, clearly, no one else could. People were walking right through those shadows as if they weren't there.

She had no intention of doing the same. With her luck, her face and hair would turn purple.

Zack squeezed her hand. "What do you see, Quinn? Something to do with Lily?"

"I'm not sure. Probably not," she replied out of habit, not about to admit to her weirdness. If Zack knew about it, he'd never said a word. And if he didn't, if he'd remained happily clueless all these years, well, there was no need for him to find out now. "Just give me a moment, Zack." She let go of his hand. "Wait here."

Quinn eased forward, dodging a couple of college kids as she neared that strange column of spotlight and shadows. It wasn't a spotlight, she realized, but sunlight illuminating the front stoop of a house that stood only about twelve feet away. Mold and mud splattered the ancient brick; glass, long since broken, left gaping holes for windows; and the front door hung askew, dangling on one hinge. On that door, a tarnished lion's-head doorknocker sat cockeyed and snarling at unwary visitors. Visitors long gone.

It looked so *real*.

The column itself was only about six feet wide, yet the house sat farther back than those six feet. To either side of the spotlighted front stoop, shadows and darkness lingered, like a nightscape cut by a beacon of sunlight. Yet people continued to flow through that shadowy column, oblivious. Unaffected.

"Lily's pen."

Quinn hadn't even realized Zack had followed her until she saw him reach for the bright green ballpoint pen lying on the sidewalk just inside the shadows.

"Zack, no."

Instinctively, she grabbed his bare forearm just as his arm . . . and her clutching hand . . . dipped into the shadows. Energy leaped at her through the hand that held him, attacking her with an electrical shock that raced over her body like crawling ants, shooting every hair on her arms and head straight up.

Her breath caught, her eyes widened. Her brain screamed, *Let go of him!* But her fingers couldn't react in time, and, suddenly, they were both flying forward.

Into nothingness.

An Excerpt from
A KISS OF BLOOD
by Pamela Palmer

FOUR MORE DAYS until Quinn Lennox's life, as she knew it, was over.

Quinn paced the lamplit living room of her apartment on the George Washington University . . . GW . . . campus, releasing her blond hair from its ponytail with restless fingers, then refastening it into a casual knot at the back of her neck. In truth, her normal life, if her life had ever been normal, had ended a month ago, when she and her brother Zack stumbled through a crack in the world and found themselves fighting for their lives in the dark vampire otherworld that, impossibly, shared physical space with much of Washington, D.C., and had for 140 years.

Washington, V.C., the vampires called it. Vamp City.

God help her, how was it possible there were vampires and werewolves and sorcerers?

She picked up her water glass, took a quick sip, then

set it back down and continued to pace. Always restless, the past week and a half she'd been positively crawling out of her skin. Because two things were going to happen on the equinox in four days.

She hoped.

One: The immortal son of the sorcerer who'd created Vamp City would renew the crumbling magic, curing Zack of the illness he'd developed.

And two: The vampires, now trapped by the magic's failure, would once more be free to come and go from the real world as they pleased. Which meant the vampire master and sadistic monster, Cristoff, would send his goons after her. She'd escaped him twice now, and she had no doubt he wanted nothing more than to make her pay.

If she could flee now, she would. Hell, she'd have left a week and a half ago, when the vampire Arturo Mazza first freed her and Zack. The trouble was, he'd warned that the two of them could possibly have become affected by the failing magic and should remain close until the magic was renewed. For once, he'd told her the truth.

Against her wishes, Zack had let his parents—Quinn's dad and stepmom—sweep him back home to Lancaster, Pennsylvania, where he'd almost immediately become ill with something the doctors couldn't explain. She alone knew what it was—magic sickness. She'd convinced Zack to come back to D.C. with her, and here they'd stay until the magic was renewed, and he was well again.

Four days.

Several days ago, she'd packed up most of hers and

Zack's clothes and given them to the Salvation Army. Everything else would remain behind. They'd each take one suitcase, no more, when they fled. But now she had nothing to do but wait for the equinox and worry.

The one thing she would never do was go back to that vampire hell.

To the vampires, of course, Vamp City was utopia—a city where the sun never shone, where they could enslave and hunt humans without fear of retribution. A place where the vampires, werewolves, and other immortal creatures could live their lives in the open. In freedom. And peace.

But even utopias have a dark side. Unbeknownst to the vampires, Phineas Blackstone, the powerful wizard they'd paid to create their dark city, had engineered a death trap instead. The moment the magic began to fail, all vampires within the city's boundaries would be trapped, unable to escape as the sunbeams slowly broke through, frying them, killing them.

Two years ago, the process began, the sunbeams breaking through, here and there, for seconds at a time. But in the past months, the process had escalated until the vampires feared they had only weeks left until the magic crumbled, and all those trapped, died.

They needed another sorcerer to renew the magic, but so far neither of Phineas's immortal sons had managed to do it. They'd been hunting for another when she accidentally stumbled into V.C. while helping Zack search for his missing friend, Lily.

And, it turned out, she was a sorceress. Apparently

the small and not-so-small weirdnesses that had always been part of her life were not her imagination after all. She might be an honest-to-God sorceress, but she was a completely ineffectual one, with little power. What power she did have, she couldn't control. In the end, Arturo had let her go, promising her that Phineas's sons would ultimately be able to renew the magic even though he'd first told her they couldn't.

Arturo Mazza was nothing if not a liar. Which of those was the lie, she didn't know and didn't care so long as she and Zack were free.

From the moment she'd stumbled into that world, the dark, handsome Arturo had been there, in turns her protector and friend, lover and betrayer. And in the end, her savior, rescuing Zack from certain death and freeing them both. As much as she hated to admit it, she missed that vampire more than she could have imagined. In a weird sort of way, they'd become friends. Perhaps more than friends. He was the only one in her life who'd known exactly who and what she was, right from the beginning, and accepted her anyway.

But that didn't mean she ever wanted to see him again. If she ever crossed paths with another vampire, it would be too soon.

Quinn glanced around the room, looking for something . . . anything . . . to do as she listened to the second hand on the replica antique desk clock ticking off the time with incredible slowness. Crossing to the window, she pushed open the lower half of the double-hung to let in the cool September air, then glanced at the dorms across the street. Half the windows were lit, like the spots on a domino, the other half dark, the students still out and about campus despite the fact that the sun had set more than an hour ago.

Zack and his best friend, Lily, both GW seniors, should have been out there with them, though more than likely they'd have been right here, side by side in front of their computers either playing some high-action fantasy shoot-'em-up or designing one. But Lily had disappeared, as so many people around D.C. had in recent months. Quinn suspected she'd fallen through the same door into Vamp City as she and Zack had, but while they'd searched for her, they'd never found her.

Lily was most likely dead. Humans didn't last long among the vampires. And Zack . . . poor Zack was suffering not only from the magic sickness but from grief and depression as well. Her sweet, easygoing brother had not emerged from Hell unscathed. Not by a long shot.

Quinn straightened, hoping her neighbor, Mike, would come over as he did most evenings and give her something to think about other than vampires, and something to listen to other than the ticking clock. In his company, she could pretend, even if just for an hour or two, that she lived a normal life in a normal world. Even if nothing could be further from the truth.

But as she turned from the window, a familiar chill skated over her skin—a feeling she knew presaged the bleeding together of the two worlds. And she was reminded, with the subtlety of a mallet to the head, just how far from normal her existence really was.

Within Vamp City, they'd feel the bleed-through as an earthquake. In daylight, the quake would be quickly followed by sunbeams bursting overhead like light through a dark piece of hole-riddled construction paper. The vampires would flee the sunlight, or die if they were unlucky enough to be standing in the wrong place when the sunbeams appeared.

But in the real world, Quinn alone felt the change, thanks to her sorcerer's blood. She alone could see through the shadowy breaks like windows into the other world. Unable to resist another glimpse of that place, she turned back and bent low, staring through the screen into that otherworld, a doppelganger of 1870 Washington, D.C.

When Blackstone created Vamp City, he'd duplicated the city of that time. But while the humans continued to upgrade and modernize the real D.C., the vampires did little with their version other than build a few castles for their vampire masters and an arena for their games. Some of the vampires had moved into the fully furnished houses, but most of the structures had been left to decay, including the line of row houses across the street from her now.

Vamp City's streets were still unpaved, its infrastructure all but nonexistent. There was electricity only in homes with generators, and few modern conveniences. Though some vampires had brought in off-road vehicles to traverse the pitted streets, most continued to live as they had in those earlier times—riding horses and driving carts and carriages. And feeding, as all vampires did, on humans.

As she peered into that strange place, she saw no one and heard nothing but the sound of the real world, which continued to carry to her ears—a car driving down the street, the tick of the clock, the banter of college kids walking along the sidewalk below her window, discussing their fantasy-football picks. This neighborhood of Vamp City, she knew from her own experience, was uninhabited and generally deserted except for the roaming Traders, who hunted for escaped slaves and humans who wandered in accidentally.

Suddenly, a young man stumbled into the scene below, a college kid appearing out of nowhere. Quinn gasped as she watched him fall to his hands and knees in the dirt. Oh, shit. One of the fantasy-football kids must have slipped between the worlds as he'd passed through the dark sunbeam. Every day, thousands passed through the breaks unaware and unaffected, but every now and then, one slipped through. As Lily probably had. As she and Zack had.

As the kid struggled to his feet in Vamp City, Quinn heard his friends' voices below, shouting for him from the real world. Shouts the kid would never hear. Only she could hear both worlds at once where they bled into one another.

She watched as the young man leaped to his feet, staring around him in stunned silence, his body language projecting disbelief, shock, and slowly dawning terror. Her heart ached for him because she'd been in his shoes just a few weeks ago. And she knew what he'd soon learn—that he had every right to be afraid.

His friends would tell the cops that he'd been right there, then just wasn't—the same story reported over and over again on the news from others who'd been with one of the missing. But the cops wouldn't find him. They didn't have a clue what was going on. And they couldn't do anything about it even if they knew.

I might be able to save him.

If she ran, she might be able to run into that world and snatch him back out before the break closed. She alone, thanks to her sorcerer's blood, could leave V.C. on a sunbeam as well as enter. And she'd managed to free others as well.

But instead of running, her body tensed with indecision. The breaks were unpredictable, some lasting many minutes, some only a minute or two. If she ran into that world to save the kid, and the break closed before she got out again, she'd be stuck, unable to return to Zack. And he needed her.

Her heart pounded. But before she could force her feet to move through the mire of indecision, she heard the sound of hoofbeats and knew any chance to help the kid was gone. As she watched, a pair of riders pulled up on horseback. Not vampires, but Traders, an inhuman race she knew little about, only that they could come and go even with the magic failing and that they were the primary procurers of supplies and humans for the trapped vampires.

As she watched, the kid stared at the riders in relief, his expression quickly turning to terror as one of the Traders threw a lasso, roping him like a steer, then hauled him onto the back of his horse. The kid's cry for help went silent, the break between the worlds closing as suddenly as it had opened, leaving Quinn once more looking at the dorms across the modern D.C. street.

Oh, God. Covering her forehead with her palm, she turned away, her skin cold, her head throbbing because she knew what awaited the kid. She'd been in that world twice and wouldn't have survived either trip if not for Arturo's intervention.

A low rap sounded on her apartment door, a knock she recognized. Mike's. Relief coursed through her, and she headed toward the door as if it provided the only measure of sanity in an increasingly insane world. Mike would not only offer her some much-needed company, but also the illusion, for however short a time, of normalcy.

As she peered out the peephole into Mike's smiling face, a sense of calm settled over her, a calm that she hadn't felt all day. The tense misery eased out of her shoulders as she unhooked the chain and unbolted the dead bolt to let him in. Mike had moved into the apartment across the hall a few weeks ago, while she was caught in Vamp City. She'd met him the first evening she got back, and he'd pushed right past her usual reserve to become a welcome, undemanding friend. A writer, he lived alone, working from home. When he was done for the evening, he was sorely in need of company and had taken to bringing over a bottle of wine about this time every night. She, in turn, always had dessert ready and waiting.

She opened the door and smiled as she stepped back to let him in. He was a good-looking guy despite his untrimmed hair, his unshaven jaw, and the three-inch scar that ran down one cheek, a scar he'd earned in a fight with his brother as teenagers, when they'd shattered a sliding glass door. Dressed in a plain black T-shirt tucked into well-worn jeans, his gray eyes alight with life and laughter, he was a welcome ray of sunshine in the dark mire that had become her life.

Mike's smile faded, his brow lowering as he studied her. "You look like you've seen a ghost."

The man was far too perceptive. "I'm fine. It's been a long day." The understatement of the year. She'd felt every single one of the day's 86,400 seconds tick by. "What did you bring tonight?" she asked, eyeing the bottle of wine in his hand.

He held it up with a flourish. "Chateau la Peyre Saint-Estephe Bordeaux." The French rolled off his tongue as if he'd been born to it.

"Will it go with banana cream pie?"

Mike's eyes crinkled with laughter. "Everything goes with banana cream pie."

They fell into their nightly routine, Mike uncorking the bottle and pouring it into the two wineglasses that Quinn had waiting, while she served up whatever dessert she'd made that day. Dessert was the one thing she could still get Zack to eat.

A glass in one hand and a dessert plate in the other, they wandered into the living room, Mike taking the sofa while Quinn sat on the reading chair across from him.

Fortunately, there was no attraction between them. If there had been, she'd have stopped these nightly visits as soon as they began. After all, she was leaving town the moment Zack was well. Hopefully, in four days. There was no sense getting involved with yet another male she'd never see again. Not that she wanted another male. The last, one far-too-handsome Italian vampire, still held her libido in thrall and probably would for months.

But Mike was good company, an easy man to like even without the gifts of expensive wine.

"How's the book coming?" she asked after she'd taken a bite of her dessert. She might not be the world's best cook, but she made a damned fine banana cream pie.

He gave her a pained smile. "Three steps forward, five steps back."

"Ouch."

"No one ever said writing was easy. I spent half the day wandering in front of the window trying to understand why my protagonist left the scene of the crime three chapters back, only to realize he wouldn't have."

As Mike launched into the details of his latest thriller novel, Quinn took a sip of wine, sinking back into her chair, enjoying the calm, mellow tones of Mike's voice. And wishing, despite herself, that it was another's. As hard as she tried, she couldn't stop thinking about Arturo Mazza, couldn't stop dreaming about him. He'd been arrogant, controlling, and manipulative. Cristoff's snake. But he'd also been charming and protective, even kind. And a gentle, passionate lover.

Heaven help her, she'd been attracted to him! An ungodly attraction that still had her waking feverish with desire almost every night. Even in her dreams, she smelled his warm, masculine scent and felt the brush of his hands over her heated skin.

Even when he'd claimed her as his slave, he'd never hurt her, not physically. Not personally. And in the end, he'd come through for her, saving Zack, rescuing her from the cruelty of his master, Cristoff, and freeing them both. Within Arturo, she'd found shades of both the hero and the villain. A male she'd trusted with her life. And a male whose word she'd never been able to trust at all.

Mike paused to take another bite of pie as he eyed her with what she'd come to think of as his writerly scrutiny, as if she were one of his characters, and he was trying to figure her out. He'd never succeed, of course. Humans didn't believe in sorceresses, or vampires, or immortal otherworlds. And she wasn't about to tell this one about them.

"How are you really, Quinn?" Mike asked, his tone compassionate, as if he could see the way she was falling apart at the seams. Every night he asked the same question, in the same way, then never pressed when she gave him her stock, trite answer, for which she was grateful. It wasn't like she could ever tell him the truth.

"I'm fine. Tired and worried about Zack, but things will be better once we get home." She'd told him that Zack's best friend was one of the many missing persons in D.C. and that Zack was suffering from depression as a result. That they were moving back to Pennsylvania to get him away from the memories. She was never sure if Mike believed her, but it didn't matter. The truth would be far harder for him to accept.

As she sipped her wine, she wished she could tell Mike everything. She wished she had someone she could confide in other than Zack, who was still too traumatized by all that had happened.

She wished Arturo were here.

No, she didn't. Not really. She never wanted to see another vampire again.

"Quinn?" Mike asked quietly, and she realized he'd quit speaking, and she'd been too lost in her own thoughts to notice.

She met his gaze sheepishly. "Sorry. I've got a lot on my mind. I'm afraid I'm not good company tonight."

He smiled at her with understanding. "You're always good company." Watching her with that studious look, he opened his mouth, then closed it slowly, as if he'd decided against saying whatever was on his mind. "Get some sleep," he said, rising. "Everything looks brighter in daylight."

Quinn snorted and smiled. "Profound."

Mike grinned at her. "That's the smile I like to see."

She said good-bye and let him out, locking up behind him, then went to check on Zack, to see if she could coax him into eating a little pie.

As she eased open his door, the light from a streetlamp lit his face, a face that had aged during his brief captivity in Vamp City, making him look older than his twenty-two years. His was still an engaging face, if harder than before, framed by overlong curly red hair. If her own hair had looked like his, instead of being blond and straight, they'd have looked rather startlingly similar, despite being only half siblings. They'd both inherited their dad's lanky height, green eyes, wide mouth, and straight nose.

"Zack?" she asked, flipping on the light. "How about a slice of banana cream pie?"

His eyes opened slowly, the circles beneath dark as bruises, the whites an unnatural, shimmery gray.

She swallowed, aching at the sight of him.

"No thanks," he murmured, then rolled away from her.

Quinn turned off the light and closed the door behind her, then sank back against the wall. He'd be fine after the equinox, after the magic was renewed. She had to believe that. But the equinox was still four days away.

And deep inside, she was terrified that Zack might not live that long.

Want to know how Violet went from
B-movie script writer to shapeshifter?
Keep reading for an excerpt from Amanda Arista's
DIARIES OF AN URBAN PANTHER,
the first in the Those Who Wander series.
Available now!

Prologue

AS I STEPPED into the crosswalk, the boy next to me ran across the white stripes to his mother's waiting minivan. His blue book bag danced wildly on his back as his hands waved in reckless abandon. Just down the road to our right, a car engine revved and the driver accelerated towards the crosswalk.

The space between my shoulder blades tingled and the scene before me slowed. The manic screams of the children on the playground across the street quieted. The breeze stopped carrying the sweet scents of fall. The police officer's stop sign rose slowly and froze just above his head. Everything faded into the background as my senses focused on what was going to happen. I knew that in five seconds, there was going to be a schoolboy pancake with a side of scrambled Violet.

Instinct took hold and I darted out in front of the car. Scooping up the small boy from the asphalt, I leapt onto the hood. The motion sent the two of us sliding, leaving a clean streak across the hot metal. We flew off the other side and tumbled to the ground.

I hit the pavement hard, almost on all fours. Kneeling, I held the boy tightly, his arms clutched around my neck. His little heart beat wildly, almost as fast as mine. I looked up to follow the driver down the street. It was the same car that had been parked outside my coffee shop. I caught a flick of blonde hair and a flash of white teeth as the driver laughed and sped around the corner out of sight. His parting shot echoed out his open window, "See you later, Leftovers."

The little boy began to wriggle in my tight grasp and pushed back to look up at me. I saw his doe-like eyes, his mouth in a small O, and the pulse in his neck. His little face puckered in panic and a small finger worked its way up to poke me in the eye.

That's when the world seemed to start up again. The wind swept through the trees carrying the scent of excited children. Doors slammed. People suddenly hovered all around us. " "Oh my god, Tomas," a woman cried out and the boy was snatched from my arms.

I leaned against the car beside me, blinking rapidly to make the sting from his grubby little finger go away.

As I pushed myself to my feet, I caught my reflection in the side view mirror. Yellow eyes stared back. Crap. Guess if I saw a monster with yellow eyes, I'd poke her in the eye as well.

"You all right?" The police officer's musky cologne and the smell of leather from his holster drew my attention as he walked closer. He was a police officer. Just a public servant. Not a threat.

"Fine." I bent over, hands on my knees, hiding my face, simply taking in long deep breaths. In through the nose, out through the mouth. I'm just a writer. And I'm fine. Just fine. Everything's friggin' peachy in Violet-Land.

My hands were shaking; my knees were weak. I heard the roar of blood in my ears and saw the pulse in my vision. My glance darted to the other side of the street where people had lined up to watch the show. Just people, I told myself. A boy nearly gets run down by a sports car and people are going to gawk. Nothing weird about that.

"I'm fine," I repeated, still taking in deep breaths, still processing everything that had flown by. Did the world actual stop moving? Had I actually just run out in front of a car? Who was that guy that called me Leftovers?

A slight chill ran down my body as the breeze cooled the sweat on my skin. My heartbeat slowed; my pulse less visible. As I turned back at my reflection in the car window, I looked like me again. Just Violet.

The boy's mother reached out and touched my forearm with cool fingers. "You saved my little boy's life."

I turned towards her quickly. I had. I had saved a life. Little Violet Jordan was a hero.

The woman hugged me, smashing the boy between us. It threw me off balance for a moment as her rose perfume assaulted my senses but I patted her back softly. She pulled away and, without meeting my eyes again, headed toward her car. Tomas's frightful eyes peered over his mother's shoulder and he stared at me until he was securely fastened into his seat.

The police officer watched silently as I tried to catch my bearings. I didn't know where home was. There wasn't a school anywhere near my house. I thought I'd run west, but with all the turns and shortcuts, I couldn't be sure any more.

"I've never seen anyone do that," the officer said with a smile as he scratched behind his ear, lifting up the edge of his hat.

"Adrenaline, I guess." I forced a half smile and watched Tomas and his mom drive away.

"You training for a marathon or something?"

"No. Why?"

"I watched you speed around the corner. It was like a woman with a mission."

I gulped. "Just running," I squeaked out.

He nodded and waved to the gathering crowd to disperse. As the people slowly retreated to their cars or back into the school building, five black dogs remained on the sidewalk, panting, staring at me.

Frozen, I stared at the motley group of mongrels. My skin crawled and the space between my shoulder blades tightened, the hair prickling down my neck. They'd found me. My vain attempt to blend into a crowd of schoolchildren three feet shorter than me hadn't worked as well as I thought and now they were waiting with baited breath.

"Is your ankle alright?"

"My ankle?" I looked down to see a gash just above

my ankle soaking my sock with deep red blood. "Where's my shoe?"

The officer pointed to the middle of the street where my size ten rested like a big white speed bump. "You clipped the front; that's what made you spin."

"*I spun?*"

He nodded and looked at the dogs, then back at me. "Do you want me to call you an ambulance?"

I tried to put pressure on my swollen ankle and fire flew up my leg. Not just bleeding, broken. I gulped but tried not to show just how painful it really was. "I've survived worse."

He pulled out a small memo pad from his breast pocket. I almost expected him to lick the tip of the pencil like in the old detective movies, but he didn't. "Did you recognize the car?"

I could only shake my head; my lips clamped shut. I couldn't positively identify it as the one that had been parked outside the coffee shop where I spent half my waking moments. I mean there were probably thousands of BMW convertibles in Dallas.

"Would you like to press charges?"

"Press charges? The guy sped off."

With an unsatisfied sigh, he put the pad back in his front pocket. "Well, I'm going to have to fill out a report anyway, but since you're refusing an ambulance, can I at least give you a ride home?"

I looked down at the empty street, then at the dogs lined up just waiting for me to be alone again. "That would be great," I said with a pain-filled smile.

I'd never been in the back of a police car but I could see the odometer from there. As I gave the officer directions, I watched the numbers tick away. Seven miles. I'd run seven miles, saved a boy's life, and broken an ankle. That was a bit more than my standard afternoon. I longed for the days when I stayed in my office to write my little stories and only ran after ice cream trucks.

We stopped outside my townhouse and the officer rushed around the front of his patrol car to let me out. He offered a hand as I gingerly slid across the vinyl seats and stood on one leg. I looked down the quiet residential street. No dogs. No speeding sociopaths.

"Thank you again." He closed the door and walked back around to the driver side of the car. "We need more heroes like you."

I watched as he drove off. Wincing with every uneven step, the walk to my house felt like another mile in itself. As quickly as I could, I found my key, unlocked my door, hobbled inside, and slammed the door shut.

Exhausted, I leaned against the door and slid down to the floor. The sock was a lost cause. I'd forgotten my shoe at the scene of the crime. There was so much pain in my leg I didn't know if I would ever move from this spot.

Now I had a reason to never leave my house again.

I hate dogs. I hate lost shoes and I really hate exercise.

And thanks to what happened two weeks ago, I'd never enjoy another Cosmo again.

BY ABOUT THE AUTHORS

AMANDA ARNOLD was born in Illinois, raised in Corpus Christi, lives in Dallas, but her heart lies in London. When not writing, she often dreams of so opening an eBakery and selling decadent desserts. She spends her weekends writing at coffee shops, listening to the hits that catch her attention, and while music good and plotting character conflicts.

IM PALEY SMITH was born in Santa Cruz, California where she wrote her first story at age five. Jt was about a Halloween craft from de store, she preceded to play card her way through school, but finally she now daydreams for writing on the Southern California coastline.

About the Authors

KERRELYN SPARKS is the *New York Times* bestselling author of a series that mimics its sexy heroes by refusing to die. Now up to book thirteen, the Love at Stake series spreads laughter worldwide. In spite of a tendency to nibble on necks or howl at the moon, Kerrelyn's vampire and shapeshifter heroes are still wonderfully romantic.

When *New York Times* bestselling author PAMELA PALMER's initial career goal of captaining starships didn't pan out, she turned to engineering, satisfying her desire for adventure with books and daydreams, until finally succumbing to the need to create worlds of her own. Pamela lives and writes in the suburbs of Washington, D.C.

AMANDA ARISTA was born in Illinois, raised in Corpus Christi, lives in Dallas, but her heart lies in London. When not writing, she often dreams of co-opening an evil bakery and selling despicable desserts. She spends her weekends writing at coffee shops, practicing for the day that caffeine intake becomes an Olympic sport and plotting character demises.

KIM FALCONER was born in Santa Cruz, California, where she wrote her first story at age five. It was about a Halloween cat! From then on, she proceeded to daydream her way through school. Fortunately, she now daydreams for a living on the beautiful Australian coast.